Barefoot

AT MIDNIGHT

The Barefoot Bay Series #14

roxanne st. claire

Barefoot at Midnight
Copyright © 2016 Roxanne St. Claire

This novel is a work of fiction. Any references to historical events, real people, or real locales are used fictitiously. Other names, characters, places, and incidents are the product of the author's imagination, and any resemblance to actual events or locales or persons, living or dead, is coincidental.

All rights to reproduction of this work are reserved. No part of this publication may be reproduced, stored in or introduced into a retrieval system, or transmitted, in any form, or by any means (electronic, mechanical, photocopying, recording, or otherwise) without prior written permission from the copyright owner. Thank you for respecting the copyright. For permission or information on foreign, audio, or other rights, contact the author, roxanne@roxannestclaire.com

Cover Art by The Killion Group, Inc. (designer) and
James Franklin (photographer)
Interior Formatting by Author E.M.S.
Seashell graphic used with permission under Creative Commons
CC0 public domain.

ISBN: 978-0-9970627-5-5

Published in the United States of America.

Critical Reviews of Roxanne St. Claire Novels

"St. Claire, as always, brings a scorching tear-up-the-sheets romance combined with a great story: dealing with real issues starring memorable characters in vivid scenes."

— Romantic Times Magazine

"Non-stop action, sweet and sexy romance, lively characters, and a celebration of family and forgiveness."

— Publishers Weekly

"Plenty of heat, humor, and heart!"

— USA Today's Happy Ever After blog

"It's safe to say I will try any novel with St. Claire's name on it."

— www.smartbitchestrashybooks.com

"The writing was perfectly on point as always and the pace of the story was flawless. But be forewarned that you will laugh, cry, and sigh with happiness. I sure did."

— www.harlequinjunkies.com

"The Barefoot Bay series is an all-around knockout, soul-satisfying read. Roxanne St. Claire writes with warmth and heart and the community she's built at Barefoot Bay is one I want to visit again and again."

— Mariah Stewart, New York Times bestselling author

"This book stayed with me long after I put it down."

— All About Romance

THE Barefoot Bay SERIES

Welcome to Barefoot Bay! On these sun-washed shores you'll meet heroes who'll steal your heart, heroines who'll make you stand up and cheer, and characters who quickly become familiar and beloved. Some are spicy, some are sweet, but every book in the Barefoot Bay series stands alone, and tempts readers to come back again and again. So, kick off your shoes and fall in love with billionaires, brides, bodyguards, silver foxes, and more…all on one dreamy island.

THE BAREFOOT BAY SERIES

Want to know the day the next Roxanne St. Claire book is released? Sign up for the newsletter! You'll get brief monthly e-mails about new releases and book sales.

http://www.roxannestclaire.com/newsletter.html

Acknowledgments

As always, this book and all that I write is the product of a group of professionals that ride with me on every book journey. Huge love to the team— content editor Kristi Yanta, who understands my characters better than I do; copy editor Joyce Lamb who knows grammar *and* math (not even fair); eagle-eyed proofreader Marlene Engel; and cover artist extraordinaire Kim Killion who has the vision I lack. Once again, photographer James Franklin had our hero in his head, and that man, gorgeous silver fox Dino Hillas, captured Law perfectly. More thanks to formatter Amy "there is no such thing as a problem" Atwell, and superstar author assistant Maria Connor. Oh, and mom kisses to the fam…especially Dante who dug out his notes from Property class to help me out, and my super lawyer brother, Gregg. If I got any legal stuff wrong, they'll represent me. Honestly, I am drowning in friends, family, and blessings.

Barefoot
AT MIDNIGHT

roxanne st. claire

Dedication

This one is for all the amazing instructors at Innovation Yoga in Satellite Beach, Florida. Kellie, Virginia, Maddie, Anastasia, Loren, Laurie, and studio owners Deborah and Stephen...thank you for giving me peace, patience, and balance every afternoon when I need it the most. You inspire and enlighten and remind me that serenity is just one breath away. *Namaste.*

Prologue

A relentless downpour made it nearly impossible to see more than five feet ahead, but Lawson Monroe gripped the handlebars of his vintage Triumph, clenched his teeth, and rocketed through the nearly deserted streets of Naples, Florida, at midnight.

C'mon, Bonnie. You can handle a little rain, old girl.

Law coaxed more speed out of a bike that had gotten him in and out of plenty of scrapes in their many years together. Under normal circumstances, he'd pull over and give her a break. He'd find a dry place to wait out the storm. He'd…quit.

But these were not normal circumstances, and for once in his life, Law wasn't going to take the easy way out. Not when a man who'd saved Law's life more times than he could count lay in a hospital teetering on the hairy edge between life and death.

The bike swerved in a puddle, a gush of rainwater spraying Law's work pants. The chef's jacket he hadn't bothered taking off when he got the call was soaked through to his skin now, and his long hair was plastered to his head since he hadn't wasted time putting on a helmet.

Jake Peterson's had a stroke.

The words of some nurse who'd been kind enough to call him still echoed in Law's brain. He'd been closing up at the Ritz-Carlton kitchen, wiping down the grill and cleaning off the remnants of a hellacious dinner rush, when his cell rang.

He never told anyone he was leaving, but marched into the rain, got on his bike, and rode.

Because that's what Jake would have done for him.

Through the rain, he spotted the red and white ER sign and pushed Bonnie to her limit, running a light to careen into the parking lot. Then he essentially abandoned the bike to charge inside. Still dripping wet, he launched the frustrating process of asking for help, directions, instructions. Down a hall, up an elevator, around a gurney, to another desk, then another, then, finally, the intensive care unit, where he was stopped cold by the fact that he wasn't family.

"I'm the closest thing he has," he said to the nurse, who didn't even soften when Law grabbed a tissue to wipe the rain dripping from his hair onto her glassy granite reception desk.

She gave him a put-upon puss. "I'm sorry, but the rules are very strict."

He huffed out a sigh and looked around the austere waiting room just as another nurse came around the corner, stopping at the sight of a man dripping rainwater all over the floor. She was older than the one behind the desk, with smooth gray hair and a piercing blue gaze that dropped to the name embroidered on his chef's coat.

"Lawson Monroe," she read out loud. "So you must be Law."

He nodded once, and she gestured toward the hall she'd come from, leaning to look around him. "It's okay. He's family."

Law gave a quick *take that, babe* face to the woman behind the desk who simply lifted a brow. "Whatever you say, Ruth."

Apparently, the rules weren't *that* strict when Ruth was calling the shots.

She came with him down the hall, her bright pink Crocs squeaking on the laminate wood with each crisp, efficient step. "He's been talking about you."

Relief washed through Law, the news easing the bits of raw pain stabbing his chest. "He can talk?"

"Oh yes."

"So it wasn't that bad?"

She didn't answer right away, making him wonder if she was choosing her words carefully. Or if it *was* that bad.

"It didn't kill him," she said simply.

"Thank God," Law whispered under his breath.

"The next one will, though."

He slowed his step. "What do you mean?"

"What I said, but you didn't hear that from me. The doctor might tell you more, but you aren't family."

"He doesn't have any," Law said. "I'm his friend."

"You're his *son*," she corrected.

"Is that what you want me to tell the doctor?" Because he had no qualms about lying his way through the health care system to get information he needed and wanted.

"That's what Jake told me."

Then he was delirious. "Okay," Law said.

"Oh, he might have said 'like a son,' but the sentiment was the same." She paused at a door with a glass insert, pulling a clipboard mounted on the wall to jot initials on a medical chart. "In any case, he begged me to contact you. You take it from here."

"Thanks, Ruth."

She opened the door and nodded for him to enter, closing it behind him.

The room was freezing, dark, and deadly quiet except for a half-dozen rhythmically beeping monitors all connected to the thin, old man lying on the bed looking about one shade lighter than his white sheet.

"Hey, Jake." Law spoke softly and moved with a deliberate step, a little terrified he'd make things worse.

Slowly, Jake turned his head and fluttered his eyes open. Without his glasses, he looked even craggier than usual, deep lines showing every one of his seventy-five years and then some.

He didn't speak but held Law's gaze, and instantly, his pale blue eyes welled up.

Oh man. Jake was a crybaby. He'd seen the old fart tear up over a McDonald's commercial. But this was different. This was fear, and Law could smell it as strong as the bitter antiseptic that hung in the air.

"Pretty crappy place to spend a Saturday night, pal." Law tried to sound light, but it didn't come out that way at all.

"Not my choice." The words were slurred and spoken through only half his mouth. The left side of his lips didn't move; they hung a little, like one would expect on a stroke victim.

The reality of a *stroke* sliced through Law like a nine-inch Wüsthof, cutting away his hope and optimism.

"I'll get you through this," Law promised. "Rehab, therapy, whatever you need. I'll run the restaurant for you, and you'll get better."

"That's why I got you here," he rasped. "Come closer. Talk."

Law obeyed, getting up to the bed and putting his hands

on the cool rail. "We'll talk about it later. Now, you just rest, buddy."

One eye narrowed. The other was hidden under a drooping lid that looked like it would take a lot more than therapy to ever open all the way again. Law's stomach tightened.

"Whatever it takes," Law said, squeezing the rail. "We'll get you better."

Jake managed to shake his head a centimeter.

"Yes," Law insisted. "We will. Don't be a quitter." He slathered the warning with enough emphasis that even a man hanging on to dear life would get the inside…well, it wasn't a *joke*. But they both got the implication.

"You are no quitter, Lawson," he managed to say on a raspy breath. "You think you are, but I know what you're made of."

"Don't talk, Jake. It's taking too much effort."

"I have to…tell you something." But his eyes closed with the effort, and Law didn't try to rouse him. Instead, he leaned over, taking in the rough features of a man who'd lived and played hard.

Law was fourteen when he met Jake, and the older man had been well into his forties back then. As he was to this day, Jake had been the proprietor of the town watering hole, a man known for lending a hand when it was needed. When Law was a messed-up teenager loaded on attitude and booze, Jake had set him straight. When Law ran away from the hell that was his home, Jake let him sleep in the room upstairs at the Toasted Pelican. When Law got out of the Army and smashed headfirst into rock bottom of a bottle, Jake had fished him out, got him into AA, and paid for culinary school.

Jake Peterson had been a father to Law. And he'd been a

hell of a lot better than the one Law had been cursed with at birth, that was for sure.

Jake's narrow chest rose and fell, making Law suspect he'd fallen asleep. He glanced over his shoulder at the door, expecting the nurse to usher him out at any minute, but she wasn't around. Grabbing a wooden-back chair, he set it next to the bed, a chill shuddering through him as his soaking-wet clothes started to dry under the intense air conditioning.

He ignored the discomfort. He wasn't leaving until they made him, and even then, he'd just sit outside. He'd talk to a doctor, he'd handle anything that arose, he'd be the son, even if he wasn't.

He wouldn't quit on Jake Peterson, the best friend he'd ever had.

Closing his own eyes and realizing they burned with unshed tears, Law let his head drop on a sigh.

"You're only as sick as your secrets."

Jake's words made Law's head jerk up, mostly because they were remarkably clear for a man who'd just suffered a stroke.

"So I've heard." Anyone who'd been through addiction recovery knew the phrase and knew it meant you couldn't get better until you got to the root of your problems, usually the secrets harbored in your heart.

But something told Law revealing a secret or two on his hospital bed wasn't going to make Jake better. Still, the concept had been pivotal to Law's victory over the bottle, and Jake knew it. It was Jake who'd gone with him to the dock on Law's first-year-sober anniversary and then to an all-night tattoo parlor to commemorate the date on his arm. It was Jake who'd listened to Law tell the story that plagued him his whole life, and Jake who—

"The Pelican. It's yours."

Law blinked at the words, taken aback as much by the sudden switch in subjects as the statement itself. He'd wanted the Toasted Pelican for years, and Jake refused to sell, give, or even let Law work at the restaurant he owned and ran forever. Yeah. Jake was definitely delirious, or the drugs had really kicked in.

"Listen, we'll figure all that out when you're home and healthy."

Jake managed a *get real* look, which was no mean feat for a man whose face was half paralyzed. But it was like he knew...he wasn't going to be "home and healthy" ever again.

"There's a will," he said.

"And a way," Law finished, happy to hear Jake thinking like that.

"No. Paperwork. Real paperwork."

"You have a will?" Of course, he *should* have a will. But it seemed strangely out of character for a man who loathed lawyers and kept his books with pen and paper.

Jake struggled as though he wanted to sit up, but the effort was too much. "You, too."

Law needed a will, too? What did he mean?

Jake moaned with frustration, or pain. Either way, Law wanted to quiet him. "Okay, listen, we don't have to pound anything out this minute. If...something happens, I'll take the Pelican. I've always wanted it, you know. I have plans."

Jake managed a smile. "Good plans. Great plans."

Then why the hell wouldn't he let Law implement those plans over the past couple of years? Instead, he'd pressed Law to take the sous chef job at the Ritz and save money to buy his own restaurant while the Toasted Pelican remained exactly what it had always been: a fifth-rate dump of a landmark on Mimosa Key, not the hip gastropub Law thought it could be.

But a visit to death's door seemed to have changed that.

"I want you to have it," Jake said, his voice low and gruff. "I have to make sure..." His words faded out, breaking Law's heart.

"Okay, we'll work that out...later." *Just don't die, you old bastard.*

Jake closed his eyes for a moment, as if to say there would be no later.

"You, too," he said, his voice fading more with every word. "Promise you'll...find it."

"I promise." He waited a beat, watching Jake's energy fade like someone had turned off the gas to his heart. *Damn it.*

"Where is it?" Law whispered.

"I still...haven't found..." He ground out each word, fighting for breath...and life. "Looking for..."

He didn't know where it was? This was crazy, but it was midnight in the ICU, and Jake was barely coherent. They'd talk about it when he got better. He *had* to get better.

"Yeah, I'll look, too. I'll find it."

"Won't be easy."

"Nothing ever is." Law leaned over the bed, the loss already gutting him. *Don't die, Jake.* "But you have to rest, man."

"I want *you* to have the Pelican. It's yours. No one else's. *Yours.*"

It wasn't like Jake had a line of heirs and siblings. His family tree was a stump, and despite his heart of gold, he didn't have a ton of friends outside the regulars and some long-term employees.

"I mean it," Jake said, growing a little agitated.

"I got you," Law said. "But I'd really rather you live, get strong, and we work together. That's a better plan."

Jake lifted a gnarled hand out from under the blanket, using all his strength to place his fingers on Law's arm, holding his gaze, and taking a deep, ragged breath that sounded a lot like someone's last. "You. No one else."

"Jake, you're going to live through this." But even as he said it, Law had doubts.

Jake exhaled long and slow. "Secrets," he murmured.

Secrets? What was he talking about?

"*You* are my son. Good as one. I always wanted..." He made face. "God, I wanted that."

The words choked Law, threatening to make those stinging tears slide out. He managed to nod, digging for composure. "You'd have been a damn good father, old man."

"I love you, Lawson." He was fighting for every syllable now, but Law let him speak. The words were a balm to both of them. "I believe in you. I trust you. I know you can do anything."

Something inside Law twisted, an ancient pain, a hollow echo of another man's slurred voice from the past. Slurred from booze and pain and grief. A voice that called him a loser. A quitter. Worse.

He silenced the hateful words of his real father and focused on the one in front of him, his heart cracking in his chest.

"You do this, Law. You'll take over and make...the Pelican yours."

"With you," Law insisted.

"*For* me," Jake gasped. "Do it for me."

"I will."

"And don't let them..." he added, his voice barely a

thread of a whisper now. "No matter what...secrets..." Jake's blue eyes closed as he fell back on the pillow, sighing as he fell sound asleep.

Not sleep, Law learned soon enough. A coma. Eight days later, after suffering a second stroke while still unconscious, Jake died and took his secrets to the grave.

And Law never found the will.

Chapter One

Eleven and a half months later

Clanging dishes, sizzling meat, and the cacophony of the controlled chaos of the Naples Ritz-Carlton main kitchen, serving four top-notch restaurants in the middle of a dinner rush, were all drowned out when Law closed his eyes and tasted the cognac demi-glace.

And wanted to spit it on the kitchen floor.

As he suspected, the sauce was broken and bitter. Law hadn't made it, but this was his steak au poivre, and he was the one who'd writhe in shame when a discerning customer sent it back. Or when a heady-with-Internet-power diner tossed a shitty review up on TripAdvisor, adding to the string they'd been getting since the new executive chef had arrived.

Grabbing a clean spoon, he took another taste of the lifeless sauce. The butter had been whisked too fast and the shallots hadn't sweat.

"You got a problem with that sauce, Monroe?"

Law met the beady brown gaze of his boss, Executive Chef Delbert Tracey-Dobbs across the stainless steel pass. "I have a better idea, Chef."

"You *always* have a better idea," Chef Del leaned closer, narrowing his eyes to pinpoints of hate. "But I'm the one in charge."

Proving that life went way beyond unfair and possibly into the ZIP code of pointless. At least this argument was. Still, Law had principles. And that sauce? It crushed his principles *and* his palate.

No, that wasn't true. This arrogant, incompetent, and clueless moron in charge had crushed him. Exactly who had this crappy excuse for an executive chef blown to get that job, anyway?

Didn't matter. Chef Del had the job, and Law had…nothing. Only a promise that died with his best friend and mentor, leaving Law stuck in this kitchen working for Satan's henchman.

He corralled some calm and faced off with his boss. "Chef, I think we should—"

"I don't care what a sous chef thinks, Monroe. Don't care what *we* should do. I'll tell you what *you're* going to do and then, guess what? You'll do it. Today, tomorrow, and for the rest of your days in this kitchen, which, if I have anything to say about it, will be few."

"One can hope," Law muttered.

"Excuse me?" Chef slammed his hands on the pass, shaking a few waiting dishes and toppling a tower of thinly sliced tuna that another sous chef had spent ten minutes building. Here it comes, Law thought. A reminder of how many people wanted his job.

"I have a hundred résumés on my desk for a sous chef position," Chef barked, right on cue. "I could have you replaced before the last dish is served tonight."

Some of the clatter around him died down as a few people nearby slowed their choreographed movements on the line to listen to the showdown, most of them probably expecting it since Chef Del arrived six months ago and decided he wanted Sous Chef Law Monroe out of his kitchen.

"Add the cognac sauce and get the order up, you scum-sucking bag of shit," Chef said between gritted teeth.

The words were as bitter and broken as the sauce. And all too familiar.

Law pushed a memory out of his head and willed himself to do what he'd done for the last eleven months: keep his smart mouth shut and cook. Just until he figured out who owned the place where he was *supposed* to be cooking now...except he'd been locked out by a nameless, faceless company claiming ownership. He had to stay here until he found a will that may or may not have been the morphine-induced ramblings of a dying man.

"The sauce, Monroe. Now!"

His whole body chafed at the order, and his hands itched to rip the chef's coat off his body and fling it in that ball-busting shithead's face.

Don't quit, Law. Don't do it. "I can have a new sauce in five—"

"Screw your sauce!" Del barked, silencing the entire kitchen now. "Order up or get the hell out, Monroe."

It wasn't quitting if he was fired, was it? And if he didn't move...

"Three seconds and you're finished," Del ground out.

Three seconds and he'd be a free man. Free to breathe, free to fail or succeed, free to devote every waking minute to finding out who took what was promised to him.

"Two."

Law closed his eyes, counted the two seconds, and tasted the sweet flavor of freedom from this hellhole, from this prick who reminded him of his father, from the prison this place had become when Chef Del showed up.

He lifted his hand and fingered the top button of his chef's coat.

"You *wouldn't*." Chef Del leaned closer, a challenge in his eyes. "Or would you?"

Law flicked the first button.

"In the middle of a rush on a Saturday night?" Del's voice rose in disbelief, and now everyone in the kitchen stilled to watch the drama unfold. "You are such a loser. A lightweight. A talentless bag of self-important air."

His eyes still closed, Law was transported back forty years to a tiny house on Mimosa Key. The smell of Jim Beam and burnt mackerel mixed with tension so thick it lay on his skin like the salty harbor air. Through it all, his father's words bounced off the walls and flattened Law's self-worth.

You worthless piece of scum, Lawson. Beckett was worth ten of you.

That made the second button slide open easily enough.

"You'll never work for a Ritz-Carlton again."

He didn't want to work *for* anyone but himself, he rationalized. So that threat was music to his ears. He unhooked the next button without taking his gaze off his boss's reddened face.

"You'll never work in this city again."

Fine. Naples, Florida, was full of old fart millionaires who didn't appreciate real cooking and their skinny trophy wives who didn't eat. The last button took no effort at all.

"You're finished, Monroe! Get the hell out of here! Go back to the twelve-step program you came from."

Law slipped the jacket off and folded it neatly next to the now-gelatinous demi-glace, the simple act giving him a rush of pure pleasure.

With every eye in the kitchen on him and most mouths gaping, Law strode down the line with his head held high.

Yes, damn it. He'd quit. And, like always, it felt about as good as the sweet burn of whiskey when it hit his gut and spilled into his veins.

Without a word, he grabbed his backpack from his locker and headed out the back door to the employees' parking lot, where the blast of a blistering August night smacked him in the face, despite the proximity to the beach.

He sucked in a mouthful of air, getting a whiff of the Dumpster where that sauce belonged.

Trying to not think too hard about the fact that he'd just walked off the job he spent years working to get and keep, he slid a leg over the side of his bike, jammed the key in the ignition, and flattened his thumb on the starter button.

With a rev of Bonnie's engine, he roared out of the lot loud enough to piss off the Ritz management. He didn't hate them, and he didn't hate the restaurant. He just hated being under anyone or anything, and the very definition of the word *sous* in his title meant "under" in French.

Well, now he wasn't under anything, including a helmet. With hot wind in hair he'd cut short for summer, he blew out onto the main road with no real destination.

He didn't have a "home"—or wouldn't by Monday. After Jake died almost a year ago, Law had moved out of the house they'd rented. That was, after he'd combed every inch of Jake's meager belongings for a will that never appeared.

Since then, Law's life had been on hold, so he'd opted for a cut in pay at his job at the Ritz and taken one of the tiny efficiency apartments they offered to the staff, deep in the bowels of the hotel.

He'd have to move out of there as soon as management

got wind of his latest stunt, making him officially homeless *and* jobless.

At least he was sober.

He waited for the kick of desire, the little tweak from a demon that resided deep in his belly and rose up on occasions just like this to whisper, "Jack and Coke, baby. That'll numb all this misery."

A year ago, that would have sent him straight over the causeway to Mimosa Key. There, he'd have slipped through the back door of the Toasted Pelican. Only a former drunk would appreciate the irony that his soft, safe place to fall was a bar and a glass of non-alcoholic beer.

A year ago, Jake would have been there, offering O'Doul's and advice, cleaning up after the last customer had left. But Jake wasn't there anymore.

Instead, the locks had been changed and the employees worked for a "shell" company that had mysteriously taken over. And Law had bruises from the brick walls he'd hit trying to figure out who had stolen the business Jake had promised to him.

He took the tight turn onto the causeway, settling into the seat as he accelerated up the long bridge over the gulf, headed to the tiny island where he'd grown up and still thought of as home, no matter how crappy that home had been.

Consumed by grief for the loss of his closest friend and the man who'd changed—no, *saved*—his life, Law hadn't cared that much about Jake Peterson's missing last will and testament at first. While Jake was in a coma, Law had looked for it in the closet Jake used as an office, but he'd never found it. After Jake died, he cleaned out the closet and everything personal in the house they'd shared, but it still never turned up.

But what did it matter, he'd thought at the time. He'd work out the legalities eventually. He called the staff and told them not to find other jobs, that he'd be taking over. Finding that will was just a matter of time and determination.

Then he showed up one morning and his key didn't fit the lock, and he realized he'd better work out those legalities sooner rather than later. That was the beginning of a long, long nightmare, starting with the appointment Law made with an attorney.

Apparently, he was too late. The Toasted Pelican had been taken over by a private company based in South Florida that claimed to have "ties" to Jake Peterson, and ownership had been approved by some judge in Collier County. No one could identify the owner, but one by one, a few of the staff had been contacted by some guy named Sam in Miami.

A manager came on board who swore to have no clue who paid the checks, and the business stayed open and hobbled on. Turnover had been rampant, and most of Law's friends were long gone, replaced by teenagers who didn't know who owned the place and didn't care as long as they got paid.

Law had even looked at other restaurants to buy, willing to give up on the Pelican just to realize his dream of owning his own gastropub. But, damn it, that's not what he wanted. Not what Jake had wanted.

He wasn't going to quit until he knew the truth.

Someone had to know, Law thought for the millionth time in almost a year. And on a Saturday night? Maybe that someone was loose-lipped at the bar.

Parking in the back, Law shut off the bike, noting that the lot was sparsely filled. Business had been lousy for months, and now it was completely in the crapper. If only he could find out who the owner was, he'd make an offer to buy it.

Forget the missing will; Law had some money saved. Not much, but he'd get a loan if he had to.

He yanked open the door and sucked in a whiff of two-day-old fry oil and stale beer. He glanced into the open door of the kitchen when he passed, noting the pimply faced nineteen-year-olds languishing in front of the grill. Down the hall to the dining area, he passed Jake's closet and paused to check out the stairs that led up to a huge storage area and sometime apartment.

Something was…different.

Frowning, he noticed that the dark stain on the stairs had been stripped off, and long boards of hardwood were lying on the landing. What the hell? They were renovating up there?

Fire and fury shot through him. Some stranger was renovating *his* property.

More determined to get hard facts than ever before, he cruised through the dining area, which consisted of mostly tables, a worthless jukebox, and a lot of dusty crap on the walls. He headed into the connected bar, where the real action was.

Only there wasn't much of that, either. He glanced around the dimly lit area, counting few booths with customers and more empty seats at the bar. This place could not be running in the black. So who had the cash to lay hardwood upstairs…and *why*?

He slid onto a barstool and looked around for the bartender. It would be one of the two guys who started working after Jake died—young guys, not locals, who also claimed to have no idea who signed their paychecks. He couldn't see around the tower of bottles and mirrors in the center of the round bar, so he twisted all the way to look back at the booths, counting the meager patrons, who included some locals he knew, a few very old regulars, and one couple.

"I thought you didn't drink, Lawless."

At the woman's question, he pivoted to the bartender and came face-to-face with...oh baby, what a face. He'd been admiring that face since he'd first seen it thirty years ago and started a cat-and-mouse chase that had yet to end with either one of them getting caught.

But they sure had fun running after each other in high school and again, a few months ago, when they'd met up at the Mimosa High reunion. Law made no effort to hide his attraction, and the beautiful lady in front of him gave a flirt as good as she got.

Only a flirt, though. Despite Law's best attempts, their contact was limited to banter and wordplay, which was fun, but frustrating.

"Libby Chesterfield, you gorgeous piece of womanhood."

She didn't smile, didn't move actually, except for the slightest tilt of her head. Blond hair—long, silky, sinful blond hair—spilled over bare shoulders. One perfectly arched brow twitched, and full lips pouted ever so slightly to remind a man that she owned a mouth that was made for one thing and one thing only. Kissing. Well, maybe two things.

"*Piece of womanhood?*" She put her hands on her hips, drawing his gaze over a formfitting red tank top, cutoff jean shorts, and about five-foot-six inches of luscious. Every stinkin' curve was pure perfection, especially the ones that rightfully earned her the name "Chesty Chesterfield" in high school. "That's the best you've got, Monroe? You are losing your touch, sweet cheeks. I expect better from you."

He took the challenge, leaning in, devouring her up and down with a hungry look, trying to remember if she was forty-four or forty-five. Better err on the side of caution.

"Lib, you're forty-four years old, and you still make mouths water, heads turn, and men rise up to praise you. How do you manage to stay so exquisite all these years?"

"Forty-*five*. I had a birthday on the Fourth of July." She leaned over the bar just enough to blind him with a glimpse of sweet, deep cleavage. "And you, too, Law, are a miracle of nature at forty-five."

"Six," he corrected. "My birthday was in July, too."

"Even more amazing."

"Because we have so much in common?"

"Because you made it all the way to forty-six years old and you still think, act, and talk like the teenager who tried to cop a feel of my left boob during a game of touch football in co-ed gym class."

"Uh, that's why they call it *touch*."

She angled her head in concession. "You did make my nipple hard."

"And you made everything hard." He winked at her. "We can have a rematch anytime you want."

She rolled her eyes. "What's your pleasure, other than your bartender?"

"O'Doul's," he said, automatically ordering his usual, but wondering…*why* was she his bartender? He'd never seen her back there before. "So, uh, when did you start gracing the poor schmucks at the Pelican with all that hotness?"

She lifted a shoulder. "Both guys who work are out and…" She turned to the fridge. "I'm helping."

Helping *who*? Law inched forward, and not merely to get a view of the flip side of Libby as she dug into the cooler for a beer. Although the back was as appealing as the front with faded denim shorts hugging a heart-shaped ass with threads skimming tight, toned thighs.

"Why would you help out here?" he asked.

"Just for something to do."

Bartending at a dive? He'd talked to her a bit at the reunion a few months ago and had discovered that Libby drove a nice car, wore quality clothes, and the rumor mill said she'd taken her last husband to the cleaners in divorce court. And he was almost positive she worked as an aerobics teacher or something. Whatever, she was smart and beautiful and belonged in a place better than this.

But here she was, so maybe she could give him the one thing he wanted most from her, at least right this minute...*information.*

"Libby, I've been in and out of this fine establishment on a regular basis for the better part of my life," he told her. "And I've seen you in here exactly once, about a month ago." He remembered it well, though. What he remembered were the sprayed-on black pants that could make a grown man weep. "You were on your way to some girlie exercise class," he recalled.

She snorted softly as she placed a cocktail napkin in front of him. "It's called *yoga*, and I'd suggest you try it, but it's really a practice for people seeking balance and wisdom." She took a look at his body, her gaze lingering on the biceps on full display under the tight short sleeves of his T-shirt. "Obviously, you'd rather throw iron around a gym and grunt like a caveman."

"Cavemen get a bad rap."

She put the drink down with the tiniest spark of appreciation in eyes that weren't quite blue or gray but a haunting mix of both, when a couple took the last two seats at the bar. "Nurse that one for a while, Law. I have to work."

"You really work here?" Since when?

But she'd slipped away to the newcomers, giving them a much friendlier smile than the sassy one he got. He heard the woman order a margarita and could have sworn Libby stiffened at the order.

While she made it, Law figured out in a few scant seconds of observation that Libby Chesterfield didn't know squat about mixing a drink or navigating her way behind the bar. So *what* was she doing here?

Law sat up straighter and looked around. Something was definitely up at the Pelican. It was damn near empty. The staff was thin at best. That ugly collection of battered Florida license plates had been taken off the wall.

And Libby was bartending.

Okay, then. The first slow burn of hope he'd felt all day—hell, in the fifty weeks since Jake died—sizzled in his gut like cast iron on high heat. If change was in the air at the Pelican and Libby was behind the bar, she *had* to know who'd assumed ownership of the establishment that had been willed to him.

And Law would use every tool in his arsenal to get the information out of her.

Chapter Two

How the hell was she supposed to know how to make a margarita? Libby didn't even drink them. The whole place was making her skin crawl with the foul stench of booze and fried dough and lost souls.

Oh, the occasional sexy customer.

She slid a glance at Lawson Monroe, a man she was determined to keep at arm's length. A dangerous man. The wrong man. A man with alluring green eyes and incredibly broad shoulders and a full head of sexy, silver hair, which, even though he'd cut it short since the reunion five months ago, was still tousled and inviting to the touch. Of course, he had just enough of a salt-and-pepper five o'clock shadow to make her wonder how those whiskers would feel against her cheeks…and thighs.

Oh boy. Those were not the thoughts of a stable, balanced woman who'd sworn off sex.

But self-imposed celibacy wasn't why she kept Law at a safe distance ever since they'd connected at the reunion and discovered their fiery chemistry hadn't died over the years. She could handle flirting with him, and honestly, she liked his wit and dry humor.

No, she needed to avoid Law because he asked way too

many questions about this wretched-smelling hellhole that she had to keep running for two more weeks before it was officially and legally and finally hers.

She took another secret peek at him as she turned to grab a bottle of beer for one of the tables. He was looking down at his phone, giving her a chance to study him longer. Study and, okay, admire.

His body wasn't like the lean rubber-band men who took the yoga classes she taught. Law was chiseled in stone with well-defined muscles under that tight T-shirt, ripped arms decorated with well-placed and subtle tattoos. Not normally a look that appealed to her, but there was something about him that made her unsteady.

And if there was anything in the world Libby Chesterfield hated, it was the loss of balance.

He caught her looking, so she didn't bother to try to pretend she wasn't. She continued to stare without, she hoped, too much admiration in her eyes. But then, she'd always looked at him with a little lust in her gaze, so why change now?

Because he attracted her like a freaking magnet, and she *had* to stay quiet and avoid his probing questions for two more endless weeks. She didn't dare ask him why he cared, because she had to stay on the DL.

Then, when the papers were signed and sealed, this dump would be gutted, cleaned, and completely renovated into Mimosa Key's first and only yoga studio for wholeness and well-being. It would be called, quite simply, Balance, as a testimony to the one thing Libby treasured the most.

He gave a half smile that actually made her stomach flutter. Great. Just what she needed. A stomach flutterer asking questions she didn't want to answer.

"Talk to me, Lib."

She shifted from one leg to the other, pretending that getting any closer to him would be downright painful. "I'm busy."

"Yeah, the place is packed." He pushed his drink aside and crooked a finger. "C'mere. I want to talk to you."

"You never want to talk, Law." But still, she stepped closer because...how could she not? "As long as I've known you, talking wasn't what you wanted from me." And that had been mutual, she thought, resisting the urge to remind him of that and fuel his fire.

He grinned. "We do go way back, don't we?"

Settling a hip against the bar, she eyed him again, looking for evidence of his hard life and forty-six years. Okay, there were a few crinkles around eyes the color of the ripe green olives she'd dropped into a few martinis that night. Of course, the gray in his hair was unfairly gorgeous, even more beautiful than the thick brown locks he'd worn way too long back in the eighties.

"You were a pretty bad boy in high school," she mused.

"And you were a pretty bad girl, as I recall. A *very* pretty bad girl. Still are pretty. Are you bad?"

"Not bad enough to do what you're thinking about." Although...

"You don't know what I'm thinking."

"I can guess." And her guess would be that he was on the hunt for information, not sex. Maybe both. "You had your shot, Lawless. That game of Seven Minutes in Heaven at Keith Hellerman's house, remember?"

"*Oof.*" He dropped his head back as if the memory hit him hard. "I was so damn happy to pull your name."

She laughed, remembering the party very well. She'd been a spitfire of a troubled junior, and he was a hot and dangerous senior. Talk about a match made in hell. "I was totally ready to let you up my bra right then and there."

25

"But you didn't."

"Whiskey breath turns me off," she said honestly. "And drunk boys in closets scared me."

His whole face changed, the flirt and fun erased and replaced by remorse and shame. "Sorry," he murmured, but kept her gaze with the steadiness of a man who'd made that apology before.

The word was so genuine and came from a place so deep, she almost reached out and touched him. Instead, she rooted around for a lighter memory. "How about that night of the Spring Fling when we slow danced? Do you remember that?"

"I don't remember the song," he said with that same sadness. "But I remember holding you very close."

"I remember the song." She remembered it all. The slow song, the bad boy, the dark gym. "It was *Blown Away* by Eddie James and the Lost Boys."

He drew back an inch, clearly surprised. "It was? You remember that?"

"I remember everything about that night," she admitted. "I especially remember that I wasn't sure if that was, uh, your belt buckle pressing against me or not."

He grinned. "Definitely not."

"It was…impressive." She grinned right back, enjoying the warmth of talking about something exciting and poignant that time had faded into a sweet moment. "Enough that I said yes to a date the next night, as you recall. But…"

"I never showed."

She studied him for a long moment. "Booze?"

"Most likely." He looked down at the bar, and she felt his embarrassment, but it wasn't shame in his eyes when he met her gaze. It was…regret. "You were probably better off I stood you up."

It didn't feel that way at the time. It stung. But she lifted a shoulder as if she couldn't possibly have cared less. "Your loss. I had big plans and a box of Trojans at the ready. I *was* a pretty bad girl."

He muttered a curse and pushed the O'Doul's away. "I've changed, you know."

Yes. He was sober. "I know."

"But I still give good belt buckle, Lib." His lip lifted in a half smile that had the same effect on her today as it had with Eddie James crooning about a storm of love.

An hour alone with Law, and she'd be toast. Celibacy would seem like the stupidest decision she ever made, and her need to stay absolutely silent about the property? Just as much at risk.

She had to remember that, at the reunion, Law had been asking if anyone knew who owned the Toasted Pelican now that Jake Peterson was dead. When he wasn't busy working on the reunion held at the Casa Blanca Resort & Spa up in Barefoot Bay that week, he'd been in town sniffing around the Pelican. She had spies on staff; she knew who was in and out of here.

Most of the spies were gone now, since they'd found other jobs on her recommendation, which was why she was stuck behind the bar tonight.

"I have to ask you a question, Chesty."

She shot him a look at the use of her high school nickname, determined to take everything back to playful flirtation. "Yes, they're real."

"Oh, I'm aware. I'm a connoisseur, you know."

"Is that so? Oh, ladies and gentlemen," she said to no one in particular. "We have ourselves a breast specialist. A regular nipple know-it-all. The champion of the chest."

"A 'brexpert,' if you will," he added. "A devotee of the double D's."

"Triple." She winked back, feeling her balance return

with the harmless sex talk. That was the safest place with Law Monroe. "Which, if you were such a discerning judge, you would know."

"I am discerning, and I believe that what we have is the rare 'high-and-mighty' triple D, which frankly belongs in the Victoria's Secret Hall of Fame."

She laughed easily. "Actually, I cheated there. Had a lift, thanks to my rich but unfaithful ex-husband number two, so they're higher and mightier than ever." She arched her back just enough to show off the goods.

Law took another lusty look at her breasts and lifted his glass in a toast. "That rack is a thing of beauty, Lib."

"Rack. Now there's a term that makes women weak with desire." She crossed her arms under that chest to plump the pillows. "Right up there with titties, ta-tas, jugs, melons, hooters, squeezers, beamers, cupcakes, sweater stretchers, and my personal favorite, mama's mammies."

He lowered the glass. "What do *you* call them?"

"My secret weapon." She leaned over the bar to torture him. "Because they have a power I'll never understand."

"But will gladly use, I imagine."

Not as often as he'd think. Not ever, really. "Don't you use that sexy smile to your advantage, Law?" she asked.

He showed off his straight white teeth and hella cute dimples. "Use what you got, my friend Ja..." He hesitated like he realized he was about to say something he shouldn't. "My friend used to say."

"Then I use my Deadly D's. They make certain yoga poses impossible, but that's a small price to pay for their potent power. Are we done talking about them?"

"You brought them up," he replied. "I wanted to ask you a serious question, and you shot a round of rapid-fire pet boob names."

"Because I already know the question." She sighed with pretend disdain, sensing he wanted to get back to a serious topic and she didn't want to go there. "The question is always the same with guys like you, Law. And my answer hasn't changed. I'm not sleeping with you."

"But you are thinking about it."

Why lie? "How could I think about anything else?"

He looked pleased with that.

"When it's all you ever talk about?" she finished.

"Not true. I talk about other things. Like..." He gestured toward the rest of the bar. "This place. Who brought you in to tend bar tonight?"

Knew it. "I told you, the bartender."

"Billy or Dan?"

Dang it, he knew them, too. He could call one of those guys and find out the entire staff had been told they should look for other jobs by the new owners...who were nothing but a name on an email.

"Libby." He leaned forward and put a hand over hers. "You know who owns this place, don't you?"

Be careful, Lib. Watch every word and commit to nothing. She could hear Sam's words in her head. But Law's touch was warm and light. It sent a shiver up her spine, making every cell scream in warning.

"Why do you want to know so badly?" she asked, since the question prevented an out-and-out lie. "Why have you spent months trying to find out, anyway?"

"Much longer than that, and I didn't realize you were noticing everything about me. Color me happy."

"Answer my question," she demanded.

He blew out a slow breath. "Jake Peterson was a friend of mine."

"Oh." She drew her hand away. "You have my sympathies."

"Thanks. Did you know him?"

"I knew...*of* him." Actually, she hadn't ever met him, but she knew enough. "Heard he was a real...piece of work," she added, because what she'd *really* heard wasn't something she'd repeat to anyone.

Law shook his head, smiling. "You know, Jake got a kick out of people assuming the worst about him, and it was his private game to not correct them."

It was a *game* to him? He got a kick out of it? She let all expression leave her face as she stared at the man who called that sorry sack of shit a friend. "Do you need anything else, Mr. Monroe?"

He leaned closer, his strong jaw clenched, the muscles in his neck corded with tense determination. "You know exactly who's running this restaurant and bar, don't you, Libby?"

She shook her head, wishing she could get the subject back on boobs and off the bar. But he wasn't going there—she could tell as Law's features hardened and he formulated his next question that would probably require her to think of another creative way not to lie but avoid the truth.

"Do you know this guy, this Sam guy who sends money and instructions on behalf of some shell company?" he asked.

Forget lying. She had to work to keep from reacting at all. No flash of surprise, no open mouth of shock. "Sam?"

"The guy paying people to work here."

Only for two more weeks. "Well, like I said, I'm just helping out Dan tonight. I don't know...everyone." She turned to busy herself with wiping down the bar, because there was a reason Sam was a lawyer and a damn good poker player. He could bluff and Libby couldn't.

"And he works for this Liberty Management company?" Law pressed.

Oh, damn it all. Law knew *way* more than he should. How long before he put two and two together and came up with...exactly who *Liberty* Management really was?

"If you say so," she said, casually pulling out a phone as if she were far more interested in checking her messages than talking about this.

"How can I reach him?" Law demanded.

"Hmm. I think that company is in..." She tried to think of a location that would send him on a wild-goose chase.

"Miami," he supplied.

Except he'd already found that goose. Automatically, her finger found Sam's name. Was he here yet? Or was he still driving over from Miami?

"Have you met anyone who works for Liberty Management?" Law practically climbed over the bar. "Do you have a phone number? Address? Anything for that company?"

"No phone number for that company." Just that man, and she was texting to it now. She tried to type, hating that her thumb quivered a little.

Need to talk to you. ASAP. Impt.

"How about a last name?" Law asked, all the lightness in their exchange gone as his questions became more demanding. "Does Sam have a last name?"

Yeah...the same as hers.

She looked up at Law, just as casual as she could be. "All I've ever heard the employees say is a guy named Sam."

"Can I see a paycheck stub?"

Dear God, he was pushy. "First of all, I don't work here. I'm doing a favor for a friend."

"For Dan, you said. Are you sure it's not for Sam?"

She could feel the blood drain from her face. "And second of all," she continued as if he hadn't spoken, "you still didn't tell me why it matters so much to you."

His eyes narrowed into menacing green slits. "Because this is my restaurant and bar. By rights. By law. By the last will and testament of Jake Peterson."

She almost fainted. Breathe, the yoga instructor in her insisted. But no breath would come. This was her worst fear. Jake had left a will after all.

"Well, you better take that up with Liberty Management," she said, marveling at her calm.

"Miss, could we have a refill, please?" a patron called, sounding like an angel sent from God.

"On my way." She gave Law a tight smile. "Good luck, hon." She walked around to the other side of the bar so she didn't have to feel his eyes boring into her, digging for answers she did not want to give.

She took her time pouring two more beers. Chatted with the customers. Refused to look around to see if he was still there. Patted her jean pocket to check her phone in case Sam texted back. And swore hard under her breath.

Her phone wasn't there. Her phone…was on the bar in front of Law.

Pivoting, she darted around the bottle stack, stopping with a sudden slam on the brakes. Her phone was right where she'd left it, but Law was gone.

She'd been so determined to ignore him that he left a ten on the bar and got away.

Grabbing her phone, she saw a text. A text that no doubt flashed when it came in and an astute and inquisitive snoop would read. What had he seen? The name of the caller: *Sammy from Miami*, punctuated by an emoji with sunglasses, the way she liked to think of that cool lawyer she loved so much. And Law had probably seen the first few words of Sam's text.

Checked in. Drinking at Junonia. Come up and talk to me.

Did Law read "drinking at Junonia?" Because he would, of course, know that was the name of the restaurant at the resort in Barefoot Bay. They'd both spent plenty of time there the week of the high school reunion.

And if she knew anything about anything, Law Monroe was on his way there right now.

With a low-grade panic spiraling through her, she tapped the phone to call Sam back, hearing it ring and ring until it dropped into voice mail. She typed a message.

Don't talk to anyone about TP!! Especially a guy named Lawson Monroe!

And then she looked around, ready to scream for the last few customers to get out. But she couldn't. People were drinking and eating. Not many, but she couldn't bring that kind of attention to herself or the bar, or her whole plan could collapse.

Suddenly, her world tilted, and balance, her precious, hard-won balance, became a thing of the past.

Chapter Three

Finally. Progress. Junonia. Hope. *Sam*.

Whoever the hell he was, Law would find him.

Following his instinct, the lead, and an uncanny ability to make friends with anyone in any bar, Law rode like hell up to Barefoot Bay.

At ten o'clock on a Saturday night in August, the parking lot of the Casa Blanca Resort & Spa was packed. Even at the height of summer, when the Gulf Coast of Florida was steamy and sweaty, this upscale jewel of a resort had a crowd.

He glanced down at his black work slacks and the T-shirt he'd worn under his chef's jacket. Ripping off the shirt, which probably didn't smell that great, he dug through his backpack for the blue dress shirt he'd picked up from the Ritz-Carlton cleaners on the way into work that afternoon.

Perfect. He shook out the folds, slipped it on, tucked it into his pants, rolled back the sleeves, and went in to find *Sammy from Miami*, who may or may not own the Toasted Pelican, but it was the first real lead Law had in almost a year.

The marble-floored lobby was cool after the hot summer night, the blast of air conditioning welcome on his face and body. The area was peppered with moneyed guests and an efficient resort staff, but he strode to the restaurant that had become a destination in the few years since it opened with the resort.

Law knew the executive chef, Ian, and had even considered moving over here from the Ritz at one point, but then Jake died, and Law figured it would make no sense to move to another restaurant unless it was the Pelican or one he bought himself. He'd looked at a few, but they weren't what he wanted.

The man who had what he wanted was somewhere on this property, and Law was going to find him.

Was Sam alone? Waiting for his sexy date and her Deadly D's? He kind of wished Libby wasn't the type to go for a guy who could afford this place. Didn't she learn anything from her "rich but unfaithful ex-husband?" Guess not.

Still, questions irked. What was her deal with the Sam dude, anyway? If he owned the Toasted Pelican, why'd he put her to work at the bar to get hit on by boozy locals?

No one was alone inside, so he stepped out to the deck, wandering over to the more casual pool bar. There was also a tiki-type thing where drinks were being served, but it was very small and on the sand. This one had far more people and activity.

Even with the proximity to the water, the air was still, heavy, and hot, making his shirt damp already. Some steel drums set a tropical beat off in the corner, the perfect side dish for the chatter, laughter, and the clink of glasses. The sounds of a bar.

When he was in AA—the first time—the conventional wisdom about a bar was simple: *you don't go there*. So he'd avoided bars for years and filled the hole in his gut by going into the Army. For fifteen years, the war Law fought was with himself, and he usually lost.

When he got out and hit what was affectionately known as "rock bottom," he walked back into the one bar he could never stay away from, the Toasted Pelican.

And Jake Peterson succeeded in pushing Law into one more AA meeting and then to a cooking-school program, all the while doling out advice that…that, well, a father would give. A real father, not the SOB Law had.

That's what Jake was to Law, and that's why he'd left him the restaurant, and that's why Law, whose weakness was quitting when things got tough, would not quit until he had his hands on Sammy from Miami's throat and squeezed the ever-lovin' truth out of him.

Fired up by the thought, he marched through the sights, sounds, and smells of people getting loose and juiced. Fact was, they didn't make Law want a drink. But when he went home tonight—which wasn't even home anymore—then he'd crave a numbing agent. But he'd make it through the night.

For Law, it wasn't one day at a time. It was one midnight at a time, when his personal demons came out to haunt and torment him.

He spotted a balding man sitting alone at a table, nursing a red wine, and walked a little closer, slowing down. When the guy looked up, Law gave him a puzzled expression.

"Sam? Is that you?"

The guy shook his head.

"Sorry," Law said, adding a smile. "You look like someone I know." He moved on, tried the trick on another guy, but failed again. Damn it. He cruised around the bar one more time, looking for an empty stool so he could possibly chat up the bartender, when a pretty blonde got up and freed a seat.

"Well, bye," she said wistfully, putting a hand on the wide shoulder of a man at the bar. "I wish my friends didn't want to leave. I hope you'll call...Sam."

Bingo.

"Of course I will, April," Sam said, adding a flirtatious smile that probably made April's panties get wet but made Law seriously doubt Libby's judgment and taste.

"You promise?" she cooed.

"I promise." The guy was handsome, in that Superman in a Suit kind of way, Law supposed, and looked to be about Law's age, with the same amount of dust on the shingles.

Well, everyone had a type. Law's type was... Libby, he admitted to himself. Libby's type must be rich cheating bastards. That was, if this was the infamous Sam of Liberty Management.

Law surreptitiously checked him out, sensing there was something vaguely familiar, but it was probably the fact that the guy looked like all the Ritz patrons. A man who had confidence and cash, wearing well-tailored clothes. He had a decent build and wore a pair of tortoise shell rimmed glasses that Law bet were clear glass to capitalize on that Clark Kent vibe.

But his name was Sam, he was hitting on women, and he looked like he might be from Miami, so Law took a chance and the barstool next to him.

"'Sup?" Law asked with a quick chin jut.

"Hey," the guy responded, reaching for his phone. Oh no, couldn't have that.

"I gotta ask you a question," Law said, his voice low and serious enough to at least slow down the guy's interest in the phone.

"What's that?"

Law paused, trying to decide what would work best. A

slow work-in during a casual conversation or a hard hit? In that second's hesitation, the phone on the bar lit up with a text, and Law glanced down to see the name. *Libby*.

Hard hit it was.

"Do you own the Toasted Pelican?"

Sam froze, an imperceptible reaction in his eyes that quickly went blank. "Excuse me?"

A ploy for time or an honest question? "The Toasted Pelican," Law said slowly, as if talking to someone from another country. "It's a restaurant and bar not far from here."

"Why would you ask?"

Answering a question with a question was just this side of lying, and Libby had used the technique plenty during their last conversation. Did she think Law hadn't noticed?

"Yes or no? Very simple. Do you own an establishment on this island called the Toasted Pelican?"

He sized Law up with interest now. "Who are you?"

Screw this. He'd have to hit really hard to get what he wanted, because keeping Jake's will a secret hadn't helped him at all this past year. "I'm the rightful owner," Law said.

The other guy gave away absolutely nothing, not so much as a flicker in his eyes, as he stared back. Finally, he asked, "Can you produce a deed to the property?"

Hell, no. *Was* there a deed to the property? Jake had owned the place free and clear for...ever. "Can you?" Law volleyed back.

"I didn't sit down at this bar and start making accusations," Sam said.

Accusations? "That's a strange word to use for a simple question."

The other man regarded him, silent for a moment before taking a breath and leaning closer. "The rightful owner of a business in the state of Florida can produce a deed to the property," he said, his voice low but each word crystal clear, even with the ambient sounds of the restaurant, bar, and steel-drum band. "And the rightful owner has the bylaws and articles of incorporation, a certificate of compliance and clearance letter, and a properly executed Form DR-835 with power of attorney. Of course, common law doctrine covers all equitable title issues, and it depends on which statute governs the interpretation of the documentation."

Law groaned noisily. "And we got ourselves a lawyer."

Sam put out his hand. "Samuel G. Chesterfield, attorney at law."

Chesterfield. Wait. That was Libby's last name. She couldn't be married to future ex-husband number three, so who was—

"Sam! Sam!" They both turned at the sound of a woman's voice, along with every male head in the place, as Libby nearly broke into a run crossing the wide patio. Her blond hair flew like corn silk in the wind, her bodacious body moving like a slow-motion beer commercial selling sex as hard as the brew.

"Libby." Sam stood as she came closer, extending his arms as if he would catch her if she fell.

She stopped just short of the other man's outstretched arms, breathless, looking from one to the other. "You met." She sounded utterly defeated.

"We were just talking about—"

Libby cut off Sam's comment by holding her hand up, catching her breath. "He claims he has a will. Jake Peterson's will."

Sam whipped around to Law, who still hadn't put two and two together and come up with anything that made sense. "Well, that could change everything," Sam said.

Precisely. Only there was one problem. He didn't exactly

have the will. "How does it change everything?" he asked.

"We'd need to see the will," Sam said.

"Why? Who are you two?" Law demanded.

Sam stood a little straighter, looking all lawyerly and official. "We're Liberty and Samuel Chesterfield, siblings, and the sole heirs to the property on Mimosa Key known as the Toasted Pelican."

Siblings. Liberty. Oh shit, now this was making sense. Except... "Jake didn't have any heirs."

"Yes, he did," Libby said. "He was our father."

"Your...*what?*" Law could barely say the word, shock bringing him off the barstool.

"Father," she repeated, sounding a little embarrassed, disgusted, and unwilling to use the word.

Law just stared at her, stunned.

"Our biological father," Sam said, as if that explained *anything*.

"And my twin brother and I are the rightful heirs to the Toasted Pelican."

No way. There was no freaking *way* this was possible.

While he was still speechless, Libby gestured from one man to the other. "Do you two remember each other from Mimosa High? Lawson Monroe was a year ahead of us."

"Vaguely," Sam said, extending his hand. "I didn't go to that reunion thing back in March, though."

Law shook Sam's hand without much enthusiasm, sort of remembering that Libby had a brainiac brother.

Jake had a daughter and a son?

Law's whole body tightened as that possibility settled over him. And, just as quickly, disappeared because it wasn't possible. Jake wouldn't hide something like that. He'd always talked about if he'd had kids and how he'd missed the boat on being a father. He'd said that on many occasions.

So, if they were telling the truth, which he doubted, Jake hadn't known. Which made Law hate them even more.

"I was really close to Jake," Law said, fighting for control. "If he had kids, I would have known it." He gave his head a firm negative shake. "No. Jake Peterson did not have offspring or heirs."

"His name is on our birth certificates," Libby said.

"Which proves nothing," Law shot back.

"Why haven't you filed the will with the state?" Sam interjected. "I have the estate in probate currently, and no will has been produced."

Because he'd need to have that sucker in his hands, wouldn't he? No way he was letting them know that. "Because I'm trying to deal directly with the owner on file, this...Liberty Management. That's you, isn't it?"

"Yes," she conceded. "I'm Liberty Jane Chesterfield," she said. "And my brother is named after Uncle Sam."

"Born on the Fourth of July," Law added, remembering what she'd told him in the bar.

Unbelievable. It had to be a con, and they were just a couple of scam artists who trolled properties of dead people and pounced.

"I'm a property attorney out of Miami." Sam produced a business card, as if reading the doubt in Law's head. "And I'm handling the estate and probate. So why don't you call this number next week, and we'll arrange a time to meet? You can bring the will, and I'll start the legal ball rolling to determine its validity." He put a hand on Libby's shoulder and started to lead her away. "Nice to meet you, Mr. Monroe."

Law grabbed Sam's sleeve without even looking at the card. "Not so fast, pal. Before I hand over a piece of paper you could destroy, lose, or discredit, why don't you get me some proof that you are Jake's rightful heirs, and I'll determine *your* validity?"

"I have no intention of doing anything to discredit said document," Sam replied, using that vague language of superiority that screamed attorney. How many stinking times had Jake griped about how much he hated lawyers? A thousand. Law never knew why, just that he did.

Because he knew his son was one?

His stomach rolled as the lawyer droned on. "…other than verifying that Jake Peterson wrote it and that it's been approved by a notary or an attorney and filed with the appropriate offices and departments."

Screw this.

"I have absolutely no reason to believe you," Law said.

"And we have none to believe you until we see a legally executed will," Libby countered. "Call Sam next week, and we'll look at your so-called will."

"So-called?" He let genuine indignation cover the truth. "Why don't we start with who is your *so-called* mother?"

She drew back as if he'd physically hurt her. "Leave my mother out of this."

"Not sure how we can do that," Law said. "Assuming Jake didn't give birth to you himself. Or is that your next claim?"

She narrowed her eyes at the sarcasm.

"Or did you two just dream this whole thing up to snag a valuable piece of property in the middle of a rapidly growing tourist destination?" he pressed, anger washing over him now. Anger and not a little bit of dread.

What if they were telling the truth?

Libby opened her mouth to reply, but this time Sam cut her off. "No, Libby," he said. "We won't have this conversation here and now. We'll make it official and on the record, not shooting off our mouths in a crowded bar. Bring us the will, Mr. Monroe."

Son of a bitch. Taking a deep breath, Law turned to Libby, trying to read the emotions in her eyes. All that playful flirtiness was gone, replaced by something he couldn't quite read. Distaste? Determination? A little dread of her own?

Or was that just the face of a swindler?

"The Toasted Pelican means everything to me," Law said, modulating his voice so that he hid just how much emotion was ricocheting through him. "It was promised to me by the owner, a man I called my closest friend. A man who should have known if he had kids."

"He did know."

"Bullshit," Law shot back. "And you know what else is bullshit? The fact that you two moved in, took over, and started renovations on my property. That can't be legal." And it sure as hell wasn't fair.

"We'll stop work until we resolve all legal issues," Sam said, as if it were a huge concession.

"You better," Law replied. "I have plans, and Jake was one hundred percent in agreement with those plans before he died. We lived in the same house and talked about it at length." He should shut up, but these two con artists needed to know he wasn't some casual acquaintance of Jake's hoping to score some prime real estate after his death.

Libby blinked at him. "You lived with Jake?" she asked, sounding more hopeful than skeptical.

"He was getting older," Law explained. "I kept an eye on him." Except Law had been at work when Jake had his stroke.

"Do you still live there?" she asked, sounding more than casually interested.

"No, but that doesn't matter."

"But you did, and that means—"

Sam cut her off with a hand on her shoulder. "We're not going to discuss this any further," he said firmly. "Call that number next week, and we'll strategize our next step."

Law eyed him with pure disgust. "The only thing Jake hated more than a liar was a lawyer. He'd roll over in his grave if someone told him his 'so-called' son was both."

He didn't wait for a response, but turned and strode across the deck with one thing pounding in his head, the sound of Jake's voice and some of his very last words.

You're only as sick as your secrets.

Holy shit. Was this Jake's secret?

Chapter Four

Libby watched Law leave, unable to take her eyes off his broad shoulders until they disappeared. Shoulders that could crush her plans. Shoulders that looked like they bore the weight of the world.

She tried to wrap her head around the fact that Law was that close to Jake Peterson. And *shared a house* with him. Not only did that mean he could have something they needed desperately, it meant...Law just dropped a few notches in her estimation. Who could he be friends with a man like that? What did it say about Law that he was?

"He doesn't have a will," Sam said quietly.

Libby whipped around. "What makes you say that?"

"Evasion, avoidance, turning the conversation around." Sam slipped back down on the barstool. "I've cross-examined enough witnesses in my life to know."

"So if you're right, that's good. Because, let's face it, Sammy. We aren't exactly bathed in an open-and-shut claim here. We have birth certificates but no other proof. And...an imaginative mother."

Sam shot her a look. "She's telling the truth."

"That's what we thought the first two times she told us who our father was. Or wasn't."

Sam puffed out a long, tired breath and picked up a flat beer. "Damn, we were so close to the one-year mark."

"Can't you use your lawyerly wiles to rush the courts a little?"

He shook his head. "When we hit the one-year mark on Jake's death, our legal wheel spins into high gear. We have to produce enough proof to win over a judge, or at least have no contest. I've pushed probate and property laws to the absolute limit, but if some dude waltzes in with so much as a few lines on a napkin and Jake's signature?"

Libby took the seat where Law had been, turning to glance back in the direction he'd gone, replaying the conversation. "He'll win, right?"

Sam snorted. "Excuse me, Lib?"

"I know you're the best, Sam, but if he has a will and we have forty-five-year-old birth certificates that have been replaced with a different father's name?"

Sam shook off the argument. "How well do you know this guy, this Lawson Monroe? Wasn't he some kind of loser at Mimosa High?"

"Hey, we were all some kind of losers at Mimosa High," she said, not quite understanding the need to defend him now. "But he was at the all-class reunion asking *everyone* if they knew who'd taken over the Pelican. I didn't want to get into details with him, so I kept him at arm's length and never answered, but he's been in the restaurant, poking around."

"If he has a will, he'd file it." Sam rubbed his square, handsome jaw, his razor-sharp brain and photographic memory no doubt calling up every property case he'd ever handled. "There's no reason to keep that secret. Especially if he lived with the guy."

"And you know what that means, don't you?" Libby asked, a new idea dawning. At the note of excitement in her voice, Sam looked hard at her.

"It means he has an even stronger case."

"And," Libby added, "it means he could have something—a hairbrush, an envelope, a damn nail clipping that we could use to do a DNA test. That would help our case. Could cinch it."

"I thought of that," Sam said. "But I didn't want him to know we're that desperate."

She slumped a little in silent agreement. "We certainly couldn't find anything in the Pelican that could be used for DNA. But, Sam, if we had access to personal belongings of Jake Peterson's, we could get what we need. And Law Monroe might have that."

"So...what are you saying?" Sam asked, smart enough to not like where she was going.

"I'm saying he has something I want, and I..." She casually grazed her fingertips over her décolletage. "Have something he wants."

Sam's jaw practically hit the bar. "What? You'd...do that? I'll kill him if he touches you, and then I'll kill you for letting him."

"Oh, Sammy, my hero of a brother. Do you think I'm so stupid to sell my body for a toenail clipping? Of course not. But I can...tease and torture and take what I want."

"Stop it," Sam said. "I won't let you put yourself in that situation."

"You won't *let* me?" She choked softly. "I'm forty-five years old, and I can do what I want." And it wouldn't be a hardship, she added silently, already anticipating the pleasure of the challenge. Nothing consummated, of course, but her pledge to stay celibate didn't include a little fooling around to get what she needed. "If I go back to his place, who knows what I could find?"

"Nothing you find there is going to help us, Lib," Sam said. "We need a legal paternity test with a witness to the collection and quality testing. You can't slip into his garage after a hot make-out session, find Jake's stuff, and grab an envelope he might have licked. That won't hold up in court."

"But what about DNA that *doesn't* hold up in court?" Libby asked.

"What good would it do?"

She leaned back and studied her brother. "Don't you want to know?" she asked. "Don't you *have* to know?"

"I know. I believe her." He looked straight ahead, silent.

"Well, I believed her when we were little and thought Mike Chesterfield was our father. Then I believed her when she got caught in that lie and some other nonexistent guy was our father. And then, wham! Hello, kids. Some guy who owns a restaurant on Mimosa Key is your father, and he's dead." She huffed out a breath of frustration and skepticism. "I'm sorry, but Donna Dearest lives her life as though the script keeps changing. While that's fine for her when she's running around Europe performing plays for underprivileged people like she is now, but it doesn't work when I would very much like to know who my birth father is. For real this time."

"She told us for real, and we have legitimate birth certificates with his name on them. Until someone else says we can't have it, his property is legally ours. If that guy has a binding last will and testament, then we have a fight on our hands."

She didn't want that fight, she thought on a sigh. "I finally have my life in order after two craptastic marriages and the challenges of motherhood. I have time, money, hope, and a future. And if I have that property, I have my dream. I want to live on this island, in the house we renovated, and run my yoga studio in town until I'm old, ugly, and Jasmine has a bunch of kids who call me Meemaw."

He slid her a smile. "You'll never be ugly, Lib."

"I can try."

"Okay," he said, patting her arm. "I'll do my legal best to make some of that happen. I hope that Law dude calls us, because if I have some time with an actual will in my hands, or even a copy of it, I might be able to build a case that says it's not legitimate and that Jake Peterson's posterity—that's you and me—get his estate in full. In the meantime, you stay away from him. I don't like the way he looked at you."

She snorted. "Like he wanted to kill me?"

"Not exactly." He finished his beer and stood up, grabbing his suit jacket. "Let's go up to the house. Is Jasmine home?"

She shrugged. "Probably not, and may not be home until morning." At his look of surprise, she added, "She's really getting serious with Noah."

"That bodyguard who works at the security firm here at the resort?" Sam asked, frowning. "She's sleeping with him? Jasmine?"

She laughed. "She's twenty-three, Uncle Sam. And I like him." But it sure got lonely at the house she and Jasmine shared on the north shore of Barefoot Bay. "Your room's ready, though," she said, her gaze drifting around and stopping when she spied shiny silver hair and a pale blue shirt over at the tiki bar.

Well, what do you know? He hadn't left yet.

Damn that vow of celibacy she'd taken when she signed her last divorce papers. If ever she were to break it, he would be the guy to do the job.

Except instead of lifelong acquaintances who'd been flirting with the idea of sex since they were kids, now they were both after the same property, and he'd probably be just another man she ended up facing in court.

"So, you coming?" Sam asked.

"Nah, I need to..." *Dig for DNA.* "Stop back at the Pelican and make sure the teenager I put in charge really knows how to lock the door and not steal any cash."

"You're down to the dregs of employees there now, I take it."

"Of course I am." Libby tried not to make it too obvious she was keeping Law in her line of vision. "You told me I had to keep the place running exactly as Jake did for one year, and I have." She'd spent as little time there as possible, but she'd had enough of a staff to keep it alive. "But I had to let those employees know their days are numbered so they'd have plenty of time to find new jobs. Most of them have."

"You still have two weeks."

"I can manage on a skeleton crew for two more weeks."

"It might be a little more than that," Sam said, leaving money on the bar. "Because when I go to court in two weeks, we have a tricky case. The provisional remedy the judge agreed to while the property is in abeyance is proving an intention to maintain the status quo through adverse possession."

Libby dropped her head back with a moan. "Speak *English*, Counselor."

"You have to run that business exactly like Jake did and cannot change a thing until it is well and truly ours, and then you can gut it, clean it, knock down walls, and build your yoga studio. But not one minute before I have that final order in hand."

"All right, Sammy." She stood and gave her brother a cursory kiss. "I hear ya. Hey, I'm teaching a vinyasa flow on the beach tomorrow morning at sunrise. Want to come and let me torture you with sun salutations?"

"I'd rather die. Or, at least, sleep. I'll have coffee with you when you get back. Will Jasmine be working or still MIA?"

"She's not exactly MIA. She's in B-E-D. With a G-U-Y."

He hammered his heart with a fist and invisible knife, grunting softly.

"You think it's bad when it's your niece?" She raised a brow. "Just wait until Ainsley is twenty-three."

"I'm locking her up when she turns twelve."

"Good luck with that."

"Anyway, I pity the man who takes on that little pistol," Sam said with an affectionate smile. "I heard her telling Chase that she was thinking the F-word really hard. Not saying it, just thinking it. Of course, he marched in to inform me that his little sister was swearing."

Libby laughed. "The bad sister and the good brother." She elbowed him. "History repeats itself."

He put an arm around her shoulders. "She could do worse than be like Aunt Liberty."

The compliment only made her feel guilty for what she was about to do. She leaned into Sam's strong side to thank him, but her gaze drifted across the deck just in time to catch a glimpse of Law heading toward the beach.

It was time. "Hey, I'm going to hit the ladies' room. You go on ahead. I'll see you up at the house later."

He gave her a kiss on the forehead and headed out.

The minute her brother was out of sight, Libby headed to the beach, a sense of anticipation tingling in her veins. Of course, that was only because she was closer to getting

Jake's DNA. That had to be the reason for all that tingling, right?

Maybe he shouldn't have walked away from that conversation, but Law had to think. At least that's how he rationalized his exit as remnants of the conversation echoed in the recesses of his brain, the words floating around like little bombs about to detonate. Deed. Bylaws. Articles of incorporation. Estate. Probate. *Legal heirs and biological father.*

It all made him want to…drink.

Law downed the ice water he'd ordered, but he was still sweating in the sticky summer humidity. He set the empty glass down on the tiki bar, resisting the urge to look across the expanse of the deck at the two people who'd just become his mortal enemies.

Instead, he kicked off his shoes and dropped them on the deck stairs and walked toward the beach, thinking about Liberty and Sam—twins born on the Fourth of July.

He could see their resemblance, even with different hair color. They both had beauty in the bones, as Jake would have said. But not a damn bit of resemblance to the man they *claimed* was their father.

But what if it was true?

Dragging his hand through his hair, he studied the crescent moon that hung over the midnight-black bay, leading him toward the low-tide surf where there might be a breeze.

Born and raised right here in the southwest corner of Florida and having spent a good part of his adult life in the kitchen, Law wasn't bothered by the heat. But tonight the oppressive humidity crawled all over him, making him itchy and angry.

No, it was this news that made him itchy and angry. And it would have made Jake cry.

Not that the old man hadn't been strong. He'd been an ox on the outside, but deep inside that crusty exterior, Jake had been as soft as melted Camembert. Finding out he had not one kid but two? He'd have bawled like a naked newborn.

But then he remembered what Libby said: *he did know.* So, he didn't care or tell anyone? Impossible. It was absolutely, categorically, out-of-the-realm-of-reality impossible. A con. A mistake. A misunderstanding.

A lie.

But who was lying? This mythical mother of theirs or…Jake?

Law stood still for a minute, the sand cool under his bare feet, the air finally drying the sheen of sweat on his forehead, feeling…something. A memory. A moment. A glimmer of the past that was, like so many of those that resided in Law's brain, faded and cracked by the years he poured too much alcohol in his body.

Hadn't Jake told him about a girl he'd loved and lost? Her name was…

Blank. Like so many pieces of Law's past, just a blank in his alcohol-drowned brain cells.

"Going skinny-dipping, Lawless?"

He spun at the woman's voice, inhaling softly at the sight of golden hair spilling over bare shoulders.

Libby walked with slow, steady deliberateness toward him, her face still shadowed from the light, but her exquisite body on full display from the skintight red top and sexy jean shorts all the way down to sweet bare feet. There was purpose in every step, and he knew exactly what that purpose was.

Sex was probably part of their scam. Maybe she thought she could screw Jake's will out of him. Well, let her try. Dear God, *please* let her try.

"Not alone." He flicked his collar and added a challenging smile. "Ladies first."

She came to a stop a few feet away from him. The lightest sheen of perspiration made her skin look dewy and soft. Sure, there might be a laugh line or three around those silvery blue eyes, and no doubt she had a few grays of her own covered with the help of a hairdresser at Beachside Beauty. But overall, this girl he'd gone to high school with twenty-eight years ago had aged to perfection as a woman.

"Don't ever dare me to do something unless you are one hundred percent prepared for the consequences," she said.

"The consequences of seeing you strip and swim in front of me?" He scratched the back of his head like he was thinking about that. "Nothing I can't handle."

She gave him a sly smile. "We'll see what you can handle, Lawless." She waltzed past him toward the waterline, but he stayed where he was, half expecting her to reach down and yank that red tank top over her head and throw it to the side.

But he knew better. She'd make him work for so much as a glimpse of her precious girls. The will, of course. That'd be her price.

If only he could pay it.

Very slowly, he walked closer to the water's edge where she stood, her back to him, her long hair floating like a golden curtain over her shoulders. Some people might say forty-five was too old for long hair, but like everything else about Libby Chesterfield, she wore it like a pro.

And he had to fight the urge to run his fingers through it.

Shit. If he couldn't resist her hair, how long could he hold out for that rack?

"Your pants are going to get wet," she warned, taking a few more steps.

"And tight," he teased, coming right up behind her, close enough for them to feel heat, but not touch. "Where's your brother? Lurking behind a palm tree ready to shoot me with a tort?"

She reached back and lifted her hair, pulling it up to expose the sinewy muscles of her back and perfect slope of shoulders. "He went to my house," she said without turning.

Which meant she wasn't inviting Law there tonight. Maybe she'd play her games on the beach. Sandy, but sexy. Hell, he'd go right into that water with her if that's what she wanted.

"Where do you live?" he asked.

She lifted her hand and pointed due north. "About half a mile past the end of the resort property."

"I had no idea you were so close. Oh, wait." He frowned, dragging his brain back over more whiskey-holed roads. "Didn't your grandparents live there or something?"

"They did, and I lived there with them, and my mother and brother, for a few years in high school. My grandparents moved away after the hurricane hit here about five years ago, which did a number on their house."

"They didn't sell to the resort owner?" he asked. "She was gobbling up all of Barefoot Bay after the storm."

"She tried to buy the property, but my brother and I talked my grandparents out of selling, and we bought the house from them and spent a few years renovating it. I live there now."

Holding her hair in one hand, she angled her head to one side, like she was stretching...or tempting him.

He studied the slant of her neck, the way her trapezius tightened and then relaxed. It was smooth, sleek, silky, and...feminine. Everything about Libby was pure *female*, and that just pulled him closer and made him want to wallow in...*woman*.

"Is that all from yoga?" he asked, letting his gaze slide down her arm the way he wanted his hand to.

She let the hair fall and started walking slowly into the inch-high water. He stayed on the hard-packed wet sand.

"That's my job, you know. I'm a yoga instructor."

So not aerobics. Something even sexier. "Does that make you a yogi?" he asked.

"Well, technically anyone who practices and certainly someone who teaches can be called a yogi," she said. "I'm still working to achieve that balance between the physical and the metaphysical, between natural and spirituality."

"Mmm. Sounds...esoteric and complex."

She laughed. "I'll put it simply, then. I'm certified as an instructor, and I teach classes right here at the resort, on the beach and inside the spa."

"Really? You work here?" Now that he hadn't known. "How come I didn't hear about that at the high school reunion?"

She flipped some water with her toes. "You were much too busy asking anyone who breathed if they knew who owned the Toasted Pelican."

"And yet you never said a word that it was you."

She slowed her step and circled her toe in the water, pointing it straight down with the precision of a dancer, then turned with her back to him again. "No," she conceded. "I didn't."

"Why not?" He got a little closer to her.

"I didn't see any reason to bring attention to the situation."

"In other words, you lied."

"By omission."

He recalled the time he'd seen her with his friends, Mark and Ken, in the Pelican. There was no "omission" in her answer that she didn't know who owned the bar. Maybe evasion, but that was lying as far as Law was concerned.

"Still a lie," he said.

"Maybe." She shrugged, bringing his attention back to her sleek shoulder. Why was it so fascinating to him, a certifiable breast man? There wasn't such a thing as a shoulder man. But Libby might make him one.

He lost the battle not to touch, lifting his hand and laying it lightly on the dip between her shoulder and collarbone, grazing lightly, just for the sheer pleasure of the contact.

Her skin was hot, damp, and as smooth as clotted cream. Without realizing it, he sucked in a soft breath just as water rolled over his feet and the hem of his work slacks.

"Aww. Did you get wet?" she asked playfully, tipping her head the other way as if to say, *Look, this side is just as hot.*

"Yeah." He kept his hand where it was, trapped between her shoulder and her ear. Getting a little closer, he flicked her earlobe with his index finger and put his mouth close to her other, exposed ear. "Did you?" he breathed.

She quivered just enough to know the answer, and then she took a few steps away, deeper into the water where she knew he couldn't follow without his trousers getting soaked.

Small price to pay, though.

Still, he held back, watching her as she waded a little farther out, the water up to her knees now. She turned slowly so her back was to him again, arms slightly outstretched, head back, hair long.

"Is that yoga?" he asked.

"Mountain pose, for balance."

"Oh, I could do that."

"Anyone can do it, but it's harder than it looks."

He snorted softly. "Standing still?"

"Maintaining balance."

He took a few steps farther, ignoring the water drenching the bottoms of his pants. "I could make you lose your balance."

She glanced over her shoulder, the slightest smile on her lips. "You already have."

Two more steps and he reached her, placing his hands on her waist and leaning her from one side to the other. "You feel pretty steady to me."

"Inside I'm all aflutter."

He laughed softly and turned her around. "Is that why you came after me? To flutter?"

She gave him a coy look and all but batted those black lashes at him. "Not sure why I came here, but I did."

He splayed his hands, enjoying the sleek lines of her waist and ribs and then sliding his palms down over her hips. "I'm glad." He searched her face, looking past the high cheekbones and big eyes to figure out what she was *really* doing here. "I always had a thing for you."

"For my body."

"That's you."

She closed her eyes, clearly not loving that comment.

"And your rapier wit and sharp tongue."

She flicked that tongue between her teeth, like a little rattlesnake teasing its prey.

"Why did you follow me here, Libby?"

She arched ever so slightly in invitation. "I always had a thing for you, too," she whispered.

"And never more than now, when I have something you want."

She flinched imperceptibly, and he knew he'd caught her. But he let her flatten her hands on his chest and take her time appreciating everything she touched as she slid them up and around his neck. "What I want is…"

"Jake's will," he finished for her.

Her eyes flashed. "Not true. I mean, I'm interested to see it, but…" She tunneled her hands into his hair. "But that's not all…I…oh!"

A wave rolled into them, just strong enough to make her tumble into him. He held tight, pulling her the rest of the way to press their bodies together, the pleasure of her curves instant and powerful.

She looked up, her lips parted with surprise. "I lost my balance." She sounded a little horrified at that.

"Don't worry," he whispered, lowering his head to kiss her. "I got you."

Chapter Five

Libby's first thought was how soft Law's mouth was, how very sweet and tender and unexpectedly gentle. But as he angled his head to intensify the kiss, that other realization hit again.

I lost my balance.

A whimper caught in Libby's throat when their tongues touched, hot and wet and fast. He sucked her lower lip and dragged his hands over her hips to add some pressure and bring her even closer to him.

But she didn't even think about backing away. No, it felt so good to be pressed against this man, to feel his muscles and relax into strong arms, to drop her head back and give him a chance to kiss a trail down her throat.

Twenty minutes ago, he was the enemy. And right now, he was...sliding his hand over her backside and adding pressure so she could feel exactly what this kiss was doing to him.

And that was definitely not a belt buckle pressing against her shorts.

Another gentle wave lapped against her bare legs, the cool water splashing some sense into her. She reluctantly broke the next kiss.

Forget balance. She couldn't *breathe* with him. Libby, a yoga instructor. Breath was her life. But he was...muscular and hard and so, so *nice*.

The world-tipping feeling was just enough to knock some common sense into her. This plan was as stupid as Sam had said. It wouldn't work, and all that would happen was...

Sex.

Libby didn't do sex anymore. It only led to heartache and reminded her that men wanted her for one thing, so what the hell was she doing using that one thing to get what she wanted?

"I lost my balance," she repeated, as if saying that might get her steady again.

"You don't need balance." Law bent over to get his mouth nearer her cleavage. "You got me."

She squeezed his arms and used real power to back away before his mouth got one inch closer to the goal.

"No, no. That can't happen."

He backed away, taking her hands in his to pull her with him. "Maybe you'll do better on the sand."

"Maybe I'll say good night."

He blinked, obviously surprised. "But we have so much to talk about, Libby."

"We're not talking."

"We can."

"We won't."

He laughed. "Sweetheart, you're the one who tore ass down the beach announcing a skinny-dipping session. I was minding my own business trying to be pissed off at you, and next thing I know, we're...fluttering. And wet."

He was right, of course. She pushed her hair back, making it to the sand and glancing at his pants, which were soaked from the knee down. "Sorry about that."

"Are you?" he challenged. "Why don't you just stop playing games and tell me what you want from me? To give up the will? Give up the fight? Give up completely?" He narrowed his eyes. "That one isn't going to happen."

She blew out a breath. "Something like that," she admitted. "And it was dumb."

"It was nice," he corrected. "But not if you're going to freak out about it. What do you want? Just ask."

How could she? How could she admit that she and Sam had a weak court case, no DNA, and their mother was given to fantasies and gifted with a wild imagination and an incredible acting talent?

She couldn't. But standing here, trying to elicit an opportunity to have access to the truth by seducing Law or even teasing him? She couldn't do that, either.

She took a deep breath, filling her lungs and then letting it out the way she taught her students. Completely, so that there was plenty of room for truth and goodness. And logic.

If she came out and asked for DNA, the admission could compromise the case Sam had worked so hard to build and win.

She searched Law's face, aching to ask him, to trust him.

But trusting men who demonstrated that they'd pretty much say and do anything to get in her pants had never, ever worked out well for Libby.

She took a few steps backward, then turned toward the resort, because the smartest thing to do was leave.

"I have to be back on this beach at six thirty tomorrow morning to teach a yoga class," she said, starting to walk. "I better go."

"Without telling me why you came after me? What you're looking for?"

She managed a shrug and kept going back toward the

resort. "I wanted to kiss you," she called over her shoulder. "Now that that's out of my system, good night! I guess I'll see you next week."

She picked up speed, but he was next to her in two strides. "You gotta be kidding."

"Look, I didn't mean to tease you, Law. It was stupid and crazy. Blame it on the moon." She gave him her best smile. "I always did have a weakness for you," she said. "But I better go. I promised my daughter I'd be home."

For a second, he froze, then blinked. "You have a daughter?"

"Yes, Jasmine. She's twenty-three and on a date tonight, but I expect—"

"So you're saying Jake Peterson had a *granddaughter*?" He grunted softly, looking down and kicking the sand under his bare foot. "That is so damn unfair, I can't even talk about it."

"Unfair?"

"That is, assuming your story about being Jake Peterson's biological daughter is true. Is it?"

"How is it unfair?" she countered.

"If you are Jake's daughter, that alone is bad enough. If Jake had a granddaughter, too? That's just heartbreaking. The man lived his whole life—his *whole adult life*, Libby—with the sense that he'd missed the most important thing a man could have. Children. And yet, all along, on the same stupid island, lived his daughter, his son"—he waved his hand in the general direction of the resort to bring her brother into the picture— "and a granddaughter? Someone made a very bad decision when they chose not to tell him that."

"Someone named Jake," she shot back. "Who the hell do you think made the decision to not have his kids in his life? He didn't *want* us."

"Now I know you're lying."

"I am not."

63

"Then you've been told lies." He started to walk away, back toward the resort. "Ever think of that?"

Too many times in the past year she'd wondered, could her mother have lied? Stretched the truth? Rewritten the script of her life? All possible, but she couldn't let Law walk away thinking that.

"Jake wanted no parts of my mother," she said, catching up with him. "And made that perfectly clear when she told him she was pregnant, or they would have gotten married."

He shook his head. "That doesn't even compute. That isn't possible. Why would he do that?"

"Good question. She was twenty years old, the daughter of a prominent doctor and a socialite wife," she told him. "In 1970, when it was still pretty damn scandalous to have a baby without a husband. He acted like it was her problem, not his. Can you imagine?"

"No." She heard him take a ragged breath and could feel a surprising amount of agony in it. Was it possible he knew a very different man than the one her mother had described?

They walked in silence for a few minutes, neither one of them giving in, but no one continuing the argument, either.

"I knew him so well," he finally ground out as they neared the parking lot. "He would never do that. He was loyal to a fault, a friend to the end, lover of anyone in trouble. He saved my life more times than I can count."

"Then he had more sides than you know."

He searched her face, thinking. "Is your mother alive?"

"Alive and performing her way through Europe this very moment. She's an actress."

He snorted. "Perfect."

"That doesn't make her a liar," she said.

"Does she say they were dating? Serious?" he asked.

"They had a...thing is what we'd call it now. In the

seventies? Maybe they'd call it an affair? A romance? A roll in the hay? Whatever, it was serious enough for them to have sex. After that, he wanted nothing to do with her."

"So what did she do?"

"She left the island and lived with my great-aunt and had us in Indianapolis," Libby said. "After we were born, my mother married Mike Chesterfield, a much older man who adopted us. He died of a heart attack when Sam and I were eight, and my mother started moving. A lot. We lived in Cincinnati, Oklahoma City, San Diego, Vegas, and that's when my proclivity for getting into a lot of trouble made her come back here to live with my grandparents for most of my high school years."

His frown deepened, as if he were digging hard through his memory banks and having trouble coming up with…

"Donna," he said softly.

Libby felt herself sway. "That's her name."

"Oh man." He closed his eyes like he'd been shot.

"So he talked about her?"

"Not exactly. He told me once that there was a girl who he…he loved."

She gave him a disdainful look. "I seriously doubt that."

"That's what he said," Law replied. "He said she came back to Mimosa Key for a few years, with two kids. She was a widow whose husband had died when they were little. She never wanted to have anything to do with him."

It was Libby's turn to feel a wave of righteous disbelief. "That's not really what happened." Although, whenever her mother came back to the island, she certainly refused to go anywhere near town.

He just stared at her. "It's coming back to me now. He only talked about her once. It was in the bar. He was cleaning. I was…sobering up."

"So your memory is not exactly reliable," she pointed out.

"No," he said. "It isn't. But I'm pretty sure I remember this. He said she was a little crazy. Very artsy. Wanted to be an actress, but her parents wouldn't let her."

Yeah, he had the right woman. "What else did he say?"

"That he loved her, but he wasn't good enough for her."

Oh Lord. "We definitely have a disconnect here," Libby said.

He nodded slowly, reaching a motorcycle parked at the very edge of the Casa Blanca lot. "I have to talk to your mother."

"If you can find her. She's part of an international acting troupe called Enter Stage Left, and right now she's in…Spain? Portugal? Norway? We aren't sure. She travels the world to obscure places and puts on plays for people who don't get to see them. We talk to her about once a month, if that."

"But she knows the truth."

"And she's told us the truth." Hadn't she?

Oh God, Libby had to know. She had to know, and there was really only one reliable way.

She took a deep breath and looked up at him. "You know what would be easier than tracking down my mother and giving her a lie detector test?"

"I don't need a lie detector, but I'd like to talk to her."

"That's impossible, so why don't we clear this up completely? Why don't you give me something of his that might have DNA on it? Then we can put this thing to bed once and for all and have no need to rely on people's ancient, booze-soaked memories."

He gave a dry snort. "DNA? I don't have anything like that."

"An envelope he might have licked? A pen he bit? A

66

brush he used? Something that absolutely without a doubt was used by him and him alone? His personal things were cleaned out of the restaurant by the time we got the judge to give us entry—"

"Cleaned out by me while my best friend was in an eight-day coma," Law said through clenched teeth. "And after he died, I kept the restaurant closed for a few weeks. Then, the next time I went to the Pelican, I was locked out. Imagine my surprise."

She could, actually, because Sam had worked fast and pulled powerful strings to get what they wanted—temporary ownership.

"Our birth certificates convinced a judge in Collier County Court," she said. "And we created the shell company to keep the place running for a year, which is part of the legal case that will be decided on in two weeks."

"What happens in two weeks?" he asked.

"The court date to get the final deed to the property, one year after Jake's death. I've had to post ownership of the Toasted Pelican in legal journals every month for a year to give anyone a chance to come forward."

"How the hell did I miss those?" he asked.

She tamped down a wave of guilt, even though they hadn't done anything illegal. Just…sly. "Sam found the most obscure journals and buried the notification. He said that's what lawyers do."

Law looked skyward with unabashed disgust. "And if no one comes forward to counter your claim?"

"The court will award us ownership on the anniversary of his death."

"Does your brother want to own half?"

"He'll sell me his half for a dollar. Sam has no interest in a yoga studio."

"A…" He choked a little. "A *what*?"

"I'm turning the property into a sanctuary for women. Rooms for yoga and meditation, and possibly a wellness spa upstairs if I can afford it."

"A…" He looked like he couldn't even say the words *wellness spa*. "Why would you do that to a local landmark that's been on Mimosa Key since the year the island was founded? Do you not know the history of the Pelican?"

Didn't know it, didn't care about it. "Those are my plans," she said simply.

"In two weeks."

"If we win in court."

He didn't reply, taking keys out of his pocket and one more step toward the motorcycle as she waited for a barrage of questions that she surely deserved. Why had they kept it quiet? Why didn't she admit she owned the place when he asked? What was Donna Chesterfield really like?

"That was it, wasn't it?"

The question threw her, and she had no idea what he meant. "That was…what?"

"What you wanted when you came to the beach and tried to…lure me. DNA."

She looked down, unable to look him in the eyes and lie outright.

"Too bad it didn't work," he said. He lifted her chin with one finger to force her gaze on him. "I'd have liked to have been lured like that." He dropped his gaze over her body. "We both would have liked it."

Understatement alert. "Well, it could never have happened, anyway," she said.

"Never say never, Lib."

"Too late. I already did. I've been celibate since my divorce a few years ago, and my plan is to stay that way."

He opened his mouth, but nothing came out, making her laugh.

"Some people do just fine without sex," she added.

"Celibate?" he finally managed to say. "Libby, that's like Michelangelo not painting. That's like Joe DiMaggio not batting. That's like Mario Batali hanging up his apron. That's like a Ferrari parked in the garage, and a—"

"I get the idea." She flicked her fingers to shut him up. "You think it's crazy."

"I think it's...not healthy."

She laughed. "I'm quite healthy, thank you very much. Take one of my yoga classes if you don't believe me."

"I might."

"Tomorrow at sunrise." She took a step back and blew him a kiss. "See you then. *Namaste*."

But he didn't move, still in shock. "Celibate?" he croaked the word again. "I guess that changes everything."

The words hit her heart, but she covered with a smile. "That's the idea, Monroe."

Of course it changed everything. And it confirmed that he was like every other man on earth who wanted one thing and one thing only. And once they had it, they disappeared.

Chapter Six

Law barely slept through the night. He hadn't received the notice that he had to be out of the efficiency apartment yet, but it would show up today or tomorrow. He needed a plan, so he'd spent the night coming up with one while he packed his scant belongings.

Since anything that mattered to him was in storage along with Jake's stuff, he could fit his stuff in two bags, but that was still more than he could throw over the back of his bike. In the middle of the night, he shot a text to his friend Ken to see if he could borrow his truck in the morning and spent a few hours digging around the Internet for some free legal advice. Then he spent the rest of the short night thinking about Jake Peterson and why he would turn away a young woman he'd gotten pregnant.

Not a single plausible reason came to mind.

He'd finally fallen asleep when a tap on his door yanked him awake before six a.m. Oh hell. Already they wanted him out?

Chef Del must have gone insane last night.

But looking through the peephole, Law saw Captain Ken Cavanaugh looking crisp and alert in a blue uniform dress shirt, not Ritz-Carlton security. Even through the concave warp of a peephole, his friend looked every bit the hotshot hero firefighter with his short-cropped military cut and I-can-save-your-life-or-your-kitten shoulders.

They'd reconnected at the Mimosa High reunion when they, along with one other guy, Mark Solomon, had been roped into being on the planning committee. None of them wanted to do that work, but all of them had their reasons. And for the other two, things had worked out nicely.

Mark's determination to keep everyone from asking questions about his late wife had him rope a lovely woman into pretending to be his fiancée and ended up engaged to her for real. And Ken had his own adventures, hooking up with an ex, a move that changed his life forever.

All Law had wanted was a chance to spend a lot of time on Mimosa Key and find out more about the Pelican.

"It's early," Law said as he opened the door.

Ken looked unfazed by the hour. "I got your text. You really quit your job?"

"Yes, I quit my job." Law opened the door to let his friend in, unconcerned that he wore nothing but boxers. "And I said anytime today, not the ass crack of dawn."

"My shift starts at seven a.m. I thought you could go with me up to the station and then take the truck for a few days if you need it. I'll be on duty, and Beth has her own car."

"Thanks," Law said, silently appreciating how great it was to have a true friend again. "Gimme a sec to get dressed." He disappeared into the bathroom, leaving Ken to wait in the apartment.

"What are you going to do?" Ken asked.

"I have a plan."

"Where are you going to live if they're kicking you out?" Ken called while Law loaded toothpaste on the brush.

"Not sure yet."

"But you're moving out today?"

"That's why I need the truck," he mumbled. He spit in the sink, washed his face, and abandoned any hope of shaving.

"So your plan is you have no plan." Even through the closed door, he could hear Ken's disapproval of the non-plan plan.

But Law did have a plan. Grabbing some loose-fitting shorts that hung on the back of the door, he went back into the efficiency. "Life on the edge, my friend. Not the way you live with a wife and baby on the way." He snapped his finger. "I meant with a baby and wife on the way. I always get that order mixed up with you because, you know, sometimes *unexpected shit happens* and you have to roll with the punches."

Ken acknowledged the reminder and settled into the desk chair, his long legs crossed in fancy dark blue pants. "The order will be right soon enough. We set a date for a Barefoot Bay wedding the first weekend in October, but ran into a funny conflict."

"Which is?"

"Mark and Emma have the night after, same beach."

Law gave a soft hoot. "What are the odds, man?" he mused. "Can I cater?"

"I'd rather you just enjoyed the party, or parties. And, damn, you should hear the A-list coming to Mark and Emma's wedding. That guy knows everybody. He's got Adam Slater coming."

"The astronaut?"

"Yeah, and Jesse MacDonald."

"Jesse Mac?" Law's jaw dropped. "The race car driver? Forget catering. I'll hang out with legends all night."

"How could you cater, anyway? You don't even know where you're going to be living."

"There's always your truck," Law joked.

"Seriously, if you need a place to crash…"

Law huffed out a breath. "You, me, Beth, and the fat dog? What a cozy arrangement. I thank you, but trust me, I have it all figured out." He hoped.

"And for a job?"

"I'll get…something." Although he had a bit of a plan for that, too. A wild-ass crazy plan, but hey. You don't know until you try, Jake would say.

Law stuffed his last few belongings into a bag and looked around the place where he'd lived for almost a year. He'd left no imprint, no real memories, nothing. Welcome to Law's life, where a quick escape was always possible.

"Come on, Captain Cav. I'll tell you the whole story on the way. Brace yourself, it's a doozy."

While they drove to Ken's fire station in Fort Myers, Law gave up that silence the one and only attorney he'd met with after Jake died had advised him to keep. He could finally fill Ken in on why he'd been so eager to find out who'd taken over ownership of the Toasted Pelican and told him all he'd learned last night.

"So, basically, there's a property without a rightful owner, and we both have somewhat of a claim," Law finished.

Ken was silent as the story unfolded, then turned to give Law a long, hard look. "Man, you need a lawyer."

Law waved it off. "My attorney is Google and Google, and they tell me that 'possession is nine-tenths of the law.'"

Ken gave him a sideways look. "Google and Google might be free, but I'm thinking you want to hire a real attorney, despite your appropriate first name."

Law grinned. "I forgot about that. Well, possession is the plan I told you about."

"Why don't I like the sound of this?"

"Because you're a strict by-the-book kind of guy, and look where that's gotten you."

"It's gotten me to the rank of captain and about to marry the woman I love."

"Because she got pregnant. You wouldn't be settling down if she hadn't."

This time, Ken's look was sharp. "Then I thank God she did, because I've never been happier. And maybe you should quit scoffing at the idea of settling down, because living like a college student at forty-six is just dumb, if you ask me."

"I didn't ask you," Law shot back. "And I choose to live like this, my friend. No roots, no ties, no family to rope me down."

"No life, no fun, no best friend to wake up with in the morning."

"What do you mean? Today I woke up, and there was my best friend at the door."

Ken laughed. "Whatever. Live your life, Monroe. Just don't screw up anybody else's in the process. What if she really is Jake's daughter, and they really do have a claim to the place, and you never produce this will? Then what's your plan?"

He was quiet for a moment, thinking of all the things that he'd remembered last night. "I do know that Jake had a thing for a woman—a girl, actually—named Donna. So there's that much to her story that's real. But the fact is, she doesn't have DNA proof, and I might be able to find it for her."

"So you'd help her win the place away from you?"

"I'll certainly let her think I'm helping her."

Ken's eyes narrowed. "That's shitty."

"No, look, if we find DNA in his stuff and she can get it sent to some testing place, fine. But it's not going to work. I did enough research to know that anything we find is going to be compromised. Also, a DNA test done by a mail-order place based on a few hairs found in a box of his crap won't work. There has to be some official third-party collector who verifies where it was from, and the results have to be more than ninety-five percent accurate and positive to stand up in court."

"So why are you helping her?"

"So she likes me."

Ken pulled into the fire station lot, shaking his head. "Just so you can have sex with her, Law? Why the subterfuge? It's not cool to do that to a woman."

"I don't want to have…well, I do, but I'm not going to. She's…" He swallowed before he said the word that was still pretty foreign to his thinking. "She claims to be celibate."

Ken reacted with a surprised expression. "Seriously?"

"That's what she said. But, whoa, she can give off mixed messages."

"Then why are you helping her if what she gets doesn't stand up in court? What do you get out of it?"

"Other than being a really good guy?"

"Or at least looking like one," Ken noted.

Law lifted a shoulder. "Well, yeah. But even more than that, she has to run the place for two more weeks before going to court. The Pelican is currently going straight to hell in a greasy saucepan, and I'm going to change that. That's all I'll ask in exchange for giving her access to all the DNA I can dig up from his stuff in storage."

"So she'll hire you if she wins?"

He puffed a breath. "I don't want to work for anybody ever again if I can avoid it. There'll be a delay, of course. There always is when lawyers are involved. And I'm going to make the Toasted Pelican so successful that she won't want me to leave. Eventually, the place will be making money, and then I'll work out some deal or make her an offer. I have the money to buy it if I have to."

"Then why don't you offer it to her and buy it now?" Ken asked.

"She won't sell. I have to convince her," he said. "Plus, she doesn't know I don't have a will. If their proof falls apart and I find what Jake says he left me, then I just saved a buttload of money, which I can put back into the business."

Ken parked, turned off the ignition, thinking and, Law hoped, seeing the plan that seemed to make so much sense in the middle of the night.

"Why would you find the will now when you couldn't before?" Ken asked.

"Because I couldn't get into the kitchen, back of the restaurant, or behind the bar," he said. "I know there are hidey-holes where he stuffed money and bills and shit. So I have a better chance of finding it if I'm working there. That's been a frustration of mine all along and one of the reasons I haven't told anyone but the lawyer I talked to when Jake died. I didn't want this mysterious owner finding that will and destroying it."

Finally, Ken nodded. "I guess, but I think you should just be upfront with her. Tell her your plan and make some kind of official agreement. Then you can relax, have a good time fixing the place up, and maybe…" He grinned. "Maybe she *will* have sex with you."

"Nah, then she'd want to get serious, and *that* official agreement would be too damn official for my tastes."

"Aren't you lonely?" Ken asked, obviously projecting the issues he had before meeting Beth onto Law.

Law smiled at Ken and slapped his shoulder. "Not lonely.

Told you, I just woke up to my best friend. And he gave me his truck."

"Don't forget Mark if you need help. He's around, you know. Working on the house with Emma, but she's really busy at doing the marketing for the resort and planning the wedding, so I'm sure he'd help you if you need it."

"If he can wait tables," Law said.

"Mark Solomon? He'd probably prefer to do it while parachuting out of a plane, but you never know. A friend's a friend."

"And you are," Law said, opening the door. "I appreciate the help, man."

"Anytime. I hope this works out for you."

"I do, too." Because if it didn't, Law was going to bounce again, and one of these days, he was afraid he'd bounce right back to the bottom of a bottle.

"Take a deep, victorious breath, hold it. Hold it. *Hooooold* it." With her back to the small group of yoga students who'd just settled on their mats for an hour of bliss, Libby lowered her arms to signal release. "And out!"

Behind her, they whooshed out their noisy *ujjayi* breath. Shifting on her backside, she lifted her right arm and placed her left next to her hip. "Follow my movement," she instructed, knowing the group behind her was likely a mix of experienced yogis and newbies trying something new on vacation. For the new ones, it would help to face the water and let them mirror her moves. "Lean all the way to the left and breathe in to fill your whole right side."

She inhaled and heard them do the same, although her

experienced ear told her someone's breathing was shallow and locked. "Now the left arm."

She demonstrated again, inhaling a deep whiff of delicious, clean morning air to clear a head desperate for more sleep. Last night's battle with the pillow finally ended at four in the morning, when Libby got up, had too much coffee and a little too much time to think.

"Now let's shift to a neutral tabletop, on your hands and knees." She turned sideways to show them what she meant by neutral, glancing at the five students lined up on the beach.

Make that *six* students.

Oh Lord. Was that even fair at this hour of the morning?

Wearing a black T-shirt, baggy shorts, and a grin brighter than the sun that rose in the east over his shoulder, Law Monroe didn't look like he'd done any battle with the bed the night before. He looked strong and handsome and so good on a yoga mat she almost cried.

"Let's move into our first cat-cow," she said, not taking her eyes off him as she took her next breath.

He winked at her, misplacing his hands, his butt in the air, his muscles bulging under the T-shirt. Okay, he looked great, but his form was atrocious.

She continued a steady, slow delivery of instructions, keeping her voice modulated and calm. Important because, on the inside, she suddenly felt anything but modulated and calm.

"Heart forward, pelvis tilted, and slowly exhale to cat. Remember to breathe with each movement." She got up to walk out of his line of vision by pretending to adjust the shoulders of an older woman at the other end of the line but stealing a look at him.

Instead of arching his back and then rounding it slowly with the beat of long breaths, he moved his back up and down with jerky speed like some kind of spastic hunchback.

Biting her lip, she worked her way down the line of students.

Law looked over his shoulder and raised his eyebrows like he needed help, but she ignored him. So he lifted his head and looked over the cats and cows being done between them, his green eyes twinkling even this far away.

No chance of inner peace today.

He cocked his head in invitation, and she shook her head ever so slightly as she returned to her mat, because her poor students had done nine cat-cows by now.

"Curl your toes, lift your bottom, and here's our first down dog."

She purposely faced away from him so that when she folded into an upside-down V, she could look through her legs and keep an eye on him.

His dog was an abject mess, with bent arms—gorgeous, ripped, ink-decorated arms, but they were bent. His feet were too close together, and his back was bowed like a rookie gym rat who didn't understand the pose at all.

Libby rose to walk through the students again. "This is your first dog, so pedal your legs and get warmed up before you straighten."

The woman next to Law was a rookie, too, and kept glancing at him to see if she was doing it right. Jeez, now they were both wrong.

Training and habit took her right over there, between them.

"May I touch you?" she said to the woman.

"Of course."

Libby pressed on the small of her back, whispering instructions so as not to bother the other students.

"You may touch me, too," Law said, smiling up at her. "Unless my form is textbook."

"If that were a textbook on function over form, you could be the cover."

He laughed as she continued her instructions. And didn't touch him because she'd never have the balance to get through the standing poses.

"Let's move to a plank." She demonstrated hers and glanced down at Law. And damn near fell on her face.

His whole body stretched out over the Casa Blanca-provided mat in a classic execution of power and strength. His muscles bulged, his back spread, and the curve of his rear end demanded intense scrutiny, which she gave it.

"That's…perfect." And then some.

He gave her a smug look, and she just shook her head because he was about to get creamed.

"Time for our vinyasa," she said, assuming the same pose to demonstrate. "Hover over the mat to *chaturanga*, knees, chest, chin, then a gentle cobra."

She glanced over to see Law effortlessly move through the flow, following her every move. Damn it. Was there nothing the man couldn't do? Once again, his look was pure cockiness.

No, this would not do.

Taking a breath, she started a sun salutation, moving through each pose with just a little more speed than usual. Then balanced it with a *kripalu* moon series that challenged many students. He struggled with the *utkata konasana*, but then, he was no goddess and the pose was easier for women.

All of his standing poses were okay, she noticed. Better than okay. So she pushed harder until she found his weakness. Eagle. Bird of paradise. Anything that required standing on one leg made him tip, but he didn't stop trying, which was endearing. And hilarious. And, somehow, still incredibly hot.

By the time they got to hip openers, she was covered in sweat, and her students were wiped out.

All but one, who wouldn't quit no matter how much difficulty he had moving that thick thigh into a pigeon pose.

And when it came time to a wheel, he just lay on his mat and watched her do the backbend with a gaze that…well, wasn't exactly how a student was *supposed* to gaze at his yoga instructor.

They all needed a nice long *savasana*, but even during that final relaxation, Libby's heart pumped and her breathing suffered.

A few moments after the last *namaste*, the students rose, thanked her, rolled up their mats, and chatted about the day ahead. She talked to them and said good-bye, and all the while, Law stayed cross-legged on his mat, waiting for her.

When the last of them left, she went back to her mat, sat down, and matched his pose, facing him. "So what did you think?"

"Easy."

She snorted. "Not a single bird pose was easy for you."

He lifted mighty shoulders, and she could see the sweat darkening the T-shirt. So, not that easy. "You call that a workout? Bunch of pretzel twists, balancing acts, and what's with the nap at the end?"

She used her hand to shade her eyes since she faced east and the sun was well over the palm trees now. "*Savasana*," she said, using the Sanskrit word. "Final relaxation. It's critical to a good yoga class."

"That one guy was snoring."

"A compliment to the instructor." She pressed her hands into the mat, narrowing her eyes. "What exactly are you doing here?"

He got on his hands and knees and slowly crawled over the sand to her, managing to be both predatory and silly. "Have coffee with me," he whispered when he was less than a foot away.

"Why would I do that, Lawless?"

He crawled one inch closer, so near to her that she could count his eyelashes and see the tiny flecks of gold the sun brought out in his green eyes. So near she could smell the heat on him and see every salt-and-pepper whisker in a beard that had grown even thicker overnight. So near she wanted to lean over and kiss that beautiful mouth.

"Three letters, yoga bear."

"S-E-X?"

"D-N-A."

She sucked in a breath. "What?"

"I got it, you want it, let's find it."

"Really? You want to get it now?"

"Let's start with a cup of coffee."

"Start with coffee," she repeated, mocking him. "Then what? Finish with another dip in the gulf? And why would you help me? How would I know it's real?"

He laughed a little. "Do you have trust issues with everyone, or is it just me?"

She let out a sigh of resignation and fell backward on the mat. He crawled right next to her, hovering over her, looking down in a way that made her want to wrap her arms around his neck and yank him on top of her.

"Everyone," she finally said. "And especially you."

He smiled and let his gaze skim her face, chest, and settle back up by looking into her eyes. "You were having more trouble in that class than I was."

"Only breathing."

"Because I make you breathless?"

"Yes," she admitted. "And you need to stop that right this minute."

He smiled like he had no intention of stopping any such thing. "Then have coffee with me and catch your breath."

As if she seriously considered saying no.

Chapter Seven

After they got coffee in the lobby, Libby suggested they walk back to the beach the long way, so they could pass by Chrysalis, the store where her daughter worked, but Jasmine hadn't come in yet.

So they wandered through the expansive Moroccan-themed lobby of the resort and talked about the last time they'd been here together, at the all-class reunion.

"Are you still in touch with the other two men from the planning committee?" she asked, thinking of the trio of fortysomething bachelors who had all the women whispering about "silver foxes" that week.

"Saw Ken this morning," he said.

She felt her brows raise in surprise. "This morning? Before sunrise?"

He just smiled as he pulled open the heavy glass door to one of the outside decks. "He told me that Mark and Emma are getting married right here in early October."

"Really? That's awesome. I'd heard they're engaged for real now and booked the resort for the wedding. Are you going?"

"Of course. And get this, Ken and Beth are getting married the night before, same place."

"What?" She whipped around, stunned by this news. "I didn't know they were that serious, though I heard they were dating."

"We've blown past dating. Baby boy Cav is due in four and a half months."

"So she's four and half months pregnant?"

"If that adds up to nine."

"But…" She did a quick calculation on a mental calendar, then her jaw dropped with the realization of when that conception had to have occurred. "They barely talked to each other at the reunion."

"I don't think she got pregnant from talking."

She laughed lightly, but something pressed on her heart…something she didn't understand and really didn't like. She wasn't jealous of Bethany Endicott or Emma DeWitt, who both found love through the high school reunion. She was just…wistful.

But Libby Chesterfield wasn't built for love, she reminded herself. She was built for sex, and every man she'd ever been with—including the two who married and divorced her—had made sure she knew that.

"Why the big sigh?" he asked.

Had she sighed? "Just so glad to see some happy ever afters come out of the Timeless reunion."

"And with the over-forty set, too," he mused, gesturing toward a table tucked into a private area of the deck and surrounded by bright purple bougainvillea. "What about you, Libby? How is it possible you can stay single?"

"I guess it's a case of been there, done that, have the alimony to prove it doesn't work. And you? How many times have you walked down the aisle and then met with a lawyer over the years?"

"Never."

She wasn't sure if this news surprised her or not. "You've never been married, Law?"

"Nope. Not even close. I don't need alimony to prove it doesn't work."

"You can get all cynical without any help, thank you very much."

"You got it," he said, pulling a chair out for her. "I just look at me and my life and know that stuff doesn't work."

She studied him as he sat down at the small wooden table in the seat across from her. He looked even more attractive in sunlight than he had in moonlight. Rougher and sweatier and sexier, he was a man who called his own shots and didn't second-guess them.

She believed that if he planned to never marry, he never would. "You're not the marrying type?" she asked.

"I'm not...a connector," he replied after giving the word some consideration. "I have a few friends, some distant relatives, the occasional work buddy."

"What about women?"

"That's the occasional work buddy."

She almost curled her lip. "That doesn't sound very satisfying."

"Neither does two ex-husbands."

She lifted her coffee in a mock toast. "Touché. I walked right into that one."

After a moment and a sip of coffee, he said, "I think a good marriage is modeled for you, to be honest. My parents did not have one." He put the cup down and eyed her intently, the unspoken question hanging in the air.

What about *her* parents? One of whom had been MIA for her entire life.

"My mother was probably not the best role model,

either," she finally said. "But it was never dull with her, I'll tell you that."

"If we have the same Donna in mind, I can tell you that Jake loved her. Enough that he remembered her and talked about her many, many years later."

"Loved?" She snorted softly. "He was twenty-nine and getting some action from a local girl almost ten years his junior. I'm pretty sure the L-word wasn't tossed around, at least not with any seriousness."

"But if this is the same woman—and it seems likely it is—he told me he never met another girl who even came close to her. And, yes, he called her a girl."

"She was twenty at the time," she said. "Qualifies as a girl."

"And, for the record, he certainly didn't know you and your brother were his," Law said. "He would have told me that. He would have…" He closed his eyes. "He would have loved that."

She tipped her head and gave him a look that she hoped communicated just how naïve he sounded. "You better reach up and take your pal Jake off the pedestal you've stuck him on, Law. Or let me tell you what my mother has told me and he'll topple right over and crack into a million pieces…just like Donna Chesterfield's heart when the father of her babies acted like he didn't know her name when she got knocked up."

"Knocked up." He sounded like the phrase was completely foreign, or at least it was where his precious Jake was concerned.

"Yeah, someone didn't wear a raincoat, but in their defense, it was 1970, and I'm sure your saintly friend promised to pull out in time."

He inched back, holding his hands up. "Stop." He looked

beyond her at the water, thinking but silent for a moment. "Why didn't you or your brother confront him about this when he was still alive? Why wait until after he's gone and can't defend himself?"

"Because we never knew Jake Peterson existed, beyond some guy who owned a restaurant we'd never walked into in high school."

"Then who did you think was your father?"

Libby took a breath and exhaled before she started her story. It was never easy talking about her mother, and with what was at stake here? She had to be very careful not to say too much. She really shouldn't even have this conversation until she cleared it with Sam, but Law had shown up and seemed…reasonable.

She could take a chance and give him some of the history.

"Growing up, I thought my father was the man married to my mother, like a normal kid. Mike Chesterfield was mistaken for my grandfather a lot because he was much older than my mother. He died when I was eight, and she never remarried and never mentioned the name Jake Peterson until almost a year ago."

He looked at her, skeptical. "She told you *after* Jake died? How? Why?"

She remembered the night Mom had sat Libby and Sam at her kitchen table to tell them news that rocked both their worlds. *Again.*

"Like I mentioned, we renovated my grandparents' house in Barefoot Bay, and we all used it as a weekend getaway when we needed a break from Miami. About a year or so ago, my daughter, Jasmine, and I had been over here for a long weekend, and on the way out of town, we grabbed a local newspaper at the Super Min. That paper was still in my car the next time I picked up my mother. I had to run into a store for a minute, and when I came out, she was reading an article about the death of a local business proprietor."

She closed her eyes and remembered the sight of her mother, deadly white and unable to speak. "I figured someone she knew had died, because she was pretty upset."

"And she told you right then? Just pointed to the paper and said, 'This Jake Peterson guy was your father'?"

"No," she said. "In fact, she didn't say a word." Her mother sometimes sat a little to the left of lunacy, but not that time. "A few days later, she wanted Sam and me to come to her house in Miami Beach. I knew as soon as we sat down that it had to do with our real dad."

"Even though you thought Mike Chesterfield was your dad."

She sighed and took a sip of the coffee, wanting to pour out the truth, but knowing when he heard what her mother had done, he'd doubt everything she said.

But he was offering to help with the DNA, so didn't he deserve the truth? Plus, what else could she tell him except what had actually happened?

"I *did* think Mike was my dad, until I was fourteen."

"Then what?"

Then hell broke loose. "We were living in Vegas, our fourth move in six years after Mike died. The great-aunt who'd taken care of my mother when she was pregnant passed away, and we all went back to Indianapolis for her funeral. One of my older cousins pulled me aside and asked me if my mother had told us the truth yet about our real father."

"Jeez. That had to be a shocker to a kid."

"You have no idea." She closed her eyes and remembered how hard that had hit her at fourteen. Forget losing balance. Libby had fallen flat on her face, and it hurt. Bad.

"It was like he died all over again that day. My mother told us that Mike married her when we were a year old and adopted us and had birth certificates made with his name. They made the decision not to tell us he wasn't our birth father because Mike loved us and didn't want that to separate us from him. But that day, when I was fourteen, Mom told us…a different story."

He looked hard at her, the doubt she didn't want to see already building like storms in his eyes. "But not about Jake."

"She told us that she'd gotten pregnant by a soldier who was in Florida on leave during the Vietnam War and that she wasn't sure of his last name, but she thought he must have died, because he never came back for her. It was, actually, the story she told her parents and great-aunt, and the one they all believed. Still, today, they believe that. No one knows about Jake but Sam and me. And the judge."

He lifted one incredibly dubious brow. "Sounds like your mother has some imagination. And maybe a few issues."

She took a slow breath, feeling like one of Sam's witnesses on the stand, uncertain of what to say to that because…her mother wasn't a liar, but she wasn't always rolling around in a great big pile of truth every day, either. One never knew what was real and what was an act with Donna Chesterfield. It was part of her charm.

And part of the reason Libby spent her life trying to be grounded.

"I think she wanted it to sound romantic and not, you know, slutty. I was fourteen and pretty impressionable."

"So how, exactly, did this news impress you?"

It changed *everything*. "Well, the notion that I was a love child from a war veteran had me spending a lot of time dreaming that a handsome soldier might knock on the door someday, freed from prison or back from battle—I don't know—and claim us as his children." She dug a fingernail into the soft wood of the table, pressing hard enough to make a fine line. "That, of course, never happened."

"So how'd you handle that?"

She gave a dry laugh. "Let's just say that was the official launch of my difficult years. I drank, I smoked pot, I spent way too much time showing my ever-growing bosom to very interested boys, and I generally made my mother's life sheer hell for committing the crime of telling me one man was my father when he wasn't."

She remembered the pain, the emptiness, the sense of abandonment. Somehow, she'd come to terms with it. However, she'd been barely twenty-one when Carlos Sanchez careened into her life. He convinced her she was not a rebound relationship after his divorce, but the real thing. So real they didn't even need to bother with birth control. This was forever.

Jasmine was conceived, born, and they got married…until Carlos went back to his ex-wife and two kids, and Libby tasted abandonment all over again.

"So she finally told you the truth—or the latest version of it—after Jake died?" Law asked.

The latest version of it. "I don't blame you for being skeptical," she conceded. "I was."

"What made you stop being skeptical?"

She managed a smile and held back the truth, which was that she was still skeptical. But who would lie three times about the identity of a biological father? Who would do that to a person? Her mother wasn't mean or heartless, just a little unstable. Which was why balance was so important to Libby.

"She told us she waited until he died, because she didn't

want us going after him and demanding…anything," Libby said.

"Why the hell not?" he shot back. "Maybe he would have liked to have known he had kids."

"He *did* know," she insisted. "He didn't want to help her. He told her to 'handle it,' whatever that means, I assume an abortion. He wouldn't help her."

With each statement, he winced like she'd punctuated the comment with a slap.

"Sorry," she said softly. "I'm just telling you this because you can't put all the blame on her shoulders. And, to be perfectly blunt, she feels we're owed something from him."

Silent, he propped his elbows on the table and his chin on his knuckles, staring ahead, thinking. "And for proof, she has some bogus birth certificates that you already said were changed when you were adopted by ol' Mike?"

"She has the *original* birth certificates from July 4, 1971, that were issued at a hospital in Indianapolis. When she arranged for new birth certificates with Mike's name as our father—which is not unusual, adopting parents do it all the time—the originals were sealed with the county, but Sam was able to get them."

"But you can't be sure they are real," he said.

"They're real. Sam had the originals verified and checked. He subpoenaed hospital records and put the certificates through whatever legal loops he had to. They're legit."

"Okay," he finally said. "Okay. You have birth certificates that say Jake Peterson is your biological father. That's not *proof.*"

"Which brings us back to the DNA."

He nodded, turning his coffee cup as if they were his thoughts, doubts, and considerations. "I have what I kept of his in storage," he eventually said. "Not a lot, and maybe not anything that could help you, but I'll take you there and you can look through it."

"You'd do that? For me? Why?"

"Uh, because I'm a nice guy?" At her look, he laughed. "I am, Libby. But the truth is, I want to know, too. If the DNA doesn't match, you can take that up with the great storyteller who raised you. If it does, we have the truth."

"The truth could cost you the Toasted Pelican."

"It won't."

"Oh, that's right, you have a will."

He crushed his empty coffee cup and stood. "And a way." Taking her empty cup, he gestured for her to stand. "I borrowed Ken's truck, so we can haul anything out of there if you want to take it home and go through it with some kind of an official taking notes. Or we can sit on the floor of a storage unit and you can go through everything yourself. Your choice, yoga bear."

She smiled at the nickname, and the opportunity. But the smile faded as she looked up at him. "There has to be an ulterior motive," she said.

"You really don't trust people, do you?"

"Would you if your mother had changed the identity of your father three times in the course of your life, the first man you married left you for his ex-wife, and the second for a new trophy?"

"Ouch."

She shrugged. "No, I don't trust easily. So why would you do this and not thwart my efforts to keep the place you've been willed?"

He braced on the table and leaned closer, getting right in her face. "What do you *think* my motives are, pretty woman?"

She met his gaze. "You truly believe I'm going to sleep with you?"

He got closer, his lips nearly on hers. "I've been waiting damn near thirty years to get you back in a closet, Lib. No whiskey on my breath this time. Maybe I'll get those seven minutes in heaven after all."

Her whole being tightened and warmed and longed to give in to the urge to kiss him.

Of course he just wanted sex. But would that be so horrible? Her eyes closed as she leaned nearer. Not horrible at all. Inevitable? Foolish? Thrilling? But not horrible.

She braced for the contact, knowing it would be as warm and wonderful in the daylight as it had been last night. Knowing, too, that it was a slippery slope, but she couldn't help herself from tensing in anticipation of a coffee-flavored—

"Hi, Mom." Her ponytail got yanked. "Whatchya doin'?"

Chapter Eight

A centimeter from pressing his lips to Libby's, Law straightened at the unexpected voice of a young woman who'd snuck up on them. He met jet-black eyes framed by dramatic brows and a cascade of raven hair. Olive-toned skin, bright white teeth, and a long, lean body that was more angles than curves completed the exotic look of someone who could easily stroll down any runway in New York.

Then her words hit him.

Mom?

"You must be Jasmine," he said without missing a beat.

"And you must be the infamous Law I've heard so much about."

Law couldn't help smiling back. "That was fast. We've only been apart six hours since our moonlight stroll on the beach last night."

"Oh, I heard about you long before that."

Libby's shoulders sank in resignation. "Not sure I'm ready for this, but Jasmine Sanchez, meet Lawson Monroe. Would you two excuse me while I pretend to go to the bathroom rather than endure what I suspect will be a discussion that will either make me cringe or cry?"

"Why?" Law asked.

"Because my lovely daughter only has one flaw. She was born without a filter."

Jasmine laughed and gave her mother's shoulder a playful nudge. "Oh, Mom, why pretend it ain't so? She talked about you after the reunion a few months ago," she told Law. "And my uncle filled me in on the latest deets over coffee this morning." She put her hands on her hips and looked from Law to Libby. "Pretty sure Uncle Sam does not know about this clandestine meeting, though, *or* the midnight stroll."

"It's not clandestine," Libby said, pushing back her chair. "Law took my yoga class."

"Looked like he was about to take more than that." She grinned and checked him out with a playful flicker of appreciation in her eyes. "She said you were smokin'. I mean, for an old guy."

He laughed. "And she said you were a beautiful young woman," Law countered. "As beautiful as your mother."

Libby looked skyward at the compliment, but Jasmine gave a cocky flip of her hair. "Different, anyway," she said. "My dad's Cuban, and I got all the Latina color but none of the Chesterfield curves." She gestured to her body, which couldn't have been more different from her mother's.

"So you take after your father."

"Only in some ways," she said.

"Jasmine, aren't you late for work?" Libby asked.

She flicked off her mother's reminder and continued like no one had spoken. "Not that he's a bad guy," she added. "Dad's heart was with his first family, and he cheated on Mom with his ex. Now, one asks, does that really make him a cheater? We debate that often, and I love the guy, but Mom is right. Cheating is cheating even if it's with your first wife when you're married to your second."

Libby slumped back in her chair. "Wake me when this nightmare is over."

Law couldn't help laughing. "The skeletons *are* flying out of the closet at a pretty impressive rate."

Jasmine shrugged and tucked a stray lock over her ear. "Hey, I decided years ago that the thing that's wrong with this world is that people don't really say what they're thinking. Did you know they did a study and found that something like eighty-three percent of everything that comes out of our mouths is not completely true? Can you believe that?"

"Not if it's part of that eighty-three percent, I can't."

She let out a musical laugh and pointed to him. "Good one." She folded herself into an empty chair, as if settling in for a long, honest conversation. "Mom said you were funny."

"Really, Jasmine," Libby said. "By now there's probably a line of people outside Chrysalis waiting for you to tell them how bad they look in a white jumpsuit."

"And guiding them to a darker, more flattering color." She gestured for Law to sit, too. "First of all, I'm early. Second of all, don't mock my superpower."

"Your superpower?" He looked at Libby for confirmation, but she just eyed her daughter with a mix of adoration and dread.

"You see," Jasmine said, "women don't like to be lied to when they're shopping. When I first started working at Macy's, years ago, I straight up laid down the truth to my ladies. That dress looks like a hay bag, I told them. Those shoes will slice your toes off after an hour, I warned them. That top makes you look like a cow, I…" She relaxed into a sly smile. "Nah. I kindly suggested something a little less snug."

"And they kept coming back for more," he surmised.

"Exactly." She grabbed her mother's coffee cup, shook it, and looked exasperated it was empty. "Next thing you know, Bloomie's stole me, helped pay for my degree in fashion merch, sent me to New York, which sucked like a vacuum cleaner, and now I work at a little shop in the resort as a buyer and personal shopper." She grinned at him. "Didn't Mom say you worked at the Ritz in Naples? I bet you could send me some customers."

Wow, Libby *had* talked about him. And how could he stare in the face of such utter honesty and lie about where he worked? "I *used* to work at the Ritz as a sous chef," he said. "I didn't interact much with the clientele, sorry."

"Used to?" Libby sat up a little. "When did you leave?"

"I quit last night, about half an hour before I walked into the Toasted Pelican."

Libby's eyes widened in surprise, but Jasmine leaned closer. "Seriously? You quit that job? A sous chef at the Ritz is nothing to sneeze at."

"Well, I sneezed pretty hard last night. All over my boss and his crappy cognac sauce."

Jasmine hooted a soft laugh at the comment, but Libby just stared at him.

"So where do you work?" Libby asked.

"At the moment? Nowhere. You have any openings?" He added a smile. "I make a mean steak au poivre, and *my* cognac demi-glace will bring you to your knees."

"Oooh," Jasmine cooed. "A man who could bring Mom to her knees is a mighty man indeed."

"Jasmine."

She ignored the warning and Law's laugh.

"You should cook at the Pelican!" Jasmine said. "We could—"

Her mother held up her hand, and Jasmine instantly closed her mouth. Apparently, even Jasmine the Truthsayer had an off switch when it came to some things.

"We actually have somewhere we have to go right now," Libby said, pushing up to a stand. "Law and I were just about to leave for a...special errand."

"What exactly is that?" Jasmine asked.

Libby turned to her. "At least one of us in this family understands the concept of discretion, and I'm practicing it now. We're leaving, you're going to work, and I'd appreciate it if you didn't mention this conversation to your uncle."

Jasmine looked from one to the other, her eyes dancing. "I'd say your secret's safe with me, but you know better. Be careful, you two, whatever you're doing." She stood, too, and planted a kiss on her mother's cheek. "You were right, Mom. He *is* a sexy silver fox."

She pranced away, leaving Libby staring at Law, her cheeks growing pinker by the second.

"And that, my friend, is why I only had one child. She is enough."

"She's awesome, Lib."

"Honest."

"Refreshing."

"Terrifying."

He laughed and reached for her hand. "Come on, Mama. Let's go on a DNA hunt. Jasmine's not the only one who likes the truth."

Libby was sweating in the first five minutes inside a ten-by-ten-foot storage unit on the third floor of a massive metal building in the warehouse district of south Naples. She could *taste* the heat.

"Glad I didn't bother with a shower." She plucked at the thin top and sports bra and cursed herself for not changing from skintight yoga pants, which were supposed to breathe, but here in the mazelike halls of hundreds of garage-doored storage units, *nothing* was breathing. "I thought you said this place was air conditioned."

"It's air conditioned enough," Law said, turning cardboard boxes piled in one corner to read the labels. "It's only about eighty-two in here, which is a good twelve degrees cooler than outside, but it is August in Florida."

She fanned her face with her hand, leaning against one of the corrugated metal walls. "Air conditioned means under seventy-eight." Or, preferably, sixty.

Law paused in the act of moving a box, glancing at her with a tease in his eyes. "Maybe you're having a hot flash, Lib."

"And maybe you want to eat those pretty teeth, Law."

He grinned, showing them off. "Have they started yet? The hot flashes?"

"Not yet. How about that erectile dysfunction?" she asked with a fake smile. "You fill that Viagra prescription yet?"

He just laughed. "Nope, and any time you want to test that out, just let me know."

When he turned to get the next carton, she let her gaze skim over his back. Law's muscles bunched under his T-shirt, and his curved, hard backside was sheer perfection in gym shorts. Even his legs were strong, dusted with dark hair, and masculine. He might be forty-six, but something told her he'd never popped a little blue pill in his life.

And that just made her warmer.

She forced herself to concentrate on the stacks of boxes in the storage pod, along with a worn leather recliner that belonged in a dump, a mattress and box spring sealed in plastic and leaning against one wall, some kind of metal exercise contraption that looked like a torture device, and a Tiffany lamp that was probably the only valuable thing here.

"What are the chances?" she mused, looking around.

"Of that test run? We can make a go of it right here, Lib. That mattress is brand new, and listen, what do you hear?"

In the silence of the enormous storage building, she heard…nothing. The halls were long, and even the ones she couldn't see had to be empty, because sounds would carry and echo along the metal walls. "I don't hear a thing."

"Exactly. We're alone here."

"And the idea of stripping down naked in a filthy storage warehouse on a bare mattress with you is so appealing, I can't even talk about it." Except that it kind of was.

"I could find some sheets."

Smiling, she knelt next to a box he'd set down, the words *JP books* written in Sharpie across the top.

"What I *meant* was what are the chances of finding DNA in…books?" She slipped her finger over the packing tape.

"Slim. Maybe none."

That had to be true. "Are books all that's in the box?"

"As far as I recall." He hoisted another carton to the floor. "I think I made five boxes for him, so this is two."

"You packed these?" she asked, surprised by that for some reason.

"Who else?"

She had no idea. "Didn't he have other people in his life? A partner? Other friends? Customers?"

"I was closest to him, and I emptied out the apartment we

shared." He reached into his pocket and pulled out a penknife, holding it out to her. "Don't break your nails."

She smiled at the thoughtfulness and took the knife, using her forearm to wipe a trickle of sweat from her brow. "I don't know," she admitted on a sigh. "This is probably a fool's errand."

"Probably," he agreed. "But if you want to find something with his DNA on it, that something is only in this little storage box."

"How long did you live with him?" she asked.

"A few years. Five, maybe. I could see he had some health issues, and I needed a place to live and..."

When his voice trailed off, she looked hard at him. "And?"

He shrugged. "He kept me sober."

She paused in the middle of opening the box, frowning at him. "Were you like each other's AA partners or something?"

"Jake wasn't an alcoholic," he said simply. "I was. I *am*, I should say, since they train you to acknowledge it's never over. But, for me, it's as over as it can be."

She studied him for a long moment, unable to see anything that she would consider classic signs of an alcoholic. He looked healthy, strong, and completely in control. Yes, he'd been wild in high school and known to party hard, but so had Libby.

"I haven't had a drop for ten years," he said as if he knew what she was thinking. "And I won't."

"Are you sure?" she asked.

He moved another box. "I guess you're never really sure, but I feel like I am. I replaced drinking with cooking as my addiction. But it wasn't easy, and I couldn't have done it without Jake."

Jake Peterson, man with a heart. That certainly wasn't how she'd thought of him since her mother had revealed this secret almost a year ago. But Law's impression of the man sure was different than hers.

She slid the penknife along a taped seam on the first box.

"How did you get to be such good friends with him?" Libby asked as she lifted the cardboard flap gingerly, half expecting a bug to crawl out.

"He caught me stealing a beer from behind the bar when I was fourteen. I was thirsty," he said matter-of-factly. "And probably needed some attention."

"Where were your parents?"

He didn't answer for a moment, gauging her as if he wasn't sure just how honest he should be. "They split when I was thirteen," he said. "My mom moved away from Mimosa Key, and my dad ran a boat-rental business down at the marina."

"Your mom left? Is that why you were already drinking that young?" she asked, fully aware of how a shaky situation on the home front could lead a teenager down the wrong path. God knew she'd had her share of booze long before it was legal.

"I was drinking because..." He paused a long time before continuing. "I was a delinquent loser who discovered at a young age that beer and wine and especially whiskey give one the ability to think they are immortal. And I needed that."

"Why?"

"Because my old man did his best to try to kill me on a daily basis." He shoved another box in front of her. "Get to work, Lib. You look like you're going to faint."

If she did, it was because pieces were falling into place, and she didn't want them to fit. She didn't want Jake to be some kind of great guy with a love for certain people. It was easier not to like him. But Law painted a picture she'd never considered before.

"So Jake really was like a father to you."

He abandoned the junk and sat down on one of the boxes. "Yes, he was. And he said as much on his deathbed and many times before."

"You were with him when he died?" For some reason, that shook her a bit.

"Not at the moment, but right before he went into a coma and didn't come back."

She considered that, and how tough it must have been. "I'm sorry for you," she said, and meant it. "But it doesn't change that, to me, he was an absentee, missing, disinterested father who rejected his children outright."

"You think."

"I think," she agreed.

"But you don't know."

She didn't answer because she'd already admitted she was on a hunt for the truth. Didn't that mean at least some part of her wasn't buying her mother's story?

"Not knowing, not being one hundred percent certain, leaves a hole in my heart," she admitted, hating that her eyes were suddenly damp with tears, but there they were. "It's like a piece of you doesn't exist."

"And you think you can find that missing piece in here." It was a statement, not a question, and the fact that he got that made her see Law a little differently. He really did want to help her find the truth.

Her heart slipped around a little, and softened, thinking of the childhood he'd had. "I guess you know a little bit about missing pieces," she said softly.

"Yeah. It sucks when shit is missing." He pointed to the boxes he'd moved close to her on the floor. "Those all came from the apartment. There's another one from the restaurant. Everything else is gone except..." He pointed to the ancient BarcaLounger. "Jake's throne."

"He sat in that?" Libby asked, a shred of hope rising. "Maybe it could be tested or scanned somehow? Maybe we could cut the leather off from the armrests?"

"If you want him to curse you from his grave," Law said. "That was his most-prized possession."

She curled her lip at the once-beige-now-brown crappy chair. If that was his prized possession, what did it say about the man who was...her father?

"Don't judge until you sit in it," Law said. "It's pretty damn comfy after a day of standing on your feet running that bar and restaurant. Come on, dig through that box."

Inside, she spied paperback novels that were so worn the library would probably have turned them away. "Why did you save these?"

Law crouched closer to look in. "I saved those because books were...I don't know, *everything* to him. He loved to read. Spy novels, mostly. But anything. Mysteries, romance, thrillers. Jake read constantly, and the ones in here were from the bookshelf he called his 'comfort' reads. He escaped in books."

He pulled out a thick, cracked, yellowed paperback. "*Shogun.*" He turned the book to her. "He must have read this book a hundred times."

"Then put it down," she said quickly. "It could have his DNA."

He angled his head, pity in his expression. "I'm no DNA expert, but I'm pretty sure you need blood, skin, hair, or nails from Jake, not fingerprints on a novel."

"Maybe there's a hair in it," she said. "Put it aside, and I'll keep looking." She carefully lifted another title, the yellowed pages threatening to part from old glue. "No chance you accidentally kept a razor or hairbrush?"

"Not in that box," he said, reaching over the open container to touch her hand. "You need to know that I've been through all of this. I did this already."

"Looking for DNA?"

"Just…looking. And packing."

So all this stuff was compromised, anyway. "I still want to look," she said, lifting her hair off her back and snagging a hair tie from her wrist to put it in a ponytail. "I still want to know what made my biological father tick. I can't help wanting to know something about him."

"Then you're looking in the wrong container," he said. "All of that is right here." He tapped his temple. "And I'm happy to tell you everything you want to know about Jake."

She pulled out the top of her T-shirt and puffed air down her chest, sweat sticking to her now. "Your memories are…biased."

He lifted another book, another historical story by the same author. "So you think you're not getting the real dirt on this guy you're determined to hate posthumously if his story comes from someone who cared for him?"

"Maybe," she said. "And maybe I just want to have a chance to figure him out for myself."

He nodded. "Then let's take the boxes to the truck," Law said. "Let's get them somewhere cooler, and you can go through every single thing and catalog everything. But you won't learn much about the man by what he read and his old tax returns." He pointed to another box. "That's what's in here, if I recall."

"And in that box?" she indicated the third.

"Some clothes, I think. His favorite Blue Angels T-shirt he got at an air show we went to."

"Why would you keep that?"

"Because he had the best time that day. I couldn't remember him ever being so happy."

She studied him for a minute, trying to imagine this rough-around-the-edges masculine man getting all tender over someone's old shirt. "Seriously?"

He shrugged. "I don't know how much clearer I can make this: Jake Peterson was my best friend. He was without a doubt the closest thing to a real father I ever had and one of the few people in the world willing to go to the mat for me when I didn't deserve it. I loved the guy. I shared meals and memories and dreams and about four hundred gallons of non-alcoholic beer. I cried when he died. Hard. And I cried again when I packed up this shit, sad that I'd never see him or hear him swear like a sailor or laugh from his belly. I'm sorry if you want to hate this man you never met, but I don't."

She studied the boxes and books, the echoes of his speech still bouncing around her head and the little room. "Okay." She couldn't think of anything else to say, because in her chest, her heart was cracking into a million pieces.

How could Jake Peterson love someone who wasn't his child, but reject someone who was?

"Let me go get one of those carts, and we can take it all down in one trip. I'll be right back," Law said, his voice still thick with emotion.

When he left, she turned back to the carton of books, stunned to realize tears were blurring her vision, her own emotions rocking her. Sadness. Regret. Frustration.

And then an unexpected wave of fury shot through her, making her grip the fat novel in her hand. She wanted to rip it apart, to just tear the thin, beloved pages out one by one and burn them along with all the rest of everything Jake ever touched.

Swearing softly, she whipped the book across the small space hard enough that it thudded against the recliner and clunked to the floor. She heard Law's footsteps and the squeak of a rusty pushcart and didn't want him to know about her little temper tantrum. On her knees, she crawled to the book and snatched it up, but when she did, something fluttered to the floor.

Great. She'd destroyed Jake's collector's edition paperback version of—

A picture. She froze as she realized it was a thin photograph, the shiny kind with rounded corners that people had developed at the drugstore when Libby was a kid. She picked it up and squinted at it, gasping softly.

"Oh my God," she whispered.

"What is it?" Law asked, coming back to the entrance.

She stared at it for a long time, vaguely aware that a tear rolled down her cheek. Did she really need more proof than a photo of a couple saved for years in the pages of Jake's most beloved book?

"It's a picture of my mother."

Chapter Nine

aw settled next to Libby on the storage room floor, taking the photograph from her hands. There were four people in the shot, two couples.

"Is that Jake?" Libby asked.

Was it? Law squinted at the profile of a young man hidden under a mop of chestnut hair and wearing tortoise shell glasses, his prominent nose sticking out as if he wore a name tag. Time had softened the young man's jaw and bony shoulders, so none of that looked like Jake to Law, but there was the nose that always looked a little too big for his face.

"Yes, it is. I recognize his nose." He glanced at Libby, wondering if he should make a joke about how lucky she was not to have inherited that. But she didn't seem in a joking mood, so he shifted his attention back to the picture that he'd somehow missed when he went through Jake's stuff. Had he missed a will, too? Was he so grief-stricken back in those dark days that he hadn't looked carefully enough?

"Is that the Super Min?" Libby asked.

"Looks like it."

"And there's a pumpkin on the door," she noted. "Must have been around Halloween."

"I wonder what year," Law said.

"Before 1971, I'd guess, since that's the year I was born. We'd have to date this picture somehow, but I doubt that technology exists." She flipped the photo over, but the back was blank. "I wonder who those other people are."

The other couple looked significantly older than Jake and Donna.

"They're not your grandparents?"

"Oh God, no. Jake's parents? They have to be in their fifties."

The older man in the picture wore an old-school golf shirt and sported mostly gray hair and the handsome face that reminded Law of a 1960's successful "Mad Men" type of executive. The woman next to him had a more matronly look, with a stiff white top and frumpy skirt. Neither of them looked too happy, but a blind man could see Jake was smitten. Donna was smiling, too, but into the camera, not at Jake. She definitely looked happy, her eyes glinting like she had a joyful secret.

Maybe she was pregnant, Law mused, but kept that theory to himself.

"It looks like he really likes her," Libby said, pointing to Jake and her mother.

"I told you he cared about her."

"Then why would he…" She swallowed, not finishing the thought.

"Maybe you don't know the whole story, Lib," he suggested gently. "Maybe what your mother thought happened wasn't exactly what really happened. How's her memory?"

She shot him a sideways look. "Her memory is not in question. Her acting skills, however, are a thing to behold."

Making her side of the story even more questionable.

"My mother is…colorful." She held out the picture of a woman who looked a lot like Libby, only she had slightly darker, wavy hair blown off her face in a style not seen much anymore. Her smile was like Libby's, though, wide and bright as she held the sides of a loose, ill-fitting minidress in a mock curtsy. Even the pose was playful and clever.

"She looks like fun," he mused.

"Fun is a relative term." She fanned herself for a second, using the picture. "She's entertaining, that's for sure."

When she stilled her hand, he took the photo, angling it so he could really study the people in the shot. "I can see it," he said.

"How entertaining she is?"

"Why Jake would fall for her."

"Pffft. He didn't fall for anything, remember? He acted like he never met her when she told him she was pregnant."

Then something didn't fit. "They are right there on the street in the middle of town," he noted. "So he wasn't hiding the relationship. How could he act like he didn't know her if he took pictures with her right in front of the Super Min?"

She studied the picture again, quiet for a moment. "He doesn't look like he would break her heart," she conceded.

"He loved her. I distinctly remember he said he loved a girl named Donna."

"Anything else?" she asked. "Did he say anything else about her? Why they broke up? When he saw her last?"

Not a chance he could remember a detail like that. "Why don't you ask her?"

She chewed on her lower lip a bit, as if contemplating exactly how to answer that. Finally, she said, "Because I don't always believe what she says, but…" She tapped the picture. "The fact that he had a picture does lend quite a bit of credibility to her story."

"And mine," he added. "Why would he keep that if he didn't care for her?"

She sighed, not arguing that logic. "Tell me something about him, Law."

He thought about that for a moment and all the ways he could go with describing Jake Peterson. Heart of gold, salt of the earth, friend to the end. But something told him she wouldn't believe any of that. At least, not without an anecdote.

"When I was a teenager, maybe sixteen or so, I spent my first night at the Toasted Pelican."

She turned and looked at him, listening.

"My dad was on a rampage, and I was pretty sure he was going to kill me."

Her eyes widened. "Why? Why was he like that?"

"Because he blamed me for some bad shit that happened in our family," he said, not wanting to get into details. "Doesn't matter," he said, even though, deep in his gut, he knew nothing else mattered quite as much. "What you need to know is that Jake risked his own life and reputation to let me stay with him, to let me hide at his restaurant, and to make sure I ate, slept, had clothes, and didn't drink…much."

"How long did you stay?"

"That time? A month or two. But there were more instances, until I was big enough to really defend myself. I took shelter in that restaurant and with that man so many times. He never did anything but help me, over and over again, and assure me that I was the son he never had."

She listened, taking it all in, her finger running over the edges of the picture she still held. "It all comes back to that damn restaurant, doesn't it?"

It sure as hell did. "I guess that place represents something," he agreed. "For me, it was a sanctuary. Still is, I guess."

"And that's what I want it to be for me," she said softly. "Exactly what I want. A place where women can go and feel safe and healthy and strong."

"How ironic that the Toasted Pelican was that for me for most of my life."

"And here I am trying to take it away from you," she said.

"And here I am helping you."

She smiled at him, those tears still glistening in her eyes. "Why would you do that? Honestly," she added before he could answer flippantly. "Don't tell me it's for sex, because I know that's not the reason."

He lifted his brows.

"Not the only reason," she added. "Why wouldn't you go all hard-ass and fight me in court, waving your will and legal rights?"

He inhaled, so ready to tell her that he had no will. All he had was Jake's last words, but all she had were her mother's words. Plus, that picture reminded him that he hadn't scoured this stuff enough, not with a clear head.

"Would you believe me if I said I'm just a flat-out good guy?"

She nodded slowly. "Yeah, I'd like to believe that, but I don't generally trust men. Especially when they think there might be sex involved."

"You just said you know that's not the reason."

"The only reason, I said. Why are you helping me?"

He looked down at the copy of *Shogun* he'd seen in Jake's hands a dozen times, practically hearing the old man launch into a lecture about honesty, one of his hot buttons. Sure, Law could be completely honest about the will, but that could cost him everything here. He had to at least have one more chance to find it.

But he also needed to be *somewhat* honest with her.

"I need a place to live, Libby," he said.

She frowned, not quite understanding.

"My job came with a small efficiency at the Ritz, and since I walked out, they're going to evict me. Not the first time I've been without a home, so maybe you could be like Jake and let me take that mattress and crash upstairs at the Pelican."

She drew back, the request obviously surprising her. "I don't know," she said. "I don't know how Sam would feel about it."

"How do you feel about it?"

She exhaled, thinking. "I have mixed emotions, I'll be honest."

"What are they?"

"Well, on one hand, I want to say it would be a really stupid idea and I'm not letting you step foot on the property."

"That sounds like Sam more than Libby."

She lifted a shoulder. "On the other hand, it has been a sanctuary to you, and you need one now."

"So much," he said.

She was quiet for a long moment before talking again. "I've been screwed, Law," she finally said. "Literally and figuratively. Loved and lost hard a couple of times. And..." She flicked her finger toward the picture. "I've lived my whole life grieving the fact that I don't really know who my father was, but still clinging to the hope that he might show up someday." She touched the corner of her eye, wiping a stray tear. "So I'm very careful with relationships and...men."

"Libby, take sex out of the equation, please. I'm not going to pressure you. I'll stop teasing you about it."

Her lips curved in a smile. "Don't," she said. "I like it. And I'd be lying if I said I wasn't, you know…"

"Interested?"

"Human. Female."

"And way overdue."

"Way," she agreed with a laugh. "But living at the Pelican?" She shook her head. "I'm already going to get my knuckles rapped by my attorney for coming here today, but I'll talk to Sam."

It was closer to the goal. Not there, but closer. He doubted Sam would go for it. He needed a more compelling argument.

"I could work there. Cook for you. Run the restaurant since you're on such a skeleton crew."

Her eyes flashed. "Now that would be pushing it."

"You need the help, Libby."

She nodded. "Let me talk to Sam. Let me think about it. I'll call you. The restaurant is closed on Monday, anyway, so if we did something like this, you could move in tomorrow."

He'd have to accept that for now.

"And what do you want to do with all this stuff?" he asked.

"Let's leave it here for the time being. I'll just take this picture, if you don't mind."

"Not at all."

It was perfect, in fact. He could come back here tonight and dig through this stuff for the will.

So he'd been honest…mostly.

Chapter Ten

Libby sipped the last of some nice Cabernet that Jasmine had brought home and put her feet up on the coffee table, looking out at the bay as evening fell. Usually, this was her favorite moment of the day. Savoring a moment on the wraparound porch that faced the water, enjoying the Victorian-style home they'd all put so much sweat equity—and real equity—into. It was especially lovely when, like tonight, she could hear Sam, who had decided to stay an extra night, joking with Jasmine while they got dinner ready.

But tonight, Libby was restless.

Maybe because the day's events had riled her up, forcing her to think about things that were difficult to face. Simple things like, *Who was my father?* Or maybe it was because she'd spent just enough time with Law Monroe to be unable to shake the achy feminine longing she felt around him. The chemistry was hot and real, and old Libby would have jumped his bones ages ago. But after her last divorce, she swore she'd never let sex muck up her life again.

Still, with Law?

She closed her eyes and thought of him, remembering…his request to live at the Pelican. That's why she was unsettled. She'd yet to broach the topic with Sam.

She'd told him she'd seen Law and that they'd gone to the storage unit, and as she'd suspected he would, Sam dismissed the effort as a waste of time. He'd shown little interest in the photo, too, immediately reminding her that it wasn't proof that would necessarily stand up in court. But it did prove they knew each other, so Mom wasn't some con artist going after some stranger's property.

And what would he think of letting Law stay at the Pelican? Time to find out, she decided. Taking one more deep drink of the oaky red wine, she pushed up and headed inside.

In the kitchen that ran the length of the back of the house, she found Jasmine on a barstool at the island, while Sam stir-fried chicken on the stove.

"But why would he have her picture in an old paperback novel?" Jasmine asked, waving the picture and using a tone that suggested she'd posed the same question ten times already.

"She's obsessing," Sam said to Libby when she came in.

"How can I not over this picture?" Jasmine replied, her big brown eyes wide with a mix of awe and confusion. "I wish I could see his face and find some family resemblance, which, thank God, does not include that nose. And can we just talk about Gran's hair? It's so…"

"Farrah Fawcett," Libby supplied. "She was always a fan."

Jasmine waved Libby closer, using the picture. "C'mere, Mom. You okay?"

Libby smiled at her daughter's question. She was honest to a fault, but incredibly sensitive, at least to Libby's moods. "I'm fine, sweetie. Tough day is all."

She sat next to Libby and took a whiff of Sam's cooking, but that only made her wonder what Law was making tonight in his studio apartment that he'd just been evicted from because he quit a great job.

Oh boy.

"What?" Jasmine asked.

Libby looked at her. "What what?"

"Why are you moaning like life is too much for you?"

Libby pointed to the picture. "Just thinking about Gran," she said as a cover for her real thoughts.

"I can't even imagine her looking anything like this."

Today, Donna Chesterfield was a sixty-five-year-old firecracker who spent most of the year traveling with Enter Stage Left, a troupe about a half step north of community theater that lived in hostels and local homes totally off the grid, bringing musical theater to the ends of the earth.

When she wasn't on the road, she lived in Miami Beach with a life chock-full of friends and fun, taking acting classes, hosting crazy-assed parties for her pot-smoking cronies, and generally causing havoc with the over-sixty set. Her hair was snow white, about three inches long, and usually full of pasty product that made it stick straight in the air. Most of the time, she wore purple-rimmed bifocals and way too much handmade jewelry. The only thing that hadn't changed since that picture was taken was Mom's penchant for a paisley hippie dress, only now they usually skirted her ankles, not her mid-thigh.

"I guess if you look hard enough, you can see the real Gran waiting to emerge," Jasmine mused. "When, exactly, did that happen?"

Libby and Sam shared a look. They knew exactly when it happened—when Donna Chesterfield's kids were raised and she didn't have to carry the burden of single motherhood anymore.

"When we were little and still living in Indianapolis with Mike, she was just a run-of-the-mill 1970s mom."

"Donna's version of normal," Sam added.

"And looking back," Libby said, "I realize that when we moved a lot, she was starting to evolve. I guess getting away from Aunt Christine and family after Mike died moved that along."

Libby never once referred to Mike as "Dad" after her mom revealed that he wasn't their father. It was a personal rebellion—one of so many.

"But what about when you lived here on Mimosa Key when you were in high school?" Jasmine asked. "Did she start to do the acting stuff? The..." Jasmine held two fingers up to her lips and noisily sucked. "Evil weed?"

Sam rolled his eyes, his mother's pot smoking a major bone of contention for him.

"She was living with her parents, Jasmine," Libby said. "And my grandmother, unlike your grandmother, had rules in this house, even for a grown woman with two teenage kids. My grandmother was vehemently opposed to the idea that anyone in the family would be an actress, so Gran was a recluse up here, biding her time until we got through high school. She followed the rules and never left the house, and now we know why."

"Fear of seeing Jake Peterson," Sam said.

"But when Uncle Sam got accepted to the University of Miami and I decided to go to a community college in South Florida, then, of course, Mom had to come with us."

"Because going to college with your kids is so normal," Jasmine said.

"Her version of normal," Libby and Sam said in perfect unison.

The three of them—the Three Cheskateers, Mom used to call them—all packed up and moved to Miami and lived in different places, but they were still together. Sam went to a four-year college, of course, because he was ten times more ambitious than Libby. And Libby had taken some classes and done some modeling, but that didn't work out because her boobs were too big to look right in clothes. And Mom went…a little crazy.

"Her not normalness really started to emerge when she got into Enter Stage Left," Sam said. "When I moved out of the dorm and you got that little apartment near the Gables, remember?"

She remembered the apartment well. Especially the man in 3C who'd been recently divorced and craved her company because he missed his ex-wife. She put her hand on Jasmine's arm, so grateful for the one great thing to come out of the union with Carlos Sanchez. "I guess because Mom wasn't responsible for us on a day-to-day basis, she threw herself into her passion for acting."

Jasmine laughed. "And getting stoned."

"Not really," Sam said. "I swear she just plays that up to get a rise out of people."

"And by people, you mean *you*, Uncle Sam."

He grinned at his niece, lifting his wine glass in a toast. "You know me too well."

"What about me?" Libby asked, ready to broach the subject she'd come in here to tackle. "Do I know you well?"

Sam looked over the rim of his glass. "Considering we spent nine months in the same womb, I figure you do. Why would you ask?"

"Because I have a question, and for the life of me, I can't imagine how you'll react."

"Fire away," he said.

"Law Monroe needs a place to stay, and he wants to crash in the space above the restaurant."

Sam frowned at her, lowering the glass to the countertop. "Why would he want to do that?"

"Because he's worming his way in?" Jasmine suggested.

That was a possibility, but Libby wanted to trust the reasons were deeper for him. "It's always been a sanctuary for him," she said. "Jake let him stay there during some pretty dark days in his teenage years. And if that's what our father did, then I wonder if that's not the right thing to do."

Sam still stared at her, legal wheels turning so fast and furious, it was a wonder she couldn't hear his brain clicking through case law.

"He said he'd help in the restaurant, too," she added. "He's a chef, you know. And all I have are two pathetic teenagers who only sometimes come to work, and we're supposed to—"

Sam snapped his fingers and pointed to her. "It's brilliant."

"Brilliant?"

"Legally brilliant. In the case he makes a priority claim, we've demonstrated *sua sponte* in *propria persona*."

Jasmine giggled. "I love it when he speaks legal."

"It's Latin," he corrected.

"Meaning what?" Libby asked.

"Meaning we look good to the judge."

"How?"

"By showing we've taken every possible step to do exactly what Jake Peterson wanted, whether or not this guy produces a will, which I still believe he doesn't have, since he would have filed it as a party in interest and made a liquidated claim." He lifted his glass again, and this time toasted Libby. "By all means, say yes."

She stared at him, trying to ignore the low grade of excitement building in her belly at the thought of Law being close and constant during the next few weeks.

"So it's kind of like keep your friends close and your enemies closer?" Jasmine asked.

"More or less."

Was Law the enemy? "I don't want him to be the enemy," she said in a whisper.

"Because you want to sleep with him."

Libby shot her daughter the dirtiest of dirty looks. "Must you?"

"Mom, he was two inches from eating your face when I found you two this morning."

Sam's eyes were getting wider by the second.

"She's just making that up," Libby said.

Sam's brow launched. "Jasmine doesn't make things up, Lib."

Libby flattened Jasmine with a warning look. "Could you *not* be the world's most honest person, just this once? Could you possibly respect the mother-daughter secret code?"

She grinned. "I think you should, Mom. He's hot and super into you."

"He is?" Sam stepped away from the cooktop, coming closer. "Never mind, he doesn't need to stay at the restaurant. That was a dumb idea."

"I thought it was…*quid pro quo* and *sua…spumonte*."

Jasmine laughed, but Sam did not find Libby's Latin-butchering amusing. "Sleeping with him is a mistake, Libby."

"I am not going to sleep with him, Sam. I want the damn restaurant, and I want to do the right thing, and if it's legally wise, then let's do it."

Sam didn't answer, but returned to the stir-fry, his temper simmering as much as the chicken and vegetables.

Jasmine picked up the picture again, flipping it over. "Does anyone know what year this was?" she asked.

"Gran might," Libby said.

"If only we could ask her," Jasmine said. "I haven't had a text from her since Stockholm or…Copenhagen. I get those two mixed up. Somewhere cold."

"She won't be back until after the court date," Sam said.

"Pretty sure she planned it that way," Libby added.

"Well, she said the troupe was thinking about breaking for a few months after a spin through Spain, but you know Enter Stage Left. There are always some diehards who want to knock out *Our Town* in a foreign country with no satellite or cell service."

Sam nodded, but Libby could tell he was still a little miffed.

"Hey," she said, putting down her drink and coming around the island to hug her twin. "I'm really not going to sleep with him," she said.

He looked down at her. "I want you to be happy, Lib."

"Oh, okay." She gave him a sly smile. "Then maybe I *will* sleep with him."

He jerked back, his eyes flashing.

"Just kidding!" She tapped his arm playfully.

"Are you?"

"Of course." Maybe. Possibly. She wasn't sure. But she couldn't wait to call Law and give him the news that, once more, the Toasted Pelican could be his sanctuary.

For now, anyway.

Law sat surrounded by open boxes in the middle of the dimly lit and dingy storage unit, listening to Libby's voice, trying to pinpoint what he detected in it.

Excitement? Interest? A genuine wish to do the right thing or somehow collaborate on this deal?

All of those possibilities made him feel a little guilty for not telling her the truth about the will. He sure as hell hadn't found it tonight.

"Yeah, I have a bed in the storage unit." He looked at the mattress, still covered in plastic and perfectly serviceable. "And not much stuff. I'll bring it in tomorrow. Thanks, Lib. Will you hang out with me and help me move in?"

"I can't," she said.

"Chicken."

"Is that what you're cooking?" she teased. "Look, I have to go to Tampa tomorrow, really early," she said. "I have a two-day Bikram certification program."

She'd be gone for two days, and he'd have the Pelican to himself? Law wanted to smile at that, but something deep inside was a little disappointed. Which was just stupid. "Can I get the keys from you?" he asked.

"Yes, and I'll be back Tuesday, late in the afternoon."

"Great, come for dinner."

"To the restaurant?"

"Of course. If you don't mind me doing a little tweaking with the menu."

"Uh, I'm not supposed to change anything significant," she said.

"You can have a chef's special," he countered. "And I'll do something spectacular. Bring some friends."

"Are you sure you can handle a rush?"

Law laughed at the question. "Bring lots of friends. I can handle anything. What's your favorite comfort food?"

"Meatloaf," she answered without missing a beat. "Which is probably beneath your culinary tastes."

"And that's where you'd be wrong." Because bacon-wrapped Angus beef meatloaf happened to be one of his specialties and perfect for a gastropub. "Buckle up for meatloaf that will make you moan with pleasure, sigh with delight, and beg for seconds."

"Are you sure we're talking about meatloaf now?" He heard the playfulness in her voice, and the sexual innuendo, and it made him press the phone against his ear to hear every little nuance and breath.

"Meatloaf and...other things."

She laughed from her throat, the sound as much of a turn-on as if she were right there lightly stroking her hand over his.

"You sure you have to leave for two days, Lib?"

"I do."

Disappointing, but while Libby was gone, he'd move in, run things, and look high and low.

"Are you sure you can manage the restaurant for two days?" she asked.

Manage the restaurant, move in upstairs, search for the missing will, shop for a new menu, and serve the best dinners the Pelican's patrons had ever had. "Yes," he said simply.

"I like your confidence."

"I like your trust, especially because I know it doesn't come easy."

Another call beeped into Law's phone, and he looked at the caller ID, recognizing the main number of the management offices at the Ritz-Carlton. Honestly? On a Sunday night they had to call and tell him to get the hell out of that apartment? No worries, he'd be out by tomorrow.

"So I'm not making a mistake, right?" she asked.

"By trusting me to make a meatloaf that will make the angels sing? No mistake, I promise."

"Okay, I'll be there Tuesday, and I'll bring Jasmine and her boyfriend. Oh, and I'll leave the keys in the back on my way out tomorrow morning," she said. "There's a brick next to the back door that—"

"Slides out and hides the key," he finished.

"Oh, right, I'm not the first person to let you crash at the Pelican."

"And I'm just as grateful now as I was then."

He heard her sigh. "Happy to help."

After he hung up, he looked around at the boxes filled with the remnants of Jake Peterson's life.

"What the hell would you have to say about this?" he mused out loud.

But Jake wasn't there, and all Law got was silence. And the sound of Libby's sweet voice in his ear, which made him feel like he'd done something wrong. Or was about to.

Chapter Eleven

L aw moved around his kitchen with nothing but purpose.
His kitchen. That didn't take long.

Essentially, it had taken less than two days. That's how long it had been since Libby left him the keys to the Toasted Pelican and gave him *carte blanche.*

Well, maybe she hadn't exactly said *carte blanche*...but he'd taken plenty of liberties. It had taken ten minutes to drag a double mattress up to the empty space above the restaurant, throw it on the floor, and dump his bags. Move-in was a breeze.

Law went straight to the dining room, paring it down, cleaning it out, making some small changes to the aging décor that he'd longed to do but Jake refused to let him.

Damn, that old guy had been stubborn about a few things. Like that sixty-year-old faded Budweiser mirror and the mismatched Formica tables. There was "vintage chic" and "ancient fugly," and poor Jake had not known the difference.

But Law did. And when this place was his, he'd work on it with the same gusto he used on the 1965 Triumph Bonneville he'd bought when he was in his twenties, refurbed to perfection, and named, somewhat uncreatively, Bonnie.

Jake, on the other hand, had refused to change, renovate, or redecorate a thing in the Toasted Pelican. As the years had slipped by, the restaurant and bar slipped from quaint, to dated, to old and dingy.

But Law saw the bones of a great gastropub, and if he got his way, it would take a little time and money to make a statement that appealed to locals and tourists.

Libby only called him three times and texted five to check on "things," which made him smile and spend every spare brain cell wondering what she'd think when she got back. He also ignored two more calls from the Ritz management offices, because they obviously hadn't gotten the message that he moved out already.

But the whole time he worked, he searched for that will, his brain going over every word he could remember from that rainy night when he had his final conversation with Jake.

Find the will.

Jake had been clear about that. But hadn't he said he couldn't find it, either? So he'd forgotten where he'd put it? Foggy about a lot of other things, but he had quite distinctly said there was a will and that Law needed to find it. And that it wouldn't be easy, but he wanted Law to have the Pelican and "no one else."

That was what had motivated Law for the past year.

Oh, and he'd also said, "You're only as sick as your secrets," so...had his secrets been two kids he refused to acknowledge?

Law looked in every nook and cranny, around dusty booze bottles, behind pictures, and he even moved the old jukebox. That thing hadn't been loaded with new music since Law was a senior in high school, ensuring that every song played was from the seventies or eighties and pissed off the patrons. He'd update that, too, once he owned this place.

He searched the kitchen, the storage and pantry, even the refrigerators in the back.

Nothing.

A little demoralized by that defeat, but psyched for his first day of business, Law spent his second day concentrating on food, starting by spending a few hours on the mainland at a local farmer's market, where he decided exactly what would be on his first night's limited, but excellent, menu. While he shopped and planned, he thought about the philosophy that would run his gastropub, the emphasis on great food and a comfortable atmosphere.

The rest of the late afternoon, he'd been in the kitchen hard at work, during which the teenage cook cruised in for his burger-slinging shift, complained when Law gave him grief for chopping the gherkins too big for the remoulade, and promptly took off his apron and quit when told his crab cakes looked like donkey balls.

Like déjà vu all over again, Law mused, checking the button on an older chef's jacket, the only thing he'd unpacked. Good riddance to bad help, he thought, as he went to work on the crab cakes.

"Whoa, you're not Brandon."

Law looked up to see the twentysomething bartender, Dan, a local who'd worked here on and off in the last year. Law had befriended him in the ongoing effort to find out who'd taken over the bar.

"Brandon quit," Law said, wiping his hands on a towel before reaching out to shake Dan's hand in greeting. "And I'm hoping you don't do the same. I'm going to be working the kitchen for a while."

"Really? Okay, that's cool, Law." He shook Law's hand and glanced around at the spread of prep. "I mean, I know you're a chef over at the Ritz, but the Pelican management has been sending out the signal that we should all be on the lookout for new jobs. I really didn't think they were hiring anyone."

"I'm not exactly hired," he said. "Got a call from Sam at Liberty Management, and he asked if I'd help out."

"That's what Libby Chesterfield did for me on Saturday night," Dan said. "I actually had a tryout at a bar up on Sanibel, and I think I'm going to take the job. But I didn't want to just not show tonight, even though it'll be a morgue in here."

"I know we have at least one small party," Law said.

Dan tucked his hands into the pockets of his khakis, leaning his lanky build against one of the prep counters. "But it looks like you have big plans for the menu, anyway. No burgers made from wood chips with a side of soggy fries?"

Law laughed. "And don't even pour the wine that takes paint off cars. I stocked the bar with a few great bottles that will go well with the limited menu and a selection of craft beers."

At Dan's surprised look, Law gestured to the chalkboard easel he'd picked up from an antique vendor at the farmer's market. "It's all there." He'd already filled it out and thought setting it outside the front door would be a nice touch.

"The Toasted Pelican Gastropub menu?" Dan choked softly. "That's a new one on me."

"Just trying to class the place up a little," Law said, returning his attention to the crab mixture to make the next patty.

"We have appetizers now?" Dan asked, reading the list. "What happened to potato skins?"

"The eighties called and demanded they die."

"Crab cakes and coconut-crusted chicken?" Dan read, adding a whistle.

"Don't be impressed," Law said. "I didn't have time to slow-cook the duck confit or smoke that pork loin for the bánh mì. Oh, and it's not on there, but if someone wants a nice brie-and-beer fondue, I know I can whip that up because I've got the brie for the burger."

"Panko-crusted brie," Dan added, but then he laughed. "An A for effort, Law, but I really think you're overestimating the average Pelican customer."

Which was exactly what Jake had always said, even though he knew what Law could do. "We'll bring in the people with palates eventually." Law finished the last crab cake and went to work on the fresh pineapple slaw.

Dan inhaled deeply, an appreciative sniff for the aroma coming from the oven. "Come to think of it, you could attract a crowd with that smell. What is that, besides amazing?"

Law gave a satisfied smile. "Angus beef meatloaf wrapped in bacon. And for the vegetarians, the signature eggplant terzetto with three sauces."

"Holy shit. You don't even have a server tonight."

"We'll wing it," Law said optimistically.

"Well, I'll take this chalkboard out front and see what we can drum up."

"Thanks." Law picked up his knife, grateful for the backup and already thinking about those three sauces. That pesto had to have the right amount of fresh basil and—

"Um, Law?" Dan was back, still holding the easel.

"Yeah?"

"We just got our first rush."

"Really?" Law put the chef's knife down and came around the prep counter, wiping his hands on a towel. "Is it Libby?" He felt a kick of anticipation that surprised him with its intensity.

"She might be one of them, but I counted at least ten other people who all want drinks. Also, they told me there's another party on the way. Maybe more. Apparently, half the damn Casa Blanca staff is coming." He had more than a little terror in his voice as he picked up a red apron and started to tie it. "They're all going to want drinks. I better get to the bar."

"We can do this," Law said, walking toward the door to step out into the hall and peer into the dining room. "You handle the bar and food orders, and I'll..."

He lost his train of thought when his gaze landed on blond hair tumbling over toned shoulders and curves from here to California in a tight white minidress.

Holy sweet hotness.

"Just take that menu out and place it where they can all see it, start the drink orders, and I'll...greet the guests."

"You're the boss," Dan said.

Law grinned at him. "You got that right, son."

From the moment she walked into the Toasted Pelican, Libby was almost speechless. How had he made this dark, sad restaurant look so much better in just an afternoon?

Not exactly different, Libby noted, but sleeker, cleaner, fresher, and the whole restaurant and bar smelled like tangy onions and fresh pineapple, not four-day-old onion rings and stale beer.

And out walked Law Monroe in a white chef's jacket with his name embroidered on the chest. He looked calm, competent, and in control.

She hadn't even tasted the damn meatloaf and she wanted more...of the chef.

Unfazed by the size of the group, Law worked his way through the crowd with warm hellos, handshakes, and easy jokes, but she couldn't help noticing that he managed to find her almost immediately and give her a sneaky, secret smile.

Law's smile widened as he approached. "You have a lot of friends."

"I have a daughter who thought half the staff of McBain Security, where her boyfriend works, needed a night out."

"You're testing me," he said.

"Possibly," she conceded.

"Explains the dress." His gaze dropped over the V-necked sheath that Jasmine just happened to bring home from the boutique as a little gift for Mom. He angled his head in a silent compliment. "You think I can't cook and drool at the same time?"

"Not in the food, I hope. Can I introduce you to everyone?"

"If you stay right by my side." He glanced at the group gathering and talking, all of them looking around as if they already noticed the differences in the dining room. "It's like a bodyguard convention. Does your daughter think you need to be protected from me?"

"On the contrary, she believes I need a nudge. She picked the dress."

"Her drinks are on me, then." He gave her another sneaky once-over. "Come back for an after-dinner drink when all this is over, okay?"

"Only to inspect the kitchen."

He winked at her. "And the chef."

Jasmine joined them, holding Noah's hand. "Hope you don't mind us crashing your first night in the kitchen," she said to Law.

"I'm happy for the chance to cook for you," Law said, extending his hand to Noah in greeting. "Law Monroe."

"Noah Tippling." Jasmine's boyfriend gave one of his rare, but dazzling, smiles, proving that tall, dark, and handsome didn't ever have to be sullen. Noah was one of the most positive guys Libby had ever met and wonderful with Jasmine. "I've never seen this joint look quite so...clean," Noah added.

Jasmine elbowed him. "He's the one fighting us for the place."

If Law was surprised Noah was up on the situation, he didn't show it. He just took Libby's hand and gave it a squeeze. "It's not a fight. It's a battle of wills."

Libby laughed. "Literally."

They shared a long look, and all the noise seemed to fade and the people to disappear as Libby got lost for a minute in his deep-green eyes. He exuded confidence tonight, and a bone-deep happiness she hadn't really seen yet. It was as subtle a change as the décor, but just as powerful and, whoa, attractive.

He needed very little help charming the party of ten, greeting each of them, learning their names, and helping move tables to make one long one in the middle of the dining room.

When they started taking their seats, Law came up behind Libby, reaching around her to pull out her chair.

"So, can you handle this?" she asked.

"Ten or twenty hungry people? Easily." He gestured for her to sit down, and as she did, he whispered in her ear, "You in a dress I'd like to take off with my teeth? Let's just say I'd love to handle that."

She cursed the shiver that ran up her spine.

"Look at that," he said, grazing the lightest, most casual knuckle over her shoulder. "She has chills instead of the usual..."

"If you say hot flash, I'll call fifty more people to this restaurant tonight."

He straightened. "Bring it. I'm ready." He gave her shoulder a light squeeze and stood to address the group, gesturing to a cutesy wood-trimmed easel with a chalkboard on one of the empty tables. "Let me tell you all about my menu tonight," he said, bringing a semblance of quiet to the group. "And my philosophy of a gastropub."

"What the hell is a gastropub?" That came from Nino Rossi, a crusty octogenarian well-known for his amazing cooking at the resort.

"The concept emerged in the 1990s in England," Law replied without missing a beat.

"The English?" The older man scoffed. "They can't cook!"

Everyone laughed, including Law.

"You'll have to forgive my grandfather," the man sitting next to him said. Libby recognized the easy-on-the-eyes consultant, Gabriel Rossi, and on Gabe's right, a stunning blonde pointed at the older Rossi with a warning.

"Watch it, Gramps," she said in a distinct British accent.

"But you know Nino," Gabe said. "If it isn't Italian, it isn't food."

"It isn't," Nino insisted, making everyone laugh again. "And I know my way around a kitchen, young man," he warned Law.

"Good, because my only sous chef quit when we had a disagreement over his kitchen skills."

"You're alone back there?" Libby asked. How was he going to manage that?

"It's fine," he assured her. "And if you all prefer, I'll set up a tasting menu for the whole table, then you don't have to make any decisions."

Most of them liked that idea, but Nino had an issue with the three sauces in the eggplant dish. "Pesto, béchamel, and red sauce?" His gray eyebrows rose. "What the hell is that about?"

"It's like the Italian flag," Law countered without so much as a second's hesitation. "And I promise you'll love it."

Dan came up to her, smiling for the first time in recent memory. "Hey, thanks again for jumping in the other night."

"I was wondering if you'd make it tonight," she said.

"I got the job on Sanibel," Dan told Libby.

"That's great," she said.

"But, I don't know..." He looked at Law, who was talking to one of the men, joking around, telling him about the quality of the beef. "If someone like that could turn the Pelican around, the tips could be a helluva lot better, and it's closer to home." His eyes widened. "I wonder if that's management's plan. They're testing this guy."

"Oh, I don't know about that," she said, throwing a look at Jasmine, who was sworn to secrecy about the ownership of the bar, but *secrecy* and *Jasmine* weren't always words used in the same sentence.

Still, with the exception of Noah, she'd been quiet.

Jasmine took a sip of water as if filling her mouth with something was the only way to keep it closed.

"Why else would he be in here with a whole new menu?" Dan asked. "I mean, you should see the kitchen. He's like a maestro back there."

Libby had a sudden urge to go back there and watch the maestro work. Maybe not so sudden.

"So what are you drinking, Libby?" Dan asked.

"Something strong. Very, very strong."

Two vodka gimlets and a lot of conversation later, the food

arrived on artfully arranged platters, somehow combining family-style with culinary chic.

The party cooed over the food, and the big guys dove in and devoured, while two more booths filled up and a couple of people took seats at the bar, checking out that chalkboard menu that was getting passed around.

"He's going to be swamped," Libby said to Jasmine and Noah. "He'll never handle a rush like this."

"He's got it under control," Jasmine said. "And if people have to wait..." She lifted a forkful of the eggplant dish, which had, indeed, gotten Nino's stamp of approval. "It's worth it."

As another four people strolled in off the street, Libby pushed back from the table. "I'm going to help him."

"Why?" Noah asked.

"Because I don't want the business to crumble."

"*Right*," Jasmine whispered.

Libby lightly, but purposely, dug her heel on top of her daughter's foot as she got up to go help out in the kitchen.

Chapter Twelve

It was past ten when they ran out of crab cakes and meatloaf, but Law had somehow managed to serve thirty-six full dinners on what was supposed to be a slow night. With help, planning, and more prep time, he could double or triple that easily. In no time, he'd have a profitable gastropub.

"Any chance you could scare up one more order of that brie-and-beer fondue?"

Law turned from the cooktop he was wiping down to see Libby across the kitchen, a maroon apron she'd tied over her white dress, a round serving tray pressed to her chest, and a few tendrils of blond hair escaping a hastily tied ponytail. Her eyes were more gray than blue in the harsh fluorescent light, but whatever color, they were bright with the satisfaction of hard work and a good time.

He felt a smile tug just looking at her.

"You used the last of the brie on that burger, didn't you?" she asked.

"No, I have enough."

"Then why do you look like you're about to disappoint me?"

"You've got disappointment confused with devour," he

joked. "And I do have brie left, but I was saving it for an after-closing treat with you."

She lifted her brows and cocked her head to the dining room. "I'll tell them we're out." She started to walk away, but he snagged her arm.

"I have enough for everyone." He slid his hand down to hers, lifting her slender fingers to his lips for a light kiss.

"What was that for?"

"Gratitude. You saved my ass, haven't complained, and look so hot in that apron I could melt the brie on it."

"Hot? With these shoes?" She held up a sneakered foot. "Although if Jasmine hadn't come back with replacements to those stilettos two hours ago, I'd have let you drown in your own terzetto sauces. All three of them. Which were a huge hit, by the way."

He grinned. "Nino really liked that dish, didn't he?"

"Yes, he did, and that's like getting a top rating from Zagat's on this island."

"And the meatloaf?"

She gave him a sexy look. "Is there such a thing as a mouth orgasm, because I might have had one?"

"Only one?"

"With every bite."

"Yes." Law gave a little fist of victory and turned to the cooler to get the last of the brie, noticing the shelves he'd stocked so carefully this afternoon were practically empty.

"You really love feeding people like this, don't you?" Libby moved closer to him to ask her question, and he could feel her gaze intently on him.

"I do," he said simply, pulling out the cheese to start one more fondue. "Just like you love teaching other people how to breathe." He turned back to her, unable to resist brushing back one of those stray strands of hair, brushing his knuckles over her cheek. "But if you ever decide to give that up, you make a helluva server, yoga bear."

"Food is not my calling," she said, not backing away from the intimate touch. "But it is clearly yours."

What was calling him were her lips, but he reluctantly returned to the cheese, taking a sliver and placing it on his fingertip for her to taste. She licked it off, holding his gaze a few seconds past casual, the sounds of the dining room fading and the kitchen feeling warmer than it had all night.

She gave a tiny whimper of appreciation at the taste, then shook her head slowly, as if confused about something. About him. About this.

After a moment, he washed his hands and went back to the fondue, nodding for her to rest against the counter. "Take a break, Lib. And spill some secrets. They say the last hour in the kitchen is made for that, you know."

"Who're they?"

"Me and…me."

"Why do you want to know secrets?"

"Because that's what makes you tick, and I want to know you."

"You want to have sex with me," she corrected.

He looked up, serious. "*And* know you."

She sighed and propped herself against the stainless counter for a moment. "Well, I don't have any secrets."

"Everyone has secrets. You're just so used to living with them buried inside, you forgot you have them."

"Maybe." She drew the word out, thinking. "I mean, I have things. Issues. History. But I don't really keep secrets."

"So tell me a thing or issue or history."

She considered that, watching him work. "I married two men who fell for my looks and body. I loved them, but when that novelty wore off, they both crushed my soul and broke my heart."

"Idiots. Both of them."

"Not really. Not Jasmine's dad. He's a good guy who never fell out of love with his high school sweetheart. The second one? Not an idiot, but not a good guy."

"What happened?"

She shrugged. "The usual. But I had the world's most cutthroat attorney, Sammy 'I Don't Lose In Court' Chesterfield, so now I have…" She rubbed her fingers together. "Security."

He stirred the fondue, thinking about that. Security was nice, but not getting it that way. "So what did you learn from your two walks down the aisle or into the Justice of the Peace or…wherever people do that?"

She laughed softly. "Country clubs. People do that in country clubs. And what I learned is that sex is the kiss of death for me. Any chance of having a good, solid, lasting relationship is ruined once the mystique is gone."

He lifted the spoon and pointed dripping cheese at her. "Maybe *marriage* is the kiss of death," he said.

"Sex and marriage are kind of related, don't you think?"

"No." He laughed lightly. "Otherwise, I'd have died of blue balls years ago."

She smiled. "Well, in my particular case, with those particular men, the love and sex and walk down the country club curved stairs were tangled up together. But the truth is I've spent pretty much every day of my adult life being looked at, ogled, chatted up, and hit on. Men see me, and all blood heads south, their brains empty out, and they think with their itty-bitty boners."

He scowled. "And you think I fall into that category?"

"Not itty-bitty."

"And these men and shitty marriages are what made you decide that cel..." He shook his head. "I can't even say the word. That *denying yourself any pleasure* is the brilliant way to handle this particular problem?"

She didn't even smile at the sarcasm. "Yes."

He huffed a sigh of disgust. "It's not. And for the record, Lib, there's so much more to you than looks, and any guy, even one with an itty-bitty *brain*, would see that."

"Oh please. If you boil it all down to facts, I'm a yoga instructor who lives off alimony from past mistakes. Yeah, I've held up well over the years, but if you get under the surface, that's what you'll find."

"Are you kidding me?" He almost choked on how wrong she was. "You don't even have to dig under the surface to see how amazing you are." At her skeptical look, he put down the utensil with a clatter on the counter and took her hand. "Libby Chesterfield, you're an incredible mother who has the coolest and most amazing relationship with her daughter I've ever seen. You're a smart businesswoman who has secretly owned and managed a restaurant under some pretty difficult circumstances. You're loyal to your family— even those who don't deserve it—and loved by your friends. To top it off, you are motivated to make something out of your life, and you have a vision to build a business unlike anything I've ever heard of."

He watched her shoulders sink with each statement of fact, as if relieved of a weight or tension. "You see me that way?"

He angled his head and shook it, aching that this remarkable woman had a second of self-doubt. "Libby, do not ever question your worth. Trust me, I've spent a lifetime doing that, and it's crippling. And don't ever think that all you are to men is a...a warm body to use and leave. You just haven't met the right guy."

"That's for sure."

"And one other thing." Very slowly, he inched closer to her, the fondue forgotten because of the need to whisper in her ear, "Sex is fun."

She gave a wry laugh. "Until it isn't."

"I'm serious. Have you ever just enjoyed it for sheer pleasure without questioning yourself or the guy or whether he's in it for the right reasons, or without worrying about…a commitment?"

"Yes," she said. "And I felt like a teenage slut."

"Then, honey, you were with the wrong guy. Now you're a woman who deserves at least five orgasms every time because *it feels good*."

"And you think you're the right guy."

"Oh hell yeah. Did you taste my food?"

"It was amazing," she conceded. "But you're not suggesting I sleep with your lasagna."

"I'm informing you, not suggesting, that I make love like I cook, yoga bear. With attention to detail and a promise of utter satisfaction from beginning to end." He brushed her lips with his. "As long as we're clear about what we're doing, and you keep those pesky marriage and love ingredients out of the recipe, because you know they muck up the works."

She inched back, searching his face, her eyes dilating with arousal right before him. "Five?"

"Minimum."

"That would be—"

"Hey, Libby, you have a check for table six?" Dan's voice from outside the kitchen silenced her, and then she sighed mightily.

"Don't worry," Law said, giving her another quick kiss before backing up to a more professional chef position over the fondue. "We'll finish this conversation when the restaurant's empty."

She picked up the serving tray. "That's not what I'm sighing about."

"Then what is it?"

"The fact that I actually know which table is 'table six.' How did this happen to what was going to be my lovely yoga studio?"

"Nothing's happened," he assured her. When she walked out, he added what he knew she was thinking. "Yet."

Three. Four. Five.

Five.

Could he really do that?

Libby shook off the thought and forced her brain back to the stack of dollar bills she was trying to count.

But the whole conversation replayed in her head over and over again. Especially that little speech about what a great mother and businesswoman she was. That was good. Hell, if he made love the way he talked, she *would* have five orgasms.

Oh, Libby, are you that desperate for validation?

Of course not, she thought as she jotted down the night's bar take, blinking in pleasant surprise at the tally. What she was desperate for was exactly what he was offering: fun sex without any of that "marriage and love" nonsense or crap or whatever he called the things she thought she believed in but only got hurt by.

She'd have to make the first move, though.

She slid the money into a pouch to lock it up in the closet safe, walking through the dining room with new appreciation.

Even that square, clumsy old jukebox looked clean and shiny.

She went closer to it to skim the double-sided cards of dozens of song titles she recognized from years gone by.

"It still plays, you know."

She turned at the sound of Law's voice, standing in the doorway of the hall to the kitchen. He'd taken off the chef's coat and wore nothing but a thin white T-shirt that clung to his muscles and showed off a few inky swirls and words. Not a lot. A date on the inside of his roped forearm. Some spiky circles around a strong bicep. His gaze was intense, his steps deliberate as he came closer.

"It does?" Her voice caught in her throat, and she cleared it, digging for composure.

"Most of the time. Want to hear something?"

She took another long look, then shifted her attention to the flat surface of the jukebox, the song titles swimming before her eyes. "Sure."

He came up behind her, close and warm, but not touching. "Of course it can only be a song from before 1988. That was the last time this thing got updated."

"Why?" she asked, not turning, because he was right behind her and if she turned around...she'd have to make that move.

Was she ready?

"Jake didn't like change. Hey, there's one you like. *Blown Away* by Eddie James and the Lost Boys."

She smiled at the choice. "Danced to that once," she said. "With a cute boy who had a nice...belt buckle."

He laughed and reached around her, pressing the letters and numbers, giving her a chance to study his hands. Wide, masculine hands with a dusting of hair and a few scars she imagined came from knife nicks. Beautiful hands. Hands she wanted...on her.

"Damn it," he muttered, stabbing a button harder, his body touching hers as he tried to make the machine work. "Like I told you, temperamental."

"That's okay."

"It's on my list to fix and update this—"

The first few notes of a wailing guitar silenced him as an old number-one hit filled the bar.

"You did it." Libby turned into him, meeting a gaze glinting with victory…and promise.

"And now we have to dance again."

She froze for a second, surprised by her own uncertainty and the tickle of anticipation fluttering inside her. "I thought I was too old for this," she whispered.

"For dancing?"

"For…crushing."

He gave her a slow smile. "Is that what you feel?"

The guitar disappeared, replaced by the inimitable rasp of Eddie James's voice.

The storm is on the inside, deep within my heart.

Every time I look at you, I'm just torn apart.

"What I feel is…off-balance," Libby said. And right then, it never felt better.

"Then find something to hold on to, Lib."

Taking a deep inhale, she reached up and wrapped her hands around his neck as the tinny speakers worked hard to deliver the lyrics.

He reached for her waist, sliding his hands all the way around her to pull her close and sway to the music, moving to a beat much slower than her heart.

Libby looked up, threading her fingers and pulling his face a little closer. "You sang to me that night in the gym," she said. "It was sexy."

He didn't say anything, but nodded a little, as if he

145

remembered, or wanted to. Then he pulled her all the way against him and pressed their cheeks together. His beard scratched like she thought it might.

"The wind is whipping outside, and the rain is falling down…" His voice was low, delicious, and endearingly off-key. "Lightning streaks across the sky and…bees are underground."

She jerked back. "Bees are underground?"

"Well, what's he saying?"

"*Bees are underground*?"

"I thought those were the words."

"It's…" She couldn't talk as a laugh clutched her. "The *bees*? What would they be doing underground?"

"I don't know. Hiding from the storm?"

She tipped her head back with another burst of laughter.

"Well, what are the words?"

She caught her breath. "'And leaves its thunder sound.'"

He gave her an incredulous look. "That's better? What the hell's a thunder sound? Why not just say thunder?"

Her shoulders shook. "Oh, 'cause 'bees are underground' is the perfect lyric for a love song."

They both laughed a little more, but that faded into smiles, and then Law gently pressed her head back on his shoulder with a strong, capable hand.

"Is that what this is? A love song?" His voice was a little tight, either from laughing or another L-word he wasn't used to saying.

"Actually, it's what you'd call a classic makeout song."

"Now we're talkin'," he whispered, lowering his face to plant a light kiss on her neck and shoulder. "And I know the next line for real."

Chill bumps tickled as his breath lightly touched her ear.

"Baby, you're a force of nature, I just got to say," he

sang. "'Cause every time you kiss me, I am blown away."

She leaned back to sing the line again with him. "Every time you kiss me…"

His lips covered hers, stopping the singing but stoking the fire that was building low inside her. His mouth was warm and sure, his hands pulling her closer.

I am blown away.

Eddie James was deep into the next verse as Law heated the kiss to let their tongues taste each other. His hands dragged up and down her sides. Each touch was warm and seductive.

And that was no belt buckle pressing into her belly.

Their breathing was tight and fast already, louder than the next chorus and the screaming guitar solo. She broke the kiss to offer him access to her throat, arching her back, moaning as pleasure tightened and squeezed, making her want…everything. Every single thing he could do to her, she wanted.

As he kissed, she turned her head to the side, seeing the wide windows facing the street. It was late, and Mimosa Key had long ago folded up, but she didn't want an audience for this.

"Come," she whispered, walking him back to the hallway between the dining room and kitchen.

He understood, kissing her as they backed away, but then he stopped. "Don't forget the cash." He snagged the bag from the top of the jukebox, barely letting her go.

Inside the hall, he stopped to kiss again and reach around to work on the tie of her apron. She felt it loosen and fall forward, and he followed, dipping his mouth right into the deep V plunge of the dress she'd worn to torture him.

Who was being tortured now?

Pleasure licked through her veins as she felt herself melt

into his arms, a hot, sweet, achy need that pulled and twisted and made her let out a soft moan of surrender.

After a moment, he stepped back, his gaze hot and unwavering.

"I need both hands for this," he said, holding up the cash pouch. "Let's put this in the safe. In the closet?"

She nodded and let him step her to the door, where he opened it and glanced around before tossing the pouch on the empty table.

"Perfect," he said, pulling her into the tiny area. "We can pick up where we left off the last time we played Seven Minutes in Heaven."

Stepping inside, she knew the space well enough to know there was no place in here for a desperate couple to make out. One wall was floor-to-ceiling shelves, completely empty but for the cash safe she kept there. A table was pushed up against another wall, and the third wall was...

Behind her back as he eased her up against it, pinned her in, and intensified his kisses.

He didn't close the door, so the light from the hall spilled in enough that she could see him. She threaded her fingers into his hair, holding his head to keep his mouth where she wanted it—on hers.

Her pulse thrummed as she finally let go so she could splay her hands over his chest, coasting over every dip and cut, moaning in appreciation.

He did the same, starting at her shoulders and working down to the rise of her chest very slowly, as if he wanted to prolong the pleasure of getting to that destination. He gave her a sexy half smile, and his hands cupped her breasts, and his thumbs grazed her already budded nipples.

"Your prize," she whispered.

"You're the prize, Libby, not these." He gave a light

squeeze. "This is all a prize." His hands continued down, over her waist and hips, over her backside. He moved incredibly slowly, as if he didn't want to miss one sensation of his first time touching her.

He reached the hem of her dress and started lifting it up her thighs so he could touch skin. His hands were everywhere at once, but everything was so slow, she was nearly breathless.

As if he read her mind, his hand moved higher on her thigh, brushing the damp silk of her panties, making her eyes go wide as she gasped with delight.

"Let's get number one out of the way," he whispered, a tease in his voice and fire in his touch.

She kept her head back against the wall, biting her lip as he stroked over her panties with his thumb.

She moaned, helpless to do anything but let him work his magic. His mouth on hers, his body hard, his thumb relentless when he knew he found her sweet spot.

"There we go," he coaxed her. "Give in to it, sweetheart. Give in."

She closed her eyes and surrendered to a quick, sweet, intense orgasm that left her shaking, holding on to his shoulders, lost for a moment. She almost swayed right to the side, but he had her.

"How did you do that?"

He laughed softly and lowered his face to kiss her neck some more. "We're just getting started, Lib. You want two and three right now, or should we go upstairs to bed?"

She couldn't answer because there wasn't enough blood in her head to think straight. Instead, she dropped her head back and blinked, her eyes adjusting to the dim light.

Looking up to the ceiling, she just let the sensations roll through her, not thinking about anything except how damn good that felt. Nothing else mattered. Not that they were in a kitchen closet, not that they were headed up to a mattress on the floor. She couldn't even think about...the brown leather bag on the top shelf of—

"What is that?"

He drew back and followed her gaze. "What is...what? I don't see anything."

She tried to clear her head as she pointed, leaning farther back to see the edge of a leather bag that had been well hidden on the top shelf. "That, up there."

"Who cares?" He went right back to kissing her throat and sliding his hand up her dress, but she pushed him back.

"I do. Isn't that a men's toiletry kit?"

His expression darkened. "It may be, but—"

"Is it yours?"

"No, it's not mine." He pressed against her. "But maybe it has a condom in it we could put to really good use."

Her eyes flashed. "It's Jake's!"

He didn't move or speak, his brain most likely as short-circuited as hers.

"Didn't you say he used this as an office?" She gave him a nudge. "Go see what it is, Law."

"All right, I will." He closed his hands around her shoulders and pulled her into him. "When we're done here."

She gave him a nudge. "If that's his shaving kit, it would have DNA in it."

"DNA?" He choked the word.

"You know, the thing I've been trying to find but we haven't even talked about for days?"

He just stared at her, the look of a man trying very hard to muster a care, but failing.

"Or maybe it's something else," she said.

He blinked, suddenly lucid. "Okay, okay." He flipped the

wall switch, flooding the little area with white light and making Libby squint against the brightness.

"How the hell did I miss that?" He yanked the table a few feet closer and, in one easy move, climbed up and stood on the tabletop, reaching for the brown leather pouch-like bag.

"Be careful," she said.

"I'm not going to fall."

"I mean be careful with that bag. It could contain incredibly important bits of DNA."

He handled the bag with care, sliding it out slowly and gingerly handing it to her. "Here you go."

She took it with two hands and set it upright on the table, staring at it while Law got down.

It was a dark brown leather Dopp kit with three initials engraved on the side.

JDP

"Jacob David Peterson," Law said, his gaze on the same letters.

"It's his," she said softly, reaching to the zipper.

"It most certainly is," he confirmed. "He kept it in here because sometimes he slept here and used the bathroom in the back of the kitchen. You want to open it, or do you want me to?"

"I will." She pulled the zipper slowly, widening the mouth of the bag and peering in to see a toothbrush, razor, shaving cream, dental floss, a few Band-Aids, and a hairbrush with at least a hundred gray hairs clinging to the fibers.

"Congratulations, Lib. You found the DNA mother lode."

Chapter Thirteen

"Do you think I need an attorney with me?" It was a rhetorical question, and Law knew it when he asked Ken. He had no intention of getting a lawyer, but he did respect Ken's opinion, and he'd spent the better part of their drive from Fort Myers to the Ritz in Naples to get Law's bike filling his friend in on the latest in the Jake situation.

Which was simple: they'd found the proof that Libby wanted, and that brought everything to a halt. At least everything they were about to do last night.

She'd left, taken her treasure trove of Jake's personal items, and then texted him to schedule an "official" meeting with her brother. She hadn't been cold or distant, just changed.

It was as if Jake himself had stepped in and stopped where they were going.

"Did you tell her you'd have a lawyer present?" Ken asked.

"No, but if what's in that Dopp kit matches her DNA, I might as well just walk away now. I don't have a will, Ken."

"And you are one hundred percent positive he left one?"

Law had replayed what he remembered of the hospital conversation a thousand times in his head. He'd been emotional at the time, caught up in the possibility of losing Jake, and sure as hell hadn't been taking notes.

"Did he look me in the eye that night and say, 'I wrote a will and left you the Toasted Pelican'? Maybe not in so many words. But that was the gist of it."

Ken pulled into the Ritz parking lot, driving through to where Law had last left his bike.

"There's Bonnie," Law said, pointing to the motorcycle he'd missed the past few days.

"Do you have a lawyer who'll come on short notice?"

"I have a guy I talked to after I got locked out of the restaurant, but..." He puffed out a breath. "I don't want to take a lawyer and make it all legal and official."

"You're trying to claim ownership of a property and business, Law," Ken said. "It has to be legal and official."

"I know, but I can't win. If that DNA matches *and* they have the original birth certificates, a judge is going to give it to them if I can't produce a will." He felt the burning urge to *quit*, and it sickened him.

"And are you sure you looked everywhere?" Ken asked. "I mean, you totally missed the shaving bag."

"Everywhere. I went through all his belongings."

"And you never saw that picture she found in ten minutes." Ken threw the truck into park and gave Law a hard look. "Listen, man, not only are you personally invested, but when you looked, you were grieving the loss of your friend and not thinking straight. Go back through the storage stuff again. You want help?"

"I did. There's nothing." He shook his head, thinking it all through for the hundredth time. "You know, having those two days in the Pelican, I got a taste, man. I loved it. That's what I want, and I know it's what Jake wanted. But I can't take what's not mine."

Ken looked hard at him. "You want my advice?"

"I don't know, do I? You're probably going to suggest I marry her and get the Pelican the old-fashioned way—as her dowry."

Ken rolled his eyes. "You won't like my suggestion any better, I suspect."

Law shrugged. "Hey, I'll try anything."

"How about the truth?" Ken asked. "Why don't you tell her you don't have the will?"

"Because she'll have yoga mats rolled up in my pantry faster than you can say *namaste*."

"They're going to make you show a will soon. Today, I'd imagine. You need to come clean with the fact that you have a verbal promise and nothing on paper."

Law just stared at his friend, a black pit growing in his stomach. "All right, thanks, Ken." He put a hand on Ken's shoulder. "Thanks for the truck. It was a lifesaver."

Ken just smiled. "You'll do the right thing."

"I'll do…something."

After Ken took off, Law walked into the office to get his last check and finalize any details for the efficiency he'd been renting, but after a quick chat with the woman at the desk, he ended up sitting for ten minutes, growing impatient and late for his appointment with Libby.

"Excuse me, Mr. Monroe?" A woman he'd never seen before came out of the back offices and smiled at him. "We've been trying to reach you for several days."

"Well, now you have me."

"Could we see you back here a moment?"

He stood, giving her a dubious look. "Trouble with my check or the apartment?"

"Not at all," she said as she gestured for him to follow her to the plush back offices. "But your timing is perfect. Mr. Phillips is here today."

Mr. Phillips? He gave his head a shake. "Don't know who that is or why I want to talk to him. I quit on Saturday."

She flashed him a smile. "It's all anyone has talked about around here."

"Really." Oh man. Was some Ritz blowhard going to rip him a new one for quitting during a rush?

When they turned the corner to mahogany row, he huffed a disgusted breath. Would he be forced to come face-to-face with that dickhead Chef Del?

Because he might try to care less, but it wasn't really possible. What could they do to him now? What did it matter?

"Look, I'm really late for—"

"Chef Lawson Monroe." A tall, older gentleman in a ridiculously expensive suit walked out of an office and extended his hand. "Clive Phillips, Vice President of Restaurant Management."

For the entire Ritz-Carlton chain?

"We've been attempting to call you, but here you are," Phillips said, shaking Law's hand. "You came right to us."

"I'm here for my paycheck. My *last* paycheck."

The man indicated that Law should go into the office, where Susan Roderick, the hotel GM, sat on the sofa, beaming at him.

"Ms. Roderick," Law said, certain he was unable to hide his confusion at this turn of events.

"Chef Law," she replied, getting up to shake his hand. "Your timing is impeccable, as always."

"Except I have no idea what I'm timing."

The other man closed the door and offered Law a seat,

then took one of his own on the plush sofa next to the GM.

"First of all, we are sorry about what happened in the kitchen on Saturday night."

They were sorry? "Look, I lost it and I apologize. If there were problems after I left, then—"

"There were problems before you left," Susan said, folding her hands on her lap and looking directly at Law. "Chef Del had...issues. He's gone now."

Holy shit. "He got canned because of that?" Law hated the guy, no doubt about it, but he didn't wish him unemployed.

"Not because of that," Susan said. "He was already on probation, but after doing some interviews with the staff, we let him go, and Clive flew out from headquarters last night to address the situation."

Next to her, Clive looked just as serious, with eyes the color of fresh sage under a shock of white hair. "We're doing some companywide restructuring, Chef Lawson, and you've walked right into the middle of our decision-making process."

Law blinked at him. "Not sure I follow how I'd fit."

"You'd fit nicely, as the chef de cuisine, and I'm here to offer you that job."

"To replace Chef Del?" His voice rose in surprise. He could do it, of course, but it was a stunning promotion.

"Oh, no," Clive said. "We immediately pulled from the Amelia Island property to put Chef Aiden McCall in that slot."

"Of course." Law had worked with Aiden when he was a sous chef in Naples. "He's terrific. Creative and fair. And I'd work for him in a minute." If he lost the Pelican. Which was a distinct possibility, so he sat a little straighter and suddenly realized that what they thought *did* matter.

"We have a better idea," Clive said, shooting a look at

Susan, who hadn't stopped smiling since Law had walked into the room. She'd always liked him, always stopped to chat with him when she was in the kitchen, and if she were a little more his type and less his boss's boss, he might have done a better job of flirting with her.

"How would you like to be chef de cuisine at our Dove Mountain location in Arizona?" Clive asked, his brows raised in expectation.

Chef de cuisine? Arizona? Law had no idea how to respond. It might be the last place on earth he wanted to live, but to run a Ritz kitchen? Yes, it would mean reporting to a long and sometimes unforgiving hierarchy, but it was some measure of autonomy. Except…Arizona. Damn, that was far away and not anything like home.

"Take some time," Clive said after a moment. "It's a huge decision, and I'm sure you have…someone to discuss this with. A significant other or family."

None of the above, he thought with an unexpected thud. Without Jake—without the promise of the Toasted Pelican—Law was free to be.

Except, this part of Florida was home. Mimosa Key was home. And Libby was…about to win the "battle of the wills."

"I'm single," he said. "And autonomous."

"I know," Susan piped in. "That's why moving you fast would be so easy. And they will have a place on property for you to live," she added. "I know how important that perk was to you."

"Still…it's sudden and unexpected." And not completely welcome, he realized. Arizona held zero appeal. Even working at the Ritz.

No, that had to hold some professional appeal. It was a career coup. Jake would have burst with pride.

Except...that's not what Jake had wanted.

"Take some time and let us put together an offer," Clive said. "I promise it will include some terrific benefits, including a signing bonus if you agree to stay two years."

Two years in Arizona? A freaking prison sentence.

When he didn't answer, Clive leaned forward. "Law, you're one of the best in our organization. It's a shame you spent the last six months under the wrong chef, but we've had our eye on you for a long time. Your time has come, and I hope you realize that."

"When do you need a decision?" he asked.

"We should have something in writing for you later today, so within a day or two?"

No, he couldn't. He needed two weeks, at least. Until that next court date.

"Do you have another job already?" Susan asked, then looked at Clive. "I told you he's an amazing chef."

Clive nodded. "You did, and so did many of your colleagues, Chef Lawson. You are quite respected in the kitchen, and I've actually heard about you from outside of the Naples property. I'm sure your talent was a thorn in Chef Del's side."

"Thanks," he said, leaning back. "But I'm not sure I can make a decision that quickly."

"We need to fill the slot fast," Clive said. "We have the chef in place until the end of the month, but I would want you to spend time with him so there's a smooth transition."

"Ten days?" he countered. By then, the DNA results would be back and his fate would be sealed.

Clive didn't look happy, but gave the slightest shrug. "You're worth the wait," he said. "And when you see the package we're putting together, you won't wait ten days, I'm certain."

More money. His own kitchen. And a prestigious title. Why wasn't his mouth watering for that? Because it wasn't what he'd always wanted. He couldn't put his fingerprint on a Ritz kitchen, not really. Not like he wanted to.

Still, Law stood when Clive did and shook his and Susan's hands. After confirming his contact information, he walked out into blistering sunshine, marveling. He'd gone in there to get his last paycheck…and left with the promise of a promotion and a *signing* bonus.

What would Jake have said to that? What did it matter? He was dead and took his secrets to the grave.

So maybe it was time to ditch the gastropub dream, the Toasted Pelican plan, and the fantasies he'd let take shape after one conversation with a man who had one foot in the grave.

At least Law could go into the meeting with Libby knowing he had a job in his back pocket. Not the job he wanted, but something.

And it would make telling Libby the truth a little easier because, in his gut, he knew Ken was right about that.

Chapter Fourteen

Libby pushed up from the kitchen table at the sound of a motorcycle in her driveway.

"It's about time," Sam said dryly, not looking up from the scads of legal documents he'd spread about. "He's only thirty-six minutes late."

Libby threw a look at her brother. "Don't be a jerk to him, Sam. He doesn't have to help us. He could make this a lot more difficult. He's being really fair."

"I'm sure he has an ulterior motive," he said. "Everyone does."

"Is it enjoyable to go through life being so cynical?" Libby asked.

"Uncle Sam's right," Jasmine piped in, coming into the room dressed in a spotless and unwrinkled pink linen shift, adorned with flawless makeup. "He definitely has an ulterior motive. And I know what it is." She sang the last few words like a playground taunt.

"Do you *mind*?" Libby asked, leaving the kitchen before the conversation went south. She peeked through the glass on the side of the front door and let out a tiny moan of appreciation. Oh, Law, really?

It wasn't fair to look that good. Except throwing him into

the lion's den that was Sam in Attorney Mode wasn't fair to him, either.

Dreading the showdown, she unlocked the door and opened it slowly.

"I know I'm late," he said instantly. "I had an unexpected meeting."

"It's all right. Everything okay, I hope?"

"Better now," he said, looking at her with the same admiration she suspected shone in her own eyes. He gestured toward the porch and the view of the bay beyond. "Your gingerbread house is stunning."

"Thanks. I'm really happy with how it came out."

"The location alone is one in a million."

"Not so much anymore, since people are discovering Barefoot Bay and vacuuming up a lot of this property. But we're lucky, and I love it."

He turned to look out to the road and the bay vista beyond it. "I've been past here many times, on the road and in the water. The canals aren't far."

She pointed to the right. "The islets and the inlets?"

"Never heard them called that."

"You mean that northeast section where locals fish? It's a mile that way. Do you go up there?"

"Not anymore," he said, a strange note in his voice. He shook it off before she had a chance to analyze it, looking past her into the house. "Yeah, wow. Really pretty, Lib. What an incredible place to live."

Considering that he was currently bunking in a room above a restaurant, her Victorian must look grand. "It's been fun to renovate it over the past few years, but I'm happy it's done, and I like living here a lot more than Miami."

"I bet," he said. "It's so...homey."

"It is," she agreed, stepping aside to let him look around, but his gaze settled on her, not the décor.

"We didn't finish last night," he reminded her on a whisper.

"We got distracted."

"*You* got distracted," he corrected. "I got hit over the head with an old toiletry bag."

"Morning, Lawless," Jasmine breezed into the room, scooping her handbag from the entryway table. "Mom slipped and used your nickname, which is now the only one I'll use."

"Still talking about me, is she?" he asked with a playful wink to Libby.

"*Constantly.*" Jasmine grinned at Libby's Mad Mom look. "And by the way, that dinner was fan-freaking-tastic."

"Thanks," Law said. "Glad to hear your friends liked everything."

"Way past like. Noah said more of the security team wants to come back tonight, and lots of customers at the boutique ask about places in town to eat, so I'm going to start recommending it."

"Thanks," Libby and Law replied in perfect unison, making Jasmine laugh.

"Well, I guess it is sort of under *co*-ownership," Jasmine said. "At least until Uncle Sam wipes the courtroom clean with you."

"Ouch," Law said. "Being the dishrag in front of a judge doesn't sound like fun."

It won't be, Libby thought.

"After last night's dinner, it'll be a shame to lose that kind of restaurant," Jasmine added. "There's an underserved market on Mimosa Key for people who can't afford the resort but really want a decent place to eat."

"I agree," Law replied.

Libby shook her head. "But what about the underserved market of women over forty who want to take yoga classes and spend time on themselves who also can't afford the resort and really want a decent place to practice?"

"Why can't we have both?" Jasmine asked. "Put the yoga studio upstairs and the restaurant downstairs. You can call it the *Twisted* Pelican." She beamed and maneuvered right between them. "You're welcome!" she called out as she glided down the porch steps to the driveway.

Libby watched her leave, then closed her eyes. "That girl."

"Is a genius," Law said, his mouth sliding into a grin.

"Don't get any ideas. My students are not doing their hatha yoga with the aroma of meatloaf floating into the studio." She poked his back, sending him in the direction of the kitchen. "Even *that* meatloaf."

"They'll work up an appetite and eat," he said. "I think it would be heaven. Or nirvana. Wherever yogis go." His chuckle faded as he walked into the kitchen and saw the sea of documents surrounding Sam, who had a cell phone pressed to his ear.

"Would you like coffee?" Libby asked as she gestured toward one of the chairs.

"I might need something stronger."

Sam held up a finger to quiet them and hear whoever he was on the phone with. "How quickly can you make a definitive match, then?" Sam looked over at Libby and mouthed, "The DNA lab."

She saw Law's broad shoulders sink a little as he took a seat and scanned the legal briefs and court docs and pages and pages of yellow papers with Sam's relentless scribbling.

"My brother had the toiletry bag we found taken by

messenger to the DNA-testing lab his law firm uses in Miami," Libby explained.

"Of course he did."

Sam stood and walked out of the room, his voice low as if he needed privacy on the call, while Libby came over to the table with Law's coffee and gestured toward sugar and milk already on the table.

"Fair warning," she whispered. "He graduated first in his law-school class and has never lost a trial. He's the overachiever of the family."

"Now you tell me." He took the coffee black and drank.

"What would you have done differently?" She slipped into the seat next to him.

"Left with your daughter the genius," he joked.

Wrapping her fingers around her own mug, she offered a look of sympathy. "Law, I had no idea anyone had any claim on the Pelican, and now I'm invested. Emotionally, financially, and professionally. I have big dreams for the place."

"So do I," he said simply.

"Sam has been working for a year so I could have it."

"Jake and I talked about what I'd do with it more than a year ago."

"Then why didn't you take over while he was still alive?"

He let out a quick exhale, as if to say that was the question of the century. "He had a…"

She waited, only realizing then that the question had been nagging her. Why had he been working at another restaurant on the mainland when his best friend had a dump that desperately needed his touch? "A what?" she urged.

"A stubborn streak," he finished. "He didn't want to give up on the Pelican being exactly what it was born to be."

"Why not?"

"I honestly can't answer that," Law said. "But I know what he told me when he died. That he wanted it to go to me so I could do exactly what I wanted with it."

"And he put that in a will." It was a statement, not a question.

Law looked down and fluttered one of the legal documents, silent.

"What else did he say?" she asked.

He swallowed and thought for a moment, then said, "He had some kind of secret."

"A secret?"

"I guess he meant you. And Sam."

She was a secret to him? Some blood drained from her head, replaced by a year-old anger. No, it was much older than that. It was…from birth. Mike was her father, then he wasn't. A dead soldier was her father, then he wasn't. Now Jake was her father…and she was his secret.

Then the pattern continued. One husband who was there, then he wasn't. And another.

Had Libby forgotten why she wanted balance in her life after all this?

"Libby, I don't have the will."

Her head shot up, and she sucked in a soft breath, trying to wrap her head around the words that had cut through her little pity party. "You mean you don't have it with you?"

"I mean I have never seen it or touched it or found it."

She felt her jaw slacken as she sank back into the chair. "Why did you lie to me?"

"I know it exists. He told me. I've been searching for it, everywhere. I can't find it."

Her head buzzed a little. A lot. "So this"—she swept her hand over the papers on the table—"is a complete waste of time? You have no will?"

"I have his verbal promise. He meant it when he said he wanted me to have the restaurant and that there was...paperwork."

"Paperwork?" Her voice cracked as she still tried to process the fact that all these days he'd been dishonest about the will.

"He said there was a will," Law insisted. "He said he wanted me to have the restaurant. He said he had secrets and that I was, in his mind, his son."

"But the fact is, *I* am his son." Sam walked into the kitchen shooting a stern look at Law as he tossed the phone on the table. "And without documentation, your claims are unsubstantiated and worthless in court."

"That may be so, but they are the truth." Law looked at Libby, nothing but honesty in his green eyes.

She stared at him for a long time, bracing for that sickening sense of instability when someone—usually a man—disappointed her. But she felt nothing except an unexpected tendril of gratitude. Law was being straight with her, and he had everything to lose by not dragging this out. This was her win. She was Jake's...

Secret.

Jake was the man who made her sick with dizziness. Not Law.

"Then we have an open-and-shut case." Sam pushed some papers around and pulled out a thick packet from the bottom. "Case law is completely in our favor. Reference *Billingsworth v. the State of Florida*, *Harris v. Harris*, and *Turner v. Schecter*, all precedent-setting cases with relevant statues and regulations pertaining to abandoned, unclaimed property in non-will probate situations."

Law glanced at Libby, a slight smile lifting the corner of his mouth. "Jake would die all over again."

"Didn't like lawyers, huh?" Sam asked.

Law gave a light laugh. "Let's just say he once asked me to go by a different name because mine reminded him of the profession he hated the most."

"That's very amusing, Mr. Monroe," Sam said. "But this—"

"Maybe that's why he doesn't have a will," Libby interjected, the words surprising her as much as they did Law and Sam. "He wouldn't have had to have gone to an attorney if he hated them."

Law nodded slowly. "That's true."

"So what does a person do who wants to leave something to someone and hates attorneys?" Libby asked her brother.

Sam looked a little put off by the question, but he shrugged. "He holds his nose and goes into the office, anyway."

"But he was sick, right?" she asked Law. "Like, literally on his deathbed when he told you he had a will."

"He wasn't sick for long. It was a stroke." Law thought for a moment, looking down at the papers, but Libby had the feeling he wasn't reading anything, just thinking. "But I know what he said to me, and he was clear. He told me there was a will and warned me that finding it, or executing it, I don't know which, wouldn't be easy."

"Could it be in a computer file somewhere?" Libby asked.

"What difference does it make, Libby?" Sam demanded. "If we don't have it when we go to court, the Pelican is yours."

But did she want something of…Jake's? Yes, and no.

"Anyway, Jake didn't have a computer," Law said.

Sam gave a condescending snort, which Law ignored.

"I want to find this damn will," Libby said to Sam.

"Otherwise, I'll feel like we somehow won unfairly. I want this to be fair." Her voice rose with the emotion that rocked her, but she didn't care. This mattered to her. "Fair and square."

Sam sighed. "Very few things are 'fair' when it comes to the law."

Law gave a dry laugh. "And that irony, my friend, is why the man hated lawyers."

Libby leaned in, looking at her brother. "How can we find it?"

He thought for a second, then, "If a will was drafted, a check would likely have been written to an attorney. Did you go through his bank statements?" he asked Law.

"Yeah, but he was big on cash and hiding money from the IRS."

"Nice," Sam muttered.

"But he did file taxes," Libby said. "How can that help us, Sam?"

He shrugged. "If he claimed any attorney fees as tax deductions, then there might be some paper trail."

"And we can go through those boxes in storage again," Libby said.

Law put his hand over hers, holding her gaze, saying nothing, except his look said everything. He appreciated the support, and he respected fairness.

Finally, she turned to Sam. "What do you think?"

Her brother sighed noisily. "Not what I think, what I know. There's powerful legal precedent for granting biological heirs unclaimed property and assets. And we'll have DNA test results in a week or so. I've asked them to do the deepest, most thorough test, so it might take a few extra days, but I'll have the results before I go before the judge two weeks from today."

"And if Law has a will by then?" Libby asked.

Sam lifted both his brows. "I'd say we'd have a helluva court fight, but you two don't seem to be very cutthroat about this."

"I want the property fair and square," Libby said again.

"And so do I," Law agreed. "No legal maneuvering."

"No courtroom dramatics," Libby added.

"No fun," Sam replied with a dry smile, looking from one to the other. "So how about a compromise?"

Law cocked a brow. "The Twisted Pelican?"

Sam shrugged, not getting the joke. "Call it what you want, but that place has to stay in business until midnight on the twenty-sixth. If it runs anything like how Jasmine described it last night, it could be profitable. Very profitable." He looked at Libby. "As long as the business remains a fully-functioning restaurant and bar, he can make menu and décor changes at his own expense. We'll wait for the DNA and, if you like, you can both look for that will. When the business is officially turned over to you, Lib, Law can keep all the profits he's made. If it's handed to him, he'll cover all your legal expenses and court costs, which aren't much, because I'm working pro bono. Is that fair and square enough for you two?"

She leaned back, waiting for Law to respond first, but Sam's phone rang, and he grabbed it, walking out of the room to take the call.

Law turned his hand over and threaded rough fingers around hers. "I have a few ground rules," he said.

She lifted her brows, curling her hand into his. "You do?"

"I do want to make some changes to the dining area and bar. Nothing permanent, but that room has to improve if we're going to make any money."

"He said you can make those changes."

"And I want complete control in the kitchen."

"No need to fear me running in to whip up a casserole, I assure you."

"And I want you to work with me. Right by my side. Every day and every night, we'll…"

"Run a restaurant," she finished.

"Together."

She leaned close to whisper, "I'm going right down that slippery slope that scares me so much, Law."

"I'll catch you."

"And drop me."

"Trust me, Lib."

She searched his face, his bottle-green eyes and promising smile. And all she wanted to do was trust a man one more time. "Okay," she finally agreed. "But I get to keep my tips."

And her heart. She got to keep that, too. But something in the way Law looked at her made her fear she might lose it….one more time.

Chapter Fifteen

Later that day, Law relaxed in Libby's comfortable Infiniti SUV as they drove down the beach road from Barefoot Bay into town. Libby had suggested she drive them to the fresh market to get supplies and ingredients, since he could hardly do that on a bike. As often as possible, he sneaked a peak at the driver, who was as nice to look at as the beach view on the other side.

Libby was a complex woman, he thought, enjoying her profile and the way she handled the luxury automobile.

"Nice whip, yoga bear," he said, patting the butter-soft leather seat.

"Not from yoga, believe me. Divorce has its benefits."

"You got the car?"

She threw him a smile. "I got a mountain of cash because that son of a bitch cheated on me right out in the open and didn't bother to hide what he was doing. Combine that with my brilliant barrister brother, a fair judge, and no prenup, and you can color me comfortable."

He laughed a little. "I see where your daughter gets her honest streak."

"Why lie about it? I didn't cheat on him, but I was foolish enough to marry him."

He eyed her again, having a tough time imagining pragmatic Libby being foolish about anything, especially a man. She had endured some crappy relationships, that was for sure.

"Did you marry him for his money?"

"*Pah*." She flicked her finger as if the idea were purely annoying to her. "Money has never been a motivator for me. I told you, I married for love." She looked skyward. "Totally foolish."

"You fell for that myth?" he teased. Well, sort of teased.

"Hey, I was thirty-six years old and *just* past my peak. Just." She winked at him. "You know, by a day or two."

He chuckled. "If this isn't your peak, I don't think I could have been able to be in the same room as you when you hit it."

She brushed a lock of blond hair over her shoulder with a playful smugness. "I was insanely hot."

"You *are* insanely hot."

"You're very sweet, but nine or ten years ago?" She whistled softly. "Peaked. And Parker Blaine was...anxious to get to the top."

"Parker Blaine? That name alone should have made you run."

"I liked it," she said. "It sounded like an old New England family to me, but trust me, it was not. He was a ruthless real estate developer who built skyscrapers in Miami and hotels in the Caribbean. But mostly, he was an insecure fifty-three-year-old man with a little dick and a big ego, and I was purchased for one purpose: eye candy."

"Come on, Lib. You're too smart to get snookered into a deal that raw."

"Love is blind *and* dumb, Law. I really, truly cared about him and thought his ego was a form of confidence."

"And his dick?"

She gave a sad smile. "I gave him a pass because you can't help what God didn't give you."

He kept his mouth shut, knowing exactly what God gave him and certain that she'd know, too, eventually. But not while she was dumping on her ex-husband.

"So how long did it last?"

"Long enough for his ambition to kick in, along with his need for the next bigger thing. A bigger deal, a taller building, a shinier trophy. He found one, and I was famously taken off the shelf."

"But well paid."

She lifted a shoulder. "That was Sam, really. He's a shark."

"He's a good lawyer, and he seems fair," Law said. "And his compromise makes sense, at least to me. You don't have to do this, you know."

"You can't exactly get all the food from that fresh market on a motorcycle," she said. "I don't have a class to teach until later this afternoon, so I don't mind going with you."

"I don't mean this drive or this trip to the market," he said. "I mean this plan to let me be so involved with the restaurant."

She kept her eyes on the road, thinking. "Don't think it's pure altruism on my brother's part. I'm sure there's some legal benefit to us opening the doors to you, with or without that will."

"But you could have said no."

"You should know by now that deep down what's really important to me is to find out if Jake was my father and...why he wouldn't take responsibility for that." Her voice hitched a little, and she threw him an apologetic look. "I like being fair about it, don't you?"

"I do, and I know you doubt your mother, but I doubt Jake sometimes. And my memory. So as long as we have doubts, why not?"

"I thought you firmly believed my mother is lying."

"What I firmly believe is that if Jake knew you and Sam were his, he'd have taken full responsibility. Although..."

"Although what?" she prodded when his voice trailed off.

Law shifted in his seat, wondering how many cards he was going to show in one day. Many, it seemed. "When he was slipping into that coma and telling me about the will, he did make a point of saying the Pelican was mine and 'no one else's.' And he mentioned that secret."

"Then he knew about us. I told you."

"And he ignored you? It's preposterous, if you knew him. Jake did the right thing, always. Maybe her version of the story is *something* of the truth, but she didn't want to marry him."

"Maybe," she agreed. "She's not changing that story, though, and there aren't very many people around who could have known them when they were younger and involved."

Traffic slowed to almost a stop as they neared town and the turn for the causeway.

"Can you even remember a time when there was more than one car on this road?" she asked, narrowing her eyes at the backup. "I came this way to and from Mimosa High every day, and there were days when this street was deserted."

"The resort changed everything on this island," he mused.

"Not everything. The town is still small, there's only one traffic light, and the Super Min is still at the heart of it all, but—"

He snapped his fingers. "Hey, I have an idea."

She frowned. "What?"

"The person who would have known them both when they were younger."

"Charity Grambling!" she exclaimed, her eyes bright as she read his mind. "That is brilliant, Law. She owned the Super Min back then, she knows everything about everyone, and she loves nothing more than gossip."

"Plus, the Super Min is in the background of that picture," he added.

"You're right. She might be able to tell us something concrete."

"Do you want to go back home and get the photo?" he asked.

She tapped her handbag on the console. "It's right here."

"You carry it around?" he asked, surprised.

"I don't want to lose it."

But something told him it was more than that. "Okay, we'll show it to her, and if I know anything about that woman, she'll spill everything she knows."

Libby cringed a little. "But I don't want her to know about my mom or anything about us," she said. "It'll be all over town before we get over the causeway."

"We won't tell her a thing," he promised. "We'll say we found it in the Pelican and wanted to know if she has any idea of the date. Historical value. She eats that stuff up with a spoon."

"Dating that might be tough."

"Don't underestimate Charity Grambling."

She gave him an appreciative smile. "Thanks, Law."

"For what? Throwing myself to the she-devil of Mimosa Key?"

"For wanting to find out the truth."

He shrugged. "It's what Jake would want."

"And I'm sorry to keep making you talk about him." She

reached over the console and took his hand. "And I'm sorry you lost your friend."

He took her hand in both of his, mostly for the pleasure of sandwiching her long, lean, smooth fingers between his palms. "I'm sorry he didn't know he had a daughter as great as you and a son who might have changed his mind about lawyers."

She smiled, a little sadness in her sweet eyes as she turned the SUV into the Super Min lot. After she parked, she grabbed her purse and climbed out. Law followed and met her at the front of the car. "Let me talk," he said.

"Why?"

"Because she likes me."

Libby snorted. "Charity Grambling doesn't like anyone."

He lifted his brows. "Trust me on this, Lib. She goes full-out cougar on me."

"This is Charity. You think she's a cougar, but she's a feral cat on the prowl for dirt and destruction."

Before they reached the door, he held out his hand. "Give me the picture."

With a skeptical look, she slipped her fingers into the side pocket of her bag and produced the photograph. He took it and placed a hand on her back and led her to the door of the convenience store that had probably been built the same year as the Pelican. "Brace yourself, Lib. Old ladies love me."

She rolled her eyes as he pushed the door in and met the gray-eyed gaze of the seventy-five-year-old Mimosa Key institution whose mother could not have chosen a less appropriate name. There wasn't a charitable bone in the woman's body, but somewhere, deep inside, she was a woman. And that woman, shriveled on the inside and out, had at least one working hormone left in her body that always came alive at the sight of Law.

"Well, look what the busty blonde dragged in." Charity pushed up from the stool she'd perched on for what had to be fifty years behind the cash register. "Lawson Monroe, where *have* you been?" She actually came out from behind the safety of her counter, as if she had to get closer to him.

"Sweet Charity, it's good to see you."

Despite the light flush of color that deepened her weathered cheeks, she managed a scowl. "If it was good, you wouldn't be a stranger." Her gaze shifted to Libby and instantly turned distrustful again as she looked up and down. "Glad to see you're not walking around in those sausage skins you call exercise clothes anymore."

Libby smiled. "You should take one of my yoga classes, Charity. It's good for the soul."

"My soul is a lost cause, and my bones are brittle." She shifted her attention back to Law. "Ever since Jake Peterson croaked, you've been MIA. What brings you back here?"

"This." He held out the picture for her. "I found it in the Toasted Pelican and thought you might like to see it. Isn't that the Super Min in the background?"

She whipped it up and adjusted her glasses. "Let me see." She squinted at the shot, angling it one way and the other. "Oh yes. That's my shop before I got the Shell franchise. Lord have mercy, that Frank Rice was a handsome man." She looked up and gave a sly smile. "Reminds me a little of you, Law, with that sleek silver hair."

"Frank Rice?" Libby asked, leaning in.

Charity barely spared her a look. "Oh, he was a fine-looking man even then, maybe fifty years old." She pointed to the other man in the picture with young Jake and Libby's mom. "Of course, he's dead now, and I heard he had dementia so bad he didn't recognize himself in the end. I hope someone shoots me if that happens to me."

Law was pretty sure half the town would line up for that job. "So you know when this was taken?"

She squinted and then looked up at Law. "Oh, that Frank was like Rock Hudson, you know? His wife left him, I recall, in an ugly divorce. Took him for every penny, and he had plenty of those." She tapped the picture, squinting as if she were looking into her memory. "Rosalind!" she exclaimed. "Rosalind Rice, that was her name. Went by the name Rosie."

She looked up at them, beaming. "Not bad for an old bag, huh? Guess no one's going to shoot me after all." She chuckled and continued to study the picture. "But I do remember Frankie and that little Rosie wife of his. He was a very important person in his day."

"Okay, thanks, Charity." Law reached for the photo, frustrated that she was concentrating on the wrong couple.

She snapped it back. "Not until I know."

"Know what?" Law and Libby asked in unison.

"Why you're asking." A smug smile looked like it would crack her peanut-brittle skin. "There has to be a reason why it matters so to you."

Law shouldn't have underestimated this woman's curiosity. "I told you, I found it in Jake's stuff," he said. "And I was wondering if you knew when it was taken."

Charity finally released the photo. "Of course I know. That picture was shot on November 5, 1970."

Libby's jaw dropped. "How can you be certain?"

She slid a blood-red nail along the photo, stopping at the outside wall under the Super Min sign. "The store was painted seafoam green right there. But see the side of the building?" She angled the picture. "Navaho white. That's the actual name of both colors. Lord, my memory is a beautiful thing."

"How does that tell you the day?" Law asked.

"Some obnoxious little pricks egged my whole building on Halloween. I had to wait three days to have it painted, which would have been November 3, 1970. They had to stop halfway, without finishing, until the following Monday because it was a Friday. And you see that little red sign on the door? That was my closed sign, and I used to be closed every Sunday back in the day when we had blue laws and such. So this had to be taken on Sunday, making it November 5, 1970." She gave a yellowed, smug-as-hell smile. "Does that help?"

"Yeah, and if I ever need an alibi for a murder, I'm calling you," Law said.

"Thanks," Libby mumbled and started for the door. As Law moved in the same direction, Charity grabbed his forearm to whisper, "Hey, did you ever find out who took over the Toasted Pelican?" she asked. "It killed me that I couldn't help you, Law."

"I did find out," he said, the bell ringing when Libby went outside alone.

Charity pointed a crimson talon at him. "Spill or die."

"Can't," he said, making her eyes go wide with disbelief. "But if you want a real treat, stop in for dinner one of these nights."

She snorted. "If I want a piece of meat that tastes like the wheel of my car, I will."

"Things have changed. I'm running a gastropub in there right now. Spread the word, will you?"

"That's like asking me to breathe."

"Then do your thing, Sweet Charity."

She put her hand on her hip. "That's the real reason you came in here, isn't it? Not trying to find out about Frank Rice. You want me to help that business."

"I admit I had an ulterior motive. Bring your whole family to dinner one of these nights. I think you'll like it."

She gave a shrug and shooed him out the door. "Get out there quick before all that makeup melts off her face."

Libby barely had any on. "You're jealous, Charity."

"You bet I am," she admitted. "If I were younger, you wouldn't have a chance."

He just laughed, blew her a kiss, and joined Libby, who stood in the blazing sun, clicking on her phone.

"Well, we got a specific date," he said.

"And an important one, if this website is correct."

"What website?" He leaned closer to see what was on her screen, but the sun was too bright.

"The one that says a baby conceived on November fifth would be born on July twenty-eighth."

He thought about that for a second, and realized where she was going. "Thought you said your birthday was July Fourth."

"It was, but my mother said a thousand times we were three weeks early and were due on..." She lowered the phone and looked at him. "July twenty-eighth."

"And that makes you think that picture was taken the day you were conceived."

She nodded. "And there she is, standing next to Jake, who's looking at her like she hung the moon." She sighed and took his hand. "Not admissible in court, but it sure feels like we're getting closer to the truth."

"That's what you wanted, Lib."

She sighed. "I don't know what I want. I mean, yes, the truth. But for some reason, I'd hoped it would be different. That he would have wanted us."

"I still think your mother might be playing with history a little bit."

"She might be." She reached the car and tapped the keyless entry. "I'll call her again tonight and see if I can shake more out of her."

"In the meantime, you and I have a restaurant to run."

"For what? Ten more days?" She opened the door and looked over the roof at him, squinting in the sun. "Doesn't it bother you that at the end of that time, you may not have that will and I'll own the property?"

"I want the experience, even if it's just for ten days. Also, it'll give me time to take that hideous bottle rack down behind the bar. Can I?" he asked.

"Knock yourself out. I certainly won't want it there when it's a yoga studio."

"Great, I'll get Mark and Ken to help me. If I leave, at least I will have done it."

"Leave? Where would you go?" she asked.

"Probably Arizona."

The squint disappeared as her eyes widened in surprise. "Why Arizona?"

"Because I have a job offer there."

He saw her swallow. "So, if I win this thing, you leave?"

"Yeah. Why do you seem so surprised?"

"I don't know. I'm just..." She slid into the driver's seat, and he waited a beat, then got in his side to find her staring straight ahead. Did his going to Arizona bother her?

"You're just what?" he asked.

She stabbed the button and brought the Infiniti to its quiet life. "I'm excited about going to the fresh market," she said with a bright smile plastered on her face.

But he didn't believe her for one minute. She was disappointed he would be leaving, which was...all the more reason to leave.

Chapter Sixteen

News traveled fast around Mimosa Key. So fast, Libby suspected Law had mentioned the changes in the menu and atmosphere to Charity Grambling. She showed up that night, with her sister, their daughters, their husbands, and some friends.

There were also a few regulars Libby had seen popping in and out over the past year, including three very old ladies who cabbed over from an assisted-living facility in Naples. She'd seen them in here before and always thought they were sweet, especially the one with a walker who had to be near a hundred. Never too old to try a gastropub, Libby mused.

Of course, when the new chef came out to say hello, Walker Woman and her prehistoric posse cooed like a bunch of teenagers at a boy-band concert.

Old ladies love me.

She smiled, watching him work his little fan club. Truth was, *all* ladies loved him.

A little while later, they got another crew from Casa Blanca and, toward the end of the night, two couples who Libby had a feeling were there in true support of Law Monroe. Of course, she knew them all from the Mimosa

High reunion that had taken place back in March. A reunion that had obviously ignited more than one happy ever after.

A little twinge of something that had to be jealousy pinched her chest, but Libby smashed it with an easy smile at people who she, too, had become friends with that week.

"Looks like we're having a reunion of the reunion," she joked as she greeted Ken Cavanaugh and his visibly pregnant fiancée, Beth Endicott, then gave Mark Solomon and Emma DeWitt another hug.

"Are we too late for dinner?" Beth asked.

"Not at all," she assured them. "Did you tell Law you were coming in?"

"I did," Ken said. "But we had a meeting up at Casa Blanca that took longer than we thought."

"Wedding planning?" Libby asked as she showed them to the roomiest booth near the bar, which was keeping Dan busy tonight, too. "I understand the resort is doing the closest thing to a double-ring ceremony that four people whose combined age is about two hundred are allowed to have."

They all laughed, taking their seats. Mark Solomon, a handsome man nearing his fifties with plenty of style and grace, let Emma slide in first. The shadow of sadness that had hung over Mark the day he'd walked into the reunion-planning committee meeting had been replaced with a sense of peace and happiness that he wore well.

And when he looked at his bride-to-be, it was easy to see she was the source.

"You can tease all you want, Libby," Mark said, "but when you hear who we just met with, you'll be begging for an invitation."

"Which I better get," she said. "I was one of the first people Lacey put on that committee, and I'm pretty sure I added your names." She pointed to Mark and Ken. "You all have me to thank for this overdose of prenuptial joy."

"Thank you," Beth said, a hand on her growing belly. "We all had no idea how our lives would change when we signed up to help with the reunion."

Their lives, she thought, leaning against the booth and smiling at them all. She was more happy than envious, she told herself. These were good people who deserved love. Everyone deserved love, right?

"So who'd you meet with? Priest? Florist? Lawyer?" She gave a playful wink. "Pardon my cynicism. I'm afraid I've been down that aisle one or two times."

"Well, you never had this band at any wedding," Mark said. "We just spent two hours with none other than Eddie James himself."

Libby felt her jaw drop wide open. "Seriously?"

Emma's golden-brown eyes danced with pleasure. "The Lost Boys were my favorite band, and the father of one of the wedding planners is Donny Zatarain of Z-Train."

"I knew that," Libby said. "Willow has taken a bunch of my yoga classes, and we've gotten to be really good friends. She doesn't go around telling the free world that she's Donny's daughter, so I'm impressed she shared that. And more impressed that she's getting Eddie James for you."

"Who's getting Eddie James?"

Libby turned at the sound of Law's voice as he approached the table, a huge smile on his face at the sight of his friends. After a round of greetings and hugs, Mark picked up the story that definitely trounced everything else.

"So it turns out that Eddie has been trying to get the Lost Boys together for some kind of reunion album," he told them.

"They broke up years ago," Libby said. "I thought they had a huge and ugly falling-out."

"They did," Emma said. "But Eddie's been talking to them and looking for a very under-the-radar way to have a few test gigs to see how it goes."

"And you want your wedding to be a test?" Law asked.

"Why not?" Emma and Mark said at the same time.

"And they'll do ours the night before theirs," Ken said. "For practice, which is fine with me." His smile widened as he put his arm around Beth's shoulder. "Gonna be a great night in Barefoot Bay."

She smiled back at him. "Another one," she said under her breath. But Libby heard the whispered comment and saw the light in their eyes as they looked at each other.

That pang of envy got a little stronger this time, and a little more difficult to ignore.

Law put an easy arm around Libby's shoulder. "Hey, we got plenty of Eddie James and the Lost Boys on the old jukebox, don't we, Lib?"

She felt a bit of warm color rise to her cheeks, remembering their sexy dance to *Blown Away*. "We sure do."

The other two couples looked at each other, not hiding their surprise.

"We?" Mark said. "You two act like you both own this place."

"Or neither one of us," Law joked. "Let me treat you guys to an amazing dinner, and then the kitchen will be closed and we can talk."

Libby got them drinks and chatted for a few more minutes as the restaurant completely cleared out. The buzz at their table was infectious, though, and Libby couldn't help pulling up a chair and talking until it was time to get the feasts Law had prepared.

She went back to the kitchen and helped him load up

trays. "This is a lot of food," she said, eyeing the beautiful bounty. He'd gone all-out for his friends, with every plate a masterpiece.

"I thought we'd join them," he said. "Everyone gone?"

"Yes, even the president of the Law Monroe Fan Club who gave me a banging good tip."

"Charity?" He grinned. "Love that old broad. Okay, let's go."

They took the trays out, set up the food, and squeezed into the booth across from each other to share the meal with friends.

They all chatted about the reunion and how it had changed their lives, talked about Emma's new job at Casa Blanca as the VP of marketing and, of course, the weddings in early October.

And with each shared look, secret touch, and spontaneous kiss, the delicious food sat a little heavier in Libby's stomach. She'd gotten everyone else's drinks but her own, so she reached for Law's O'Doul's with a question in her glance.

She needed something to quench the thirst for…what they all had.

Oh, Libby, have you not learned your lesson about forever love?

Law gave a little nod and then frowned as if to silently ask if she was all right.

The conversation was flying, and it was no time to say, *Well, gee, Law, I'm feeling kind of blue with all these about-to-be happily married people, longingly looking at yet another man who all but wears his expiration date stamped on his forehead.*

But he kept his gaze on her, then stood, reaching out his hand. "C'mon, Lib, let's put some music on."

She let him pull her out of the booth and didn't mind at

all when he put his arm around her and walked her to the jukebox, certain the others were noticing the affection.

"You look like a woman who didn't love her duck confit flatbread," he whispered.

"I adored every bite," she assured him, a little touched that he was so in tune with her feelings and a little terrified he'd figure out they were deepening.

"So what's the matter?"

"Nothing," she said, letting him stand her in front of the jukebox and press himself against her back. He'd shed his chef's coat, and she could feel the warmth of his body through a thin T-shirt. "Let's pick an Eddie James song to get them in the mood for their weddings."

"Not our song," he whispered into her ear, the words and air sending a million chills down her back.

"No underground bees?"

He laughed. "Not for them. When I hear *Blown Away*, I want to be alone with you. Soon. Tonight." He added a kiss on her neck that had its usual impact on her balance.

Holding the edge of the jukebox, she let her eyes skim the song titles. "Um, *Broken Vows*? One of my favorites."

"Maybe not the right message for this crowd," he joked.

"Nah. They're too far gone to think about the inevitable broken vows."

He tsked in her ear. "Such a pessimist."

"You're the one who called love a myth."

"Did I?" He slipped an arm around her waist and settled her back against his chest. "Well, those four might be an exception."

"Hey, we're waiting for our Eddie James music," Mark called.

"Unless you two want to just make out for a while," Ken added.

"Annnnd...I'm in high school again," Law said on a laugh. He let go of her long enough to press a few buttons on the box, and the beat of a fast rock song started, getting a cheer from the table. "Bon Jovi. Can't go wrong."

"*Livin' on a Prayer*," Ken called out. "Great choice."

Law danced her back toward them just as Ken brought Beth out of the booth, ignoring her protests that pregnant women shouldn't dance. Mark and Emma joined them, and before Libby realized what was happening, the six of them were dancing to a song that hit the charts when almost all of them were in high school.

Law took her hand and moved to the beat, holding her gaze, laughing, belting out the words with everyone else, surrendering to a moment of craziness Libby was certain they'd all remember.

When the song ended, Mark pulled Emma close and kissed her like no one else existed on the earth, let alone watched in the room. Beth and Ken hugged and laughed and kissed as well and rubbed her baby bump together.

And Law looked at her like...like something was so missing in their lives.

Oh God, Libby, don't make this mistake again. It's sex and nothing else.

An ancient pain crept up from her stomach and tightened her throat. When would she learn that for some people, forever wasn't in the cards? Not for her and certainly not for this man whose entire belongings fit in a room upstairs and who casually talked about moving to Arizona the way other people talked about going to the store.

The next song started, with the now familiar notes of *Blown Away*.

He smiled and pulled her all the way into him for a kiss, already starting to slow dance.

"I thought that was just for us," she said.

"As fate would have it, our song played."

"Fate and you hit that button."

He laughed, but suddenly stopped at the bit of static and then nothing.

"Damn jukebox," Law said as the protests and complaints rose. "We're going to have to fix that," he added to Libby.

"Yeah," she said, but deep in her heart, she knew there was no fix for what would happen if she let herself fall for Law. It would end and it would hurt.

And she was starting to not care how much it would hurt.

Was it worth it for, what? Five orgasms and a truckload of tears?

Maybe.

Something had changed with Libby. She was a little distant after the kiss, quiet after their friends had left and they cleaned the kitchen and closed for the night.

Oh, they talked about the success of the evening and a few menu changes Law was mulling over. She shared some anecdotes from the dining room and, as always, relayed numerous compliments to the chef.

But something was different, and Law could feel his high hopes of ending the night horizontal and wrapped in each other's arms, preferably naked and in bed, slipping away with each soft sigh she must have thought he didn't hear.

When she came back into the kitchen from closing up the bar, she had a glass of wine.

"That looks good," he said, rinsing a pan he'd just washed.

"I'd offer you one, but…" She angled her head. "Do you ever miss it? I mean, when all your friends are having a party, and beer and wine are flowing?"

He shook his head slowly. "Not really, not in the way you'd think. I miss how booze could erase the things I didn't want to think about, but not how it made me feel."

"I've never had a drink to try and forget something," she said, taking a sip as if testing the wine for those kind of magical qualities. "I usually drink to unwind or take away inhibitions, but since I already danced like a tenth-grader at the prom, I've proven I can do that sober."

"Maybe you don't have things you need to forget." He lifted a platter from the sideboard and started to wash it.

She gave a dry laugh. "You forget about my two miserable marriages. Plenty to forget."

"I still can't believe Jasmine's father really left you and her for his ex-wife." Talk about stupid.

"Well, he did. He should never have divorced her in the first place, and I shouldn't have rushed into marriage and a baby at that age. But it all seemed so…stable to me."

He paused in the act of scrubbing the porcelain, studying her. "That's what you were looking for."

"Always," she said. "I hate that feeling that the world is out of control. I felt it when I found out Mike wasn't my father, and then with my first marriage, and my second. And then…Jake."

She put the wine down as if she just realized it loosened her tongue too much.

"You've been looking for men to balance you, when all this time you could do it yourself."

She nodded. "I'd like to think that. But…I can't do everything myself."

He smiled, catching her drift. "Some things do require

help. Like…" He handed her a towel. "Dishwashing. Takes two."

She took the towel and the clean platter to dry it. "Yeah, I have a long history of bad decisions where men are concerned." She rubbed the water off. "Long. Ugly. And I really wanted to put a stop to that."

"Why do I hear a 'but' lingering?"

She looked up. "But then I met you."

"Is that what I am? Another bad decision?"

"Not yet."

"The night is young. We could make many bad decisions." He took the platter from her and set it on the counter so she'd put her arms around him. Normally, he wouldn't wait to kiss a woman this close and willing and beautiful. But after the vibes he'd been getting for the last hour or so, taking his time seemed like a good idea.

"What are the things you wanted to erase?" she asked. "The stuff with your dad?"

He stared at her, wanting to kiss so much more than talk.

"You've said enough for me to know it was bad, Law. Will you tell me more or does it hurt to talk about it?"

He didn't answer right away, mostly because he was trying to think of the right way to respond. He could tell her what happened, of course, and what he endured. But would she understand? And what would she think of him?

"Law?"

He studied her for a second as an idea landed in his head. "You need long sleeves," he said.

"Excuse me?"

"You can wear my chef's jacket. It smells like the kitchen, and that will actually ward off mosquitoes, because there are a lot of them out there." The more the plan settled over him, the better it felt.

They shouldn't have sex—at least not yet. Not until she knew what she was getting into and what he was all about.

Libby frowned, shaking her head, her blue-gray eyes clouded with confusion. "What are you talking about?"

"And I only have one helmet, but you can wear it."

"Wear it…*where*?"

"Up to—what did you call them?—the islets and the inlets."

"Why would we go there?" she asked.

"To talk." He turned and grabbed her wine glass, handing it back to her. "Gas up, yoga bear. I'm taking you for a ride, and you might want to lose a few of those inhibitions. After that, you can tell me what happened to you tonight."

"Nothing happened tonight."

"Drink it or toss it. I want to go." He went to grab his chef's jacket and the keys to his bike, happy with the decision.

Blessedly, she didn't argue, but finished the wine in a few impressive gulps. She put the glass in the sink and took his jacket, still eyeing him suspiciously.

"Why are we going up there? I mean, if you just want to go back to my house and, um, *talk*, Jasmine most likely won't be home tonight and Sam's left for a deposition in Sarasota."

"Good to know, but we're not going there yet."

She walked with him out the back door, waiting while he locked up and following him to where he'd parked Bonnie in the back. Then she stopped.

"You're not scared of motorcycles, are you?" he asked, unhooking the helmet.

"I'm scared of you," she said softly. "I'm scared of how much you could hurt me and how little I care."

The wine worked, he thought with a smile. "You don't have to be scared of me, Libby. But come with me and let me show you exactly who and what I am. Then, if you still want to go down that slippery slope, I'll go with you. But not until you know everything about me."

She took the helmet and nodded. "That's fair. Let's go."

Chapter Seventeen

Even with a helmet and long sleeves, a warm, summer breeze covered Libby enough to make her feel hot and reckless and daring. The little bike was in great shape but had to be as old as she was...but still roaring, she thought with a smile. Law skillfully guided them through the streets of Mimosa Key, then up the far back roads of the eastern side of the island.

There, they rode along the water and dark, mysterious canals that had yet to be touched by eager developers. A midnight half-moon lit their way, and for a time, a short, free time, Libby didn't think about anything but the strength of the man in her arms, the feel of his muscles and thickness of his torso, and the rough, hot, noisy engine between her legs.

She pressed her lips to his shoulder and closed her eyes, inhaling the lingering smell of the food on him and the briny air from the brackish canal water.

Coming around a corner on a darkened road, he slowed a little, then veered to the side, bringing the bike to a stop. He put his feet on the ground to balance them, then shut off the ignition.

She squinted into the darkness, not sure exactly where

they were, though she knew the area well enough. As her eyes adjusted to the darkness, she could see a blackened waterway and some islands beyond it, then past that, the Gulf of Mexico.

He pushed the kickstand down and climbed off the bike, holding it steady for her to do the same. "Come with me."

She reached up and unsnapped her helmet, shaking out her hair. The closest thing to cool air that anyone would feel on an August night in Florida kissed the little bit of skin she'd left exposed, and almost immediately, a mosquito buzzed by her ear.

She flicked at it, and Law tossed her an *I told you so* look, taking her hands and walking her to a long, weathered dock she hadn't seen in the moonlight.

"Oh, I know where we are," she said, getting her bearings now. "We used to bring kayaks to this dock when we were teenagers."

"Mmm." He nodded. "Lots of people do. There's parking over there, and it's the start of a good run through these islands."

"Does this dock have a name?" she asked.

"Might. But I think of it as Beckett's dock."

She glanced at him as they walked toward the wooden planks. "Who's Beckett?"

"My brother."

She looked up at him, surprised. "I didn't know you have a brother."

"Had," he corrected.

"Oh, I'm sorry." She studied him for a moment, then the darkness beyond. "Is that why you brought me here?"

"I brought you here because you need to know who I am. What I am."

He took her hand and walked along the wooden platform

to the dock that extended out about twenty-five feet into the canal. They walked in silence to the end.

"Right here," he said, pulling her a little to sit down. "Right here."

They sat on the end of the dock, and he crossed his legs. "Don't hang your legs in," he warned.

"Best not to feed the gators?"

"Yeah, but we're safe up here." He leaned back, bracing himself on two hands, looking up to the moon, quiet. She watched him for a moment, then scanned the still, black water and clusters of small islands.

"I liked kayaking up here with Sam," she said, a memory floating back to her. "And my grandfather liked to come up and fish."

"Good fishing here," he agreed. "Except..."

"Except what?" she asked, sensing they were getting to the root of why they were there.

He didn't answer, staring straight ahead.

"Law?" she finally asked, putting a hand on his arm. "Tell me about your brother."

He focused his attention on her, coming back from wherever he'd gone. "He died here in a boating accident. And it was my fault."

She sucked in a little bit of air, the statement so direct and unexpected and...sad. "I'm sorry."

"Me, too," he said with a wry laugh. "But you can never be sorry enough when you're the reason the far better, smarter, and more amazing son is dead."

Oh. She squeezed his hand in sympathy, not arguing with what sounded like an old, old pain. Instead, she tried to wrap her head around losing Sam, and failed. "I can't imagine that."

"No," he agreed. "You can't. It's crippling. The only way

I ever numbed it was with alcohol. It deadened the guilt and killed the memories. For a while at least. And then it started killing me, which is when Jake Peterson stepped in and saved my life."

"How did he do that, Law?"

"He..." He looked directly in her eyes, a world of hurt in his. "He loved me. And at that point in my life, I didn't know what that even was. Never knew it before or since."

"Your parents didn't love you?"

He opened his mouth to answer, then shut it again, turning away, silent.

"They must have," she said, as if the question begged some kind of answer.

"They probably did, before September of 1980. After that? I was nothing but a source of pain. My mother was wrecked and eventually moved away to be with her family in Tennessee. She died a few years ago, and I can honestly assure you that she never once forgave me or said she loved me in the thirty-some years between Beckett's death and hers."

Libby winced at the thought. And no one had loved him since then? She couldn't imagine her mother not loving her, or, for that matter, not loving a child. She might sleep in an empty bed, but her heart and life were full with family love.

"My dad raised me, more or less, and did his best to introduce me to the joys of drowning your sorrows in the bottom of a bottle. He also beat the crap out of me, reminded me every day that if I hadn't given up, I might have saved my brother, and then he died, too, of cirrhosis. He didn't really recognize me the last time he saw me. He called me...Beckett."

She sighed, still holding his hand, feeling like a little window to his heart was opening, and getting a chance to peek in was frightening and humbling. And just made her care for him more, and something told her that was not his intention at all.

On the contrary, he was ripping back the curtain and expecting her to recoil.

"We shouldn't have been out that late," he said, looking at the water again, drifting away in his thoughts. She knew better than to prod for details. She had to wait until he was ready.

It took a full minute until he spoke again. "Beckett was fearless, you know? Four years older than I was, bigger than life. Loud, funny, smart, athletic, and nothing scared him. We should have gone home, but we didn't. Fish were biting, and he...he'd stolen some beer from my dad. I didn't drink it, since I was only ten, but Beckett had a few, and he got crazy."

He narrowed his gaze, locking on something...out there. She didn't let go of his hand as she waited for more of the story.

"He was acting like an idiot, throwing the net out too far, and we were only on a skiff with one shitty engine. It was dark, and I wanted to go home so bad, but Beckett was drunk. Maybe for the first time in his life. He threw the net off the bow, and it got caught on something, and he fell in. I wasn't even looking. I just heard the splash and then...nothing. Silence. Just...nothing."

She tried to put herself in the body of a ten-year-old boy whose brother had just fallen into black, gator-filled water at night. The terror must have been paralyzing.

"It was so damn quiet. That was the scary part. One second he was there, the next, gone." He let out a slow sigh, steadying his voice and, she suspected, his heart. "I kept calling and looking. We had one flashlight that was almost out of batteries, and I was so nervous and scared I couldn't steer the rudder. I just kept screaming his name over and over, but...nothing."

He dropped his head and let it shake from side to side, and Libby moved closer, putting an arm around him. She wanted to tell him it was okay, but that kind of pain couldn't be brushed away with a platitude.

He swallowed and composed himself. "I left," he said softly. "I finally got the boat to steer right, and I came right back here and stood in the road wailing until some stranger drove by and found me, and I honestly don't remember the rest of the night. They found his body the next day, and no, a gator did not kill him. He must have hit his head on something and died instantly or drowned quickly. Really, the details never stuck in my head, because I knew the truth." He closed his eyes, the pain etched on every feature of his face. "I quit. I gave up. I left too soon."

"No!" She sat up straight, shaking her head. "What could you have done? Jumped in the water and had the same thing happen to you?"

He exhaled again. "I shouldn't have left, and my dad told me that every day I saw him for the rest of his life. He ingrained it in me—Lawson Monroe is a quitter. I believed it, I lived it, and I drank to escape that truth."

"But you're not drinking now, so you must have come to terms with this accident by now, at least to some degree."

"I have," he said. "Going into the Army helped a lot, finding my skill in the kitchen, but Jake was the one who got me off booze and made me face the fact that my dad needed someone to blame for the loss of his favorite son. But it doesn't change who I am, deep down. Not really good enough for...anything."

"Anything?"

"Anything that really matters. Ninety-nine percent of the time, I'll quit. When the going gets tough, Law gets going. In the other direction."

She shook her head, not buying that at all. "Your dad said you were a quitter, you think that trait is why your brother died, but now you can't or won't have relationships because of it?"

He stared at her, the slightest misting in his eyes. "Something like that."

"Is that why you've never married? Or settled into a home? Or one long-term job?"

"That's a lot of questions," he said with a laugh, picking up a dried leaf from the dock and slowly breaking it into small pieces as he looked out to the night.

"Then take them one at a time."

"Okay. Why I never married? I suppose if you dig deep enough, the accident shaped every relationship I ever had."

"Shaped them into what?" she asked.

Another mirthless laugh as he cracked the leaf. "I guess I asked for this when I brought you here, huh?"

"Really." She leaned into him and gave a nudge. "We should be in bed right now, Lawless, not having deep, introspective talks on a bug-infested dock in the middle of the night."

"No kidding. What was I thinking?"

"Too late now. Answer my questions."

He shot her a smile, about to say something, but then he shook his head.

"What?" she asked.

"You," he replied.

"What about me?"

"I thought you were all..." He hesitated again. "I had you all wrong, that's all."

Her heart did a little squeeze at the admission, and she wanted to ask how he had her wrong, what he thought, but she didn't. "Why don't you live somewhere permanent?" she asked instead. "Why are you moving about and bunking in spare rooms at your age?"

The little light of warmth disappeared from his face, and he turned away again, silent for a long beat before he answered. "I guess the same reason," he eventually said. "A home, like a long-term relationship, is just...well, it feels wrong to me."

"Wrong? How is that possible?"

"Like it's for other people, not me."

She drew back. "How can having a home be for other people and not for you?"

He didn't respond, silenced either by emotions or secrets too deep to share, even here.

"Law." She whispered his name, sympathy welling in her chest. "Everyone deserves a home."

He just flicked his brow and let the broken leaf fall back to the dock. "I don't even get the concept, to be honest. Mine was crap as a kid, then in the Army I never had a home, then I sort of bounced around and lived with Jake. And what was your last question? Oh, the job. Well, chefs jump jobs unless..." He narrowed his eyes at her. "They own a place."

He was trying to tease, but guilt squeezed. "So that's what the Pelican would be to you. Your first long-term job."

"My first long-term anything. And at forty-six, that's saying a lot."

She gave a grunt of guilt. "God, I'm sorry."

"Don't be. It means something important to you, too." He searched her face for a moment, as if he were trying to get inside and find out what that something was.

"Balance," she whispered.

"Yes, that's what you're going to name the place. I remember."

"No, that's what I'm looking for," she said. "My whole life has been tilted by the need for…a man to validate me." Even as the words came out, they surprised her. She hadn't ever thought about it quite in those terms, and the concept was both unspeakably true and shameful.

But, really, wasn't that at the core of everything that troubled her? "Without that, I feel unstable. So I think the business would replace that and bring balance into my life."

"You don't need a man to validate you," he said. "To make sweet love and give you pleasure and enjoy all that beauty and brilliance, yeah. But you're valid, Libby Chesterfield."

She smiled at him, but her mind was whirring through this new revelation. "I have an issue with casual sex."

"So I've heard."

"No, not just since I decided to be celibate, but always. I don't like the way it makes me feel."

"That's because—"

"I know, I've been with the wrong guy and I'm putting too much meaning on the act. Let's just say I've had enough meaningless hookups to know they don't work for me, no matter the circumstances. That's always been my downfall and why I married the wrong men. But men look at me, and that's what they want. Sex and more sex and then…they move on."

To Arizona, she thought glumly.

She took a deep breath to finish the speech. "I would like to change that."

He stared at her, waiting for her to elaborate.

"I would like to…be with you and have no expectations," she said. "You know why?"

"I'm going to guess it's not the five orgasms I've promised."

"I trust you."

He just looked at her some more.

"I trust you to make love to me and make me laugh and feel great and have fun, and I know, I *know* without a shadow of a doubt, that we're both going into it with our eyes wide open."

"You might close your eyes."

"The fifth time. Exhaustion, you know."

He gave her a sly smile. "I can do that, and I think I've made it clear how much I want to. But are you sure? You're not going to wake up, freak out, and run screaming into the night?"

"Nor will I demand you love me forever and take the trash out on Tuesdays."

He laughed softly. "But isn't that kind of a contradiction? You have these issues with men who only want you for sex, and now you want sex with one who's made it perfectly clear what he wants, why he wants it, and how it won't lead to anything except the next round."

"Yes." She took a slow, deep, cleansing breath. "It's like yoga. Sex with you will be like yoga."

"Ooh." He hooted softly. "I promise you, Libby, it will be *nothing* like yoga."

"One of my best instructors once told me that it's not yoga until you fall out of the pose. That's when you realize what you're doing wrong, and that's when you reap incredible benefits. Obstacles fall away. Conflict disappears. Things that tripped you up your whole life suddenly make sense."

He studied her for a moment. "Yoga really does that?"

"Absolutely," she said. "It could help you."

"I don't need help," he replied quickly, starting to get up as if she might change her mind.

"But you do." She didn't rise with him, but kept his hand in hers. "You need to let go of the thing that has you coming back to this dock."

"My brother? Never."

"Your guilt. Your shame. Your regret. Your firm belief that you aren't worthy of a home or a relationship or a long-term job."

He shook his head and tugged her hand to bring her up with him. "I can't *yoga* that stuff out of my life. But…" He pulled her all the way up and into him for a kiss. "I'm happy to help you have sense-making sex if you're sure that's what you want."

She nodded, firm in her conviction. "That's exactly what I want. I want to enjoy sex and not have it all wrapped up with things that…don't matter."

He took her hand and brought it to his mouth. "They matter to you, Lib."

"But I don't want them to," she insisted, meaning every word. "And you are the perfect lover to do the job. Tonight. Now. My house is ten minutes away."

He just looked at her for a few moments, a bit of wonder and amusement in his eyes. "Okay, yoga bear," he whispered. "Let's fall together."

Chapter Eighteen

Law was drunk. He remembered the feeling and recognized it immediately. The erratic and chest-cracking hammer of his heart when the first sip hit his blood. The numbness in his fingers as they reached for another drink. The slack jaw, heavy limbs, the single-minded focus on pleasure, even the ringing in his ears that screamed more, more, *more*.

Holy hell, Law was *plastered* on Libby Chesterfield.

He'd felt a little tipsy during a long, wet, grabby kiss in her driveway. He'd gotten slammed as they started stripping each other before the door was locked behind them. And he was downright wasted on the feel of her breasts and the taste of her mouth as he and Libby staggered helplessly up the stairs to her bedroom.

And now, standing at the foot of her bed, naked and hard and desperate as she lay down and beckoned him with the crook of her finger, Law knew that as soon as he had her, as soon as he plunged into paradise and surrendered to the sheer intoxication of Libby, it wouldn't be enough.

Just like that first sip of Jack and Coke, when it had slid down his throat and warmed his veins, he'd want her again and again and again.

Then he'd be addicted to Libby, and hadn't he just made some kind of promise that this would be nothing but a hedonistic, indulgent pursuit of pleasure that would happen once or twice or maybe three times and then it would be over?

Except, he knew himself too well.

And he didn't care.

"What's taking you so long?"

"Using all my senses, starting with my eyes." He knelt on the bed and let his gaze do what his hands and mouth were about to. "You are a damn work of art, Libby."

She gave him a soft half smile that didn't reach her eyes.

"Oh, sorry," he added. "You hate that, don't you?"

Then she reached for his hand to pull him onto the bed with her. "What I hate is talking and looking and thinking when I want to be kissing and touching and coming."

"So demanding."

"*Now.*" She yanked him on top of her.

He started with a kiss to her mouth, but worked his way south, hungry to taste the budded nipples of her succulent, abundant breasts. He inhaled the smell of one of his favorite places in the world, the depth of a silky cleavage, but he'd never caught a scent quite as glorious as Libby's. Spicy and sweet at the same time, like the perfect combination of a savory dessert.

She moaned and responded instantly, her hips rising and falling as if they called for his attention, too. Reluctantly, he left his treasure and went searching for more, kissing slick, tender skin, exploring every curve with hungry hands, and shifting to his side to let her do the same.

He kissed her, suckled her tongue, and slipped a finger between her legs, making her moan and shudder.

"You are ready to come," he observed with a laugh.

"You promised five. And the closet didn't count for tonight."

"Take one now, sweetheart." He thrust his finger in and out and stroked her with his thumb, rising up to watch her pretty features lost in the pleasure of his touch.

"Law, that's...amazing." She worked to steady her breath, but gave up and groaned, turning her head from side to side as she came in his hand. He held her tight as she whimpered and strained, then kissed her mouth some more. "That was pretty easy, Lib."

"I've been practicing in the shower," she said, making him chuckle.

"As long as it was me, I'm okay with that."

"It was," she admitted, sounding a little defeated. "Ever since the reunion, you've been my fantasy of choice."

He lifted his head from her throat and chest, smiling. "That's the nicest thing you've ever said to me."

"You turn me on," she said simply. "I guess that's stating the obvious."

And it just made him want to turn her on more. He gave her another orgasm with his mouth, enjoying the taste of her, drunk on that, too, then found his wallet and the condoms he'd been carrying for a few days now.

As she recovered, she stroked him with two hands, her gaze intent on his erection as scorching as her touch.

They rolled a few times, letting their legs wrap around each other, caressing all the skin, tasting, touching, and tenderly whispering all the things they'd been thinking for days.

Sexy, secret, hoarse confessions of what they'd been wanting to do...and then doing exactly that. Every whisper she made was as delicious as the mouth that uttered it. Every dirty, shameless plea more intense than the last. And every touch of her skin was like gulping a gallon of full-bodied Cabernet.

By the time she slid a condom on him, spread her legs, and welcomed him deep inside her, he couldn't remember his name and the whole room spun mercilessly.

Drunk.

She met every stroke, grew hotter and more impatient, dug her nails into him, and let him carry her to another sweet orgasm, and another, growing frantic with each rush up to the peak and shaking as she caught her breath for the next. His blood like hot lava, his hard-on ready to explode, he finally shut his eyes and scooped her whole body into his arms as he thrust furiously into her.

As he shuddered and lost control, she did, too, with perfect timing, strangled breaths, and precious pleas for more and more.

His exquisite release came from somewhere deep inside and didn't end until there was nothing left to give.

While they lay gasping for breath, covered with sweat and each other, Law remembered something else about being drunk. That sickening, broken, miserable feeling of a hangover.

It wasn't supposed to happen. He wasn't supposed to care. He was in this for the pleasure and fun, with his eyes on the prize of the restaurant. What the hell was he doing wanting more of Libby? Why was he opening his eyes, looking at this pretty room, and aching to wake up here often…always…with this woman in his arms?

Oh man, he was past drunk on Libby. He was out of his freaking mind.

"Oh, Law."

He turned when Libby sighed the words, watching her eyes blink open slowly and the smile pull at her lips. "Yeah," he agreed. "That was amazing."

She sneaked a look at him. "Five times, too. Truth in advertising."

He wanted to laugh, but it would take too much energy. "Five more where that came from. Hell, fifty. Five hundred." Lost for a moment, he reached for her face, stroking her flushed cheek. "Baby, I want to do that to you for…for…"

Forever. What the ever-lovin' hell was he saying?

"For the rest of the night. At least," he added.

"Oh…really." She sat up, the loss of her body warmth making him suck in a surprised breath. "I think we're…good."

Good? "Lib, we haven't even started. That was the first round."

She lifted a brow. "At your age?"

"I'm good with some rest, a shower, a bite to eat." With her, it might take less time than ever. "I get a whole night, Libby." He hated that he wanted it so much, hated that he was begging…but he absolutely loathed the idea of leaving her.

She stared at him for a beat or two, a storm brewing in her eyes, turning them more gray than blue, more scared than satisfied. "My daughter will be home early in the morning," she said.

"It'll be nice to see her."

Her eyes flashed. "And we have to work late tomorrow."

"I can stay tomorrow, too." Did he just say that? Oh, what the hell. What was one more night? Two more? Ten more? He wanted to be with her.

"But…you can't."

"I can," he replied, then stroked a strand of silky blond hair. "I want to."

He saw her visibly swallow. "But wasn't that the whole idea of this?" she asked. "A chance to see if I could simply let go, have sex, get all out of balance, then resume life without any desperate need for more?"

Damn it. She was right. "Yeah," he said. "Like yoga, I think you called it."

"Which lasts an hour or two at the most." She inched out of his touch. "So our practice is over."

He didn't move, letting this sink in. "Libby, I want to spend the night with you. I want…more." Way more than he'd ever admit, but he knew when to shut up.

"We'll see each other tomorrow at the restaurant. And if the spirit moves us, we'll do this again. But probably not. We *agreed*."

"To cutting it short after an hour?" Frustration zinged up his spine.

"If you spend the night, then I'll want you to do the same thing tomorrow. And the next night. And the next. And then…" She shook her head.

Then they'd be connected, and he didn't do that. Except… "Then what?"

"Then there's going to be this thing in court and the DNA tests, and one of us is going to win the Great Pelican Race, and then…"

"Then what happens next?" he demanded again.

Since when did *what happens next* with a woman even matter to him? Since about an hour ago. Maybe more.

"Then I'll—" Her eyes widened. "That's a car pulling into the driveway."

He frowned, listening to the engine and nodding in agreement. "Yeah, someone's here."

"Oh, Jasmine's home early." She shot out of bed and started scooping up clothes on the floor. "You have to leave."

"Libby, you're a grown woman. You can have a lover if you—"

She whipped around, fire in her eyes. "You *have* to leave, Law."

Oh, so *this* was Donna Chesterfield.

She pushed in, passed him, and looked up the stairs where her daughter stood buck naked, except for an expression of pure exasperation. "Libby, I'm so glad you gave up that stupid vow of celibacy. It's for priests, not gorgeous fortysomethings." She turned to Law. "Don't leave on my account, sweetheart."

"If you insist, I can—"

"He was just leaving." Libby was the one doing the insisting. "Weren't you?"

Not if he finally had a chance to talk to the ever-elusive Donna Chesterfield. But he looked up at Libby and read the abject plea in her eyes, visible even fifteen stairs away. She wanted him to leave. She was *begging* him to leave.

And, damn it, he actually cared about her too much to stay and make things worse for her. He didn't know when that happened, but it had.

"Yeah," he said. "I was on my way out. See you tomorrow, Libby." He paused in the doorway and searched Donna's face, which was smooth for her age and as pretty as her daughter's. "I'd like to talk to you sometime, though."

"We'll find you that agent," she said with a wink. "I may take a commission, too."

He stepped outside, and she closed the door behind him.

On the front porch, he took a deep inhale of soggy summer air, but that still didn't clear his head. Well, it wasn't the first time he'd wandered drunk into the night, shirtless, shoeless, and wanting…just one more.

He'd long ago conquered that problem. Now he'd have to do the same thing with Libby. One midnight at a time, just like always.

Chapter Nineteen

"I don't know if it's morning or night." Libby's mother closed the door behind Law slowly, watching him leave as long as she could, then turning to give Libby her brightest smile. "Jet lag is killing me. Do you have any of that chocolate raspberry truffle coffee I had last time I was here?"

Libby stayed frozen, trying to come to grips with her failed experiment. No grips were forthcoming. Not a single one even on the horizon.

"Libby?"

It was actually funny how spectacularly she'd failed at casual sex. Five orgasms and she was looking at her next marital mistake.

"Libby! The coffee?"

And there stood the reason at the bottom of her stairs.

"What are you doing here?" she asked her mother, still sounding as dazed as she felt. "I thought you were in Europe doing...*A Streetcar Named Desire*."

"They switched to *The Importance of Being Earnest*. I don't like Oscar Wilde, so I left early. When I realized Sam wasn't in Miami, I drove over here."

Libby still didn't move, but rubbed her arms as the chill set in.

Mom looked up, dragging her purple specs down to get a better look. "That doctor did an amazing job on your lift, honey. Those are the tits of a twenty-year-old. Or is that yoga? All the actors rave about it. Would it get me a hunk and a half like you just had?"

Oh Lord, she'd been gone so long, Libby had forgotten just how weird Donna Chesterfield could be. "I don't know," she mumbled, turning back toward her room.

"How about that coffee?" Donna called up.

"In the top drawer under the coffeemaker. I'll be down in a second."

"No hurry. I'll be up all night."

Great.

In her room, Libby stared at the bed and took the deepest breath her lungs could handle and let it out slowly and with a lot of noise so she could be completely empty.

Like that bed.

Oh God. That was the most amazing sex she'd ever had, bar none. That was the most generous, delicious lover she'd ever imagined. And that freak-out at the end? The most over-the-top and ridiculous post-coital she'd ever pulled off.

And her mother's arrival was just icing on the stupid cake.

But she'd have to deal with Mom now and face her pathetic personal imbalances later. She walked to the closet and flipped it open, grabbing her raggy old bathrobe, desperate for the comfort of the fluffy turquoise wrap.

She tied it tight, glancing at the bed again, feeling the siren call to just lie down and remember the things her body had just done and felt. Her body, at least, had been on its best behavior, cooperating, responding, melting, and exploding. Five freaking times, and there could have been more.

He wanted more.

And she wanted...*a different kind of more*. Yeah, her body had been all in for the meaningless smashup. It was her brain and soul and mind and spirit that had fallen apart when she looked into Law Monroe's eyes and longed for...him. Him in a way that he didn't do.

Once again, Libby Chesterfield had blown casual sex to bits.

Still, she perched on the edge of her bed, so not ready to deal with the human whirlwind that was her mother, aching to lie down and think about Law. She stroked her hand over the pillow where his head had been, barely dented from their coupling. They'd moved around, mussed the covers, but hadn't pressed any heads into pillows or cuddled until dawn or exchanged more secrets and dreams and fantasies about forever.

Because Law had been clear he wasn't a forever guy. And Libby had attempted...but the intimacy they'd shared made her want to wrap him up in her bed and...keep him there. Which was why when he suggested that very thing, she realized that if she didn't shove him out the door, she'd be clinging to him like a barnacle on a boat by morning.

He'd openly scoffed at the idea of a relationship that lasted longer than a standing-tree pose, and she'd sworn she could have a hookup and walk away unscathed, and now she was all...scathed. Touched and kissed and satisfied. Held and trusted and...loved.

Oh, Libby, when are you going to stop seeking the myth of love?

She'd looked into those green eyes and tilted sideways, all the way, dizzy and wobbly and *needy*, like she always was with a man who mattered.

What had she been thinking?

That she could be a normal woman of the new millennium who could fall into bed with a hot, willing guy and not immediately start thinking about some happily ever after that didn't exist anywhere but romantic comedies and fiction?

She stood quickly, waiting for the rush of imbalance to threaten, but she was as steady as ever. Because it wasn't balance she lacked in her life, she realized with a start, it was *permanence*. Something—someone—who would last forever.

"I can't find the raspberry kind!" Donna's voice floated up from the kitchen.

Because of her. Donna Chesterfield and her constant movement and changing stories and desire to float through life with no anchor except her two kids. She was the reason Libby longed for stability and balance and something that lasted a lifetime.

"Is the chocolate coconut any good?"

Oh, for crying out loud, what was wrong with that woman? Suddenly, urgently, Libby wanted to know the answer to that question. She pushed off the bed and marched out of the room, fueled by something she hadn't ever really wanted to confront before, but now she had to.

She'd just sent a dreamy lover packing because she wanted something so badly that she couldn't even put it into words, and someone had to be blamed. Donna Chesterfield had just stepped on a land mine.

"The chocolate coconut is awful." She made a lot of noise on each step, like a drumbeat to the argument she wanted to have. "And so are you for barging in here at midnight and interrupting my night without even a phone call of warning."

Mom turned from the coffee drawer when Libby entered

the kitchen. "Honey, you know I'm a night owl, and when you and Jasmine moved back here, you gave me a key and said this house was my house whenever I wanted it, and tonight, I wanted it." She shifted back to the drawer and plucked out a K-Cup. "Oh, cinnamon pastry. Perfect! Want one?"

"No coffee for me." She yanked open the fridge, spied an open bottle of Chardonnay, and seized it with a little too much desperation. "This is what I need."

"He *was* leaving, right? I mean, he wasn't answering the door carrying his shirt and shoes. Did I read that right?"

"Yeah, more or less." Libby slid onto a stool at the island and poured a large glass, then took a healthy swig. "I just booted him out," she said after swallowing. "Would you like to know why?"

"Not for his bad looks."

Libby watched her mother get a cup and then find the milk, sugar, and spoon, her brain ticking away on all the possible routes this conversation should take. Was she going to blame her mother? Demand an apology? Just talk about it and work it out? Get help?

"I kicked him out because I wanted him to stay."

Mom crossed her arms and narrowed her eyes to a dramatic squint, as if some imaginary director had said, *Donna, give your best dubious look and make sure they see it in the back row!*

"You see, I have a problem, Mom," Libby said. "I can't seem to have casual sex or easy flings or one-night stands or anything that doesn't end up with a visit to a wedding planner followed by another to a lawyer. Why do you think that is?"

"I know exactly why it is," she said, dumping too much milk in her cup. "You married a wuss, and then you married a prick. Please don't try and blame your bad choices on some silly notion that you attach too much significance to sex." She lifted the cup to her lips. "You didn't place much worth on sex in high school, as I recall finding condoms in your room when you were barely sixteen."

"Because I was reeling from the fact that my father wasn't my father."

Mom looked away, suddenly interested in rinsing her spoon at the sink, her back to Libby. "Yes, well, you know what a difficult spot I was in."

Actually, she didn't. "Twice? So difficult you had to make up another lie?"

"We've been over this," she said on a sigh. "Old news. And now you know the truth."

"Do I?"

She whipped around as if the words had hit her right in the back. "Yes, Liberty, you do. And that is going to get you the thing you are owed, a lovely piece of expensive real estate in the middle of a town poised for growth and success."

"Maybe. Maybe not."

Her mother drew her brows together, another practiced stagelike expression, and Libby sighed, wishing Sam were here to deliver this particular blow as legal news. And that her mother had bothered with basic communication during her flights of fancy to act in other countries.

"Law Monroe was Jake Peterson's closest friend and, when Jake died, his roommate."

The frown softened to something more genuine, something a little more like…fear. "That man who just left? He knew Jake?"

"He knew him, loved him, and was promised the Toasted Pelican when Jake died."

Donna's jaw dropped, also unscripted. "What?" she croaked. "But Sam said he'd checked all those possibilities, and he filed that notice in the legal journals. I thought we were months and months past the possibility of this happening."

"He doesn't have a physical will, just a verbal promise that Jake made on his deathbed."

"Oh." She huffed in relief, folding herself onto another barstool at the island. "Then screw him. We have birth certificates. Does he have anything else? Anything...else?"

"We're about to have DNA, which will obviously be in our favor."

Her eyes popped. "Excuse me?"

"Law and I found a men's toiletry kit in the restaurant. It was full of personal items that contained his hair and skin. Sam has it at one of the best DNA-testing facilities in Florida, comparing it to ours. He used a courier as a witness to take our samples and sign an affidavit that the kit belonged to Jake—"

"But you can't be sure!"

"Pretty sure. Sam thinks it has a good shot at holding up in court."

"Only if it's a match." She slipped off the barstool and leaned closer. "You can't take that chance and have the whole thing blow up in our face."

"Why wouldn't it be a match?" Unless her mother had lied.

"Because you can't trust those labs. Plus, how do you know that thing you found really belonged to Jake?" she demanded.

"It had his initials on it, it was in a closet he used as an office and personal space, and Law recognized it right away as Jake's when we found it."

"Law?" She lifted one brow like a single arrow shooting north. "The man who says the Toasted Pelican was left to him."

"Yes, that same Law."

"Hah." She snorted with derision. "How convenient that he was with you when you found it, this man who has no will but claims Jake left him the Pelican."

Libby stared at her. "He's not lying."

"And he's sleeping with you."

"Once," she said. "We slept together once." And all Libby really wanted to do was wallow in that right now, not defend a man she hadn't seriously considered would lie to her about this.

She rolled her eyes to the ceiling and shook her head vehemently, all Drama Mama again. "Isn't that just perfect, though? He finds the thing that you think will help your cause and hurt his, but it turns out it'll hurt you and help him."

She blinked at her mother, heat rising. "Even Sam didn't go there," she said.

"I'm sure this Law character made it seem very natural and probably even let you think you'd discovered this alleged toiletry kit."

"Nothing alleged about it," Libby said softly. "It was definitely a toiletry bag, and I did discover it."

"How?"

"I told you. It was in the closet Jake used for an office."

"When did you find it?"

"A few days ago."

Her mother's eyes narrowed. "After you'd been in that restaurant for a year and, I assume, in that closet more than once."

Every night. She just looked down.

"Had he been there alone before you?"

She didn't have to answer, because her mother, who clearly had given Sam the cross-examination gene, was absolutely right.

"And did he guide you straight to this discovery, or did you just come upon it by yourself?"

Don't forget the cash. I need both hands for this. In the closet?

And she'd thought he was just being thoughtful. And desperate for sex. But maybe he was being cunning and distracting her while guiding her right to the actual discovery…that he planted.

Oh Lord. They'd never even considered that. Even Sam believed him!

"I see you agree," her mother said, calmly seated again, sipping her coffee.

"I don't know. Sam honestly didn't even think about that angle since I was sure…" She closed her eyes, hating that the idea had ever been planted. She'd *trusted* him. The hardest thing in the world for her to do. Well, after casual sex.

"Libby, we have to get this DNA test pulled." Mom popped off the seat to grab her handbag on the counter. "Let's call Sam and tell him to cancel it and not file any kind of motion, or whatever he does, because this could ruin everything I want for you." When Libby didn't answer, her mother took out her phone and pointed it at her. "That son of a bitch owes you an inheritance after ignoring you for your whole life."

Jake wasn't a son of a bitch, was he? Not the Jake she'd come to know from Law. But maybe that was part of Law's…game.

"Don't call Sam now," Libby said. "It's late, and he's in

some hotel for a deposition this week. We'll call him tomorrow, if I decide to pull that DNA test."

"What's to decide?" Mom demanded. "You know I'm right, and I would bet a million bucks it's going to come back without the remotest match because it's probably some fake thing he made so you look like fools in front of the judge."

"Law wouldn't do that."

She sniffed, as if that said so much more about her opinion of "this Law character" than words did.

"He's trying to help me," Libby said. "He wants this decision to be fair and square. And so do I."

"Fair and square is giving a man's property to his biological offspring, and that is you and Sam. And is that why he's sleeping with you, because it's fair and square?"

God, Libby hoped that wasn't true. But if it was, she was glad she booted him out. Except, it wasn't true.

Was it?

"Has he found anything else? Or should I say, have you with his help?"

Libby frowned. "What else would he find?" But even as the words came out, she remembered the picture. But Libby had found that, right? Libby had thrown that book across the room and it fell out.

Or had he planted it?

Sighing, she dragged her hand through her hair, trying to even think of why he would do that. Because that picture supported her mother's story. And if Charity's date was right, it *really* supported it.

"What?" her mother demanded. "What is the other thing that you conveniently found that will ruin this for me? For you," she corrected quickly.

Libby picked up the wine glass, drained it, and put it back

down again before standing up to get the photo out of her bag. "Well, I can prove you wrong," she said as the wine hit the black pit of fear lurking in her stomach.

"How?"

"Because *I* found this in Jake's belongings." Belongings that Law had packed and had access to the night before, knowing he'd convince Libby to go there with him the next day, but she kept that to herself. "He certainly wouldn't hand me a photograph of you and Jake together, which would be something else that would help us in court and hurt him."

"A picture of us together?" Her mother's voice rose and cracked. "Where would he get something like that?"

"From Jake, who kept it, because..." She found the photo in the side pocket of her bag, but held it to her chest like a poker player saving the winning card for last. "According to Law, Jake talked about you and said he loved you."

Color drained from her mother's face. "He...what?"

"He has a take on Jake, Mom. He says he was a guy who helped people, especially Law. He says he knew you came back to town with kids and had absolutely no idea we were his."

She was as white as the coffee cup in her shaky hand now. "Let me see that," she ordered on a strained whisper.

Libby took a step closer, still clutching the photo and holding her mother's gaze. "Why would he set this up and have Charity Grambling confirm the date it was taken, which was, by the way, exactly the date you would have conceived if July 28, 1971, was your due date, which I'm pretty sure it was."

She slowly set the cup down and took a step closer. "Let me see that, Liberty."

"Why would he help me discover that if he was playing me to steal my inheritance, Mom?"

She swallowed and reached out her hand, and Libby gave her the picture. Adjusting her glasses to see through the bottom of the bifocal lens, she held the photo in front of her face, dead silent as she stared.

Mom's shoulders rose and fell in a silent sigh. Her throat moved with what had to be a painful swallow. Her shoulders dropped in resignation.

Thank God, Libby was right and Law could be trusted.

"I'm sorry, Libby. I know you care for the man. You yourself said you don't sleep with someone unless you're falling for him, and that's certainly the case with that handsome and, I have to say, shrewd and scheming man."

Libby frowned, the entire sentence making absolutely no sense at all. "That's all you have to say about this picture? It's proof you and Jake were together, and Law gave it to me and even took it to Charity to confirm the date, which adds up to him being my father. Law's *helping* me."

She lifted a brow. "Oh, right, because Charity could never be paid off or charmed by a man that delicious."

Trust me, Lib. Charity goes full-out cougar on me.

"What...do you mean?"

Her mother smiled. A practiced smile. A well-directed smile. But a smile of complete victory nonetheless. "This man in the picture is not Jake Peterson, honey. I don't remember his name, but I agreed to go to some Halloween pumpkin patch thing just to make Jake jealous, which was a complete failure, I might add. Did Law tell you this was Jake?"

"He thought it was him. His...nose."

She nodded and glanced at it again. "Lots of people with noses, even prominent ones. I'm sure he'll be able to prove in court that it's not Jake, right after Sam files it as evidence or something, all designed to ruin our case. If I were you, I'd tear this to shreds. In fact—"

"No!" Libby reached for the picture, but it was too late. Donna ripped it in two, right down the middle. "Why would you do that?"

"Because this picture will blow up in your face, I promise you. Don't take it to court. And don't be fooled by someone who wants to steal what's yours. And don't let him near you or your business or your family."

Libby just stared at her, stunned by the reaction, which, even for her mother, was over the top. "It's too late," she said. "He's living and working at the Pelican."

Her mother crossed her arms, still holding the photo. "Have you never heard the expression 'possession is nine-tenths of the law'? Can't you see how he'll use that against you, worm his way into the place, and put his stamp all over it, making it his, not yours? Probably making money, too. Can't you see that?"

Apparently, she couldn't see anything, because her mother was right about all of that.

"Sam thought it was a good idea," she said, sounding weak to her own ears. "He had some legal Latin term for why it would help us."

Mom choked softly and turned back to the island, grabbing the open bottle of wine. "I'll take this to bed with me. It'll help my jet lag."

Libby stood stone still as Donna Chesterfield executed the perfect exit stage right, closing a killer scene that was supposed to have been Libby's big confrontation about the origin of her issues…but had ended up churning up nothing but doubt and broken trust.

God, that woman was a good actress. But was she right about Law?

It didn't matter. The seed of distrust was well planted and already taking root.

Chapter Twenty

"Come on, Solomon. Aren't you a tech type? Fix this bastard so I can update the songs." Law turned the screw he was working under the jukebox lid, glancing across the bar to where Mark Solomon was perched on a ladder.

"High tech, not transistors."

"These aren't transistors," Law said. "I did some research, and this is a 1971 Rowe MM6 with a solid pre-amp and tube-type amplifiers. I'm pretty sure the problem is in the search unit on the records, if I can just get to it."

From his ladder, Mark yanked a shelf out and handed it to Ken, who stood below him, ready to retrieve. "Anyway, I happen to like the music that thing plays. The eighties were good years, right, Cav?"

Ken added the shelf to the pile of rubble they were creating as they dismantled the bottle stacks. "I just think it's a waste of time, Law."

The two men had come over to the Pelican that morning to help Law with some heavy lifting, including taking down the eyesore that blocked the view from one side of the bar to the other.

They were almost done now, and while they finished up

the last few shelves, Law had turned his attention to the jukebox, which had gotten even wonkier in the past few days. But he was determined to make the damn thing work.

"That jukebox is as ancient as the vinyl inside and pretty damn ugly," Ken added. "I don't even think it's worth refurbing it, let alone making it play all the songs again. If you want a jukebox, get something hip and cool that's been rebuilt to play digital music with touch-screen pads at each table."

"Touch-screen pads?" Law made a face. "Not the vibe I want in here. I'd want to keep some things and honor the history." He went back to work on the next screw. "Did you know there was actually a pelican living in here while they were building this place and they fed it toast?"

Mark snorted. "Mimosa Key folklore."

"Also not true," Ken said. "Beth's grandfather was one of the island founders, and he told her they gave the pelican booze and it wobbled around the job site, and that's how the place got its name."

Law gave a dry laugh, finally getting the top free and slowly lifting the heavy glass piece that held yellowed tabs with old song titles. "Anyway, maybe I would want to get a new one in here if I were going to be the owner and proprietor, but once that DNA comes back and Perry Mason proves his case, I'll be packing up and taking that job in Arizona. But I'd like a functioning jukebox for the rest of the time I work here. Music is important to the ambience."

But then, maybe Libby would waltz in here this morning and kick him out of the Pelican the way she kicked him out of bed. Then there'd be no ambience. And no Libby.

He shook off the thought and peered into the belly of the jukebox and—what the hell? It didn't look anything like the YouTube video. This one had been modified, heavily. Did it work the same?

Reaching around the open lid, he scanned the bright yellow buttons, a list of the alphabet and a row of numbers, to pick a random song. How about...L for Libby. And five for...*don't think about it, Law.* There wasn't going to be a sixth.

The cylinder turned, a metal prong searching for a song on the round record stack, but it got stuck after moving an inch. He reached in and tried to help it move, but it didn't budge as it had in the video he'd watched.

Swearing under his breath for what was probably the twentieth time that morning, Law pushed away. He'd deal with it later. These guys had been here all morning and had lives to get back to.

He walked back to the bar to help them finish, his gaze traveling over about fifty bottles of booze he'd taken down himself from the rack.

"That couldn't have been a pleasant job at seven thirty in the morning," Ken mused, following Law's gaze.

Law shrugged. "It was a great victory."

"How's that?" Mark asked.

"Handling all those bottles and not feeling a thing. It's like seeing an ex and not even twitching to touch her. That stuff..." He jutted his chin toward the bottles. "Has no hold on me."

"Then what does?" Ken asked. "Or should I say who?"

Mark slowed his screwdriver, eyeing Law as if the answer interested him, too.

"Nothing. No one."

They shared a look that said they thought he was lying. Damn, was he that transparent about her? Law flicked the air to ward off more questions, looking around the bar. "You know, it's a shitty job to work on a restaurant and doubt it will ever be mine."

"You don't know the outcome yet," Ken said. "You

could still find that will, or the judge could put some kind of delay in place and you could be here for another year."

"Great. Libby torturing me for a year. Just what I need."

"Didn't look like torture last night," Mark said. "You two can't keep your hands off each other."

Law snorted. "She can."

He saw the other two men exchange another silent look.

"I take it you've talked about this already," Law said.

They didn't answer, and he choked softly, grabbing a rag to start wiping off the bottles he wanted to keep to display on the new lower back bar.

"Guess you got all curled up with your 'fiancées' and shared secrets and opinions about poor, miserable Law, destined to live alone and pop from restaurant to restaurant."

Ken chuckled. "You're the one who scoffed at the idea of having a fiancée, bro. You practically spew venom every time either one of us reveals that, hey, we're happy and satisfied and content with these amazing women we've found."

Ken's words seared his chest like hot oil on a cast-iron pan. Law swiped the rag over a bottle of Jose Cuervo Silver, the faint whiff of tequila making his stomach turn a little. "God, I hate this shit."

"The booze or the conversation?" Mark asked, pulling the last shelf out and climbing down the ladder to dispose of it himself.

"Both," Law admitted. "Addictions suck."

"You just said you're not addicted to the booze anymore," Ken said. "Is it Libby?"

He closed his eyes and fought the urge to howl. *Yes, it's Libby! Of course it's Libby!* He breathed out, the way she did when she got tense. Noisily. "I didn't expect this to happen," he ground out.

"Lose the restaurant?" Mark asked.

Law shot him a look.

"Or lose your precious solitude?" Ken fired back.

Law swore again under his breath, and the other two laughed. "I'm really glad you think this is funny."

"Watching you topple from your mighty 'love sucks and is just for idiots' soapbox?" Ken asked.

"Yeah, it's pretty entertaining," Mark agreed. He came around the bar and brushed his hands on his jeans. "But it isn't easy. I've been there."

"We both have," Ken added.

"You were itching for a wife," Law said to Ken. "You made no bones about the fact that you wanted to hook up, settle down, and breed."

Ken smiled, shaking his head. "It wasn't a hookup." At the look both men gave him, Ken shrugged. "Okay, it was a hookup. And an unplanned pregnancy. But, damn, I didn't realize life could be this good. You, too, Mark. Right?"

Mark grabbed one of the rags on the counter and used it on his hands, considering his response as he wiped. "I knew life could be this good. I found love as a kid and lost it as a man. But I didn't think I could find it again, or that it would be so different. But it's…" He nodded, looking from one to the other, fighting a smile. "It's damn good stuff, Lawless. If you can't break the habit of Libby, I say that's one addiction that can only make you stronger and better."

Law eyed his friend, the oldest of the three of them, and maybe the wisest. But Ken was no dummy—a hero and a firefighter. He'd be a great father, too.

While Law? What the hell would he be, but…

He waited for the old voice, Dad's voice, to remind him what a piece of shit he was and always would be. He waited for Jake's voice, always there with something positive to say. Even his own internal ghost who nudged him to find the easy way out. In this case? That would be a one-way ticket to Arizona.

But the only voice he heard was Libby's. Sweet words. Sexy words. And *get the hell out* words.

"Why are you fighting it so hard?" Ken asked, confirming that Law was probably doing a lousy job of hiding his emotions.

"I'm not," he said gruffly. "She is."

"Because of this fight over who owns the restaurant?" Mark asked. "Too complicated?"

"She's just, you know, independent."

Ken snorted softly. "You gotta work with that, my friend. It makes a woman damn attractive."

"I mean, she's had a few crappy marriages, and I...well, I've never entertained the idea, so—"

"Marriage?" They said it at exactly the same moment, with matching faces of sheer incredulity. Law couldn't help but laugh at the reaction.

"Well, a *relationship*," he said, picking up another bottle to clean. "Something steady. Something longer than...the hour in the sack I got last night before being unceremoniously shoved out the door."

"Got a taste of your own medicine, huh?" Ken needled.

Law glared at him over a half-empty bottle of rum.

"Just take it slow," Mark said. "You know, like you learned. One day at a time."

Or one night. One lonely night like last night after he left Libby's.

"I have to make a decision about a job at a Ritz-Carlton in Arizona," he said, realizing just how heavily that was weighing.

"You want to go to Arizona?" Ken made a face. "I mean, I heard it's pretty and the Ritz is awesome, but...damn. That's far."

"Really far," Law agreed.

Mark stood and put a friendly hand on Law's shoulder. "Listen, Emma's waiting for me down at the house. We're going to finish that new kitchen today if it kills us. Just don't fight it, okay? If Libby feels right, trust that."

Law nodded. Libby felt right, that was for sure. Every inch of Libby felt right, inside and out. "Thanks for the help, man," he said to Mark.

"Yeah, I gotta go, too." Ken lifted the toolbox he'd brought over for them to use, then held it out. "You want me to leave this in case you want to work some more on that jukebox?"

Law almost said no, but then he glanced at the broken machine in the corner. It wouldn't even play *Blown Away* anymore. God knew he'd tried to listen to it last night when he came home to lick his wounds.

"Yeah, leave it. I'll bring it over to you in a day or two."

"I don't need it now. We finished building the shelves in the nursery."

"The nursery." Mark grinned at them. "Man, things have changed since that reunion."

"Changed for the better," Ken said.

"Damn right." Mark gave a quick salute and headed to the front door, a bounce in his step that Law watched with no small amount of envy.

"You'll figure it out, Law." Ken grabbed his wallet and keys from the bar.

"Or I'll go to Arizona."

"But, man, that's far away," Ken said again.

"From what?" Law looked hard at his friend.

"From my kid. I want him to know Uncle Law."

Law gave a rueful laugh, ready to disparage his uncle-ing skills...but then he realized how much he wanted to know Ken and Beth's little dude. Damn it. This was the life he wanted. Here, on Mimosa Key. Here, in the Toasted Pelican. Here, with Libby Chesterfield.

Son of a bitch. "I'll visit," he said quickly. "Because why stay here? If she wins this place, and something tells me she will, then what? I can't even work for her if she turns it into a stupid…yoga studio."

"You can't be sure that's going to happen," Ken said.

"Oh, it's happening. She's on a mission to have this place called Balance and make an *oasis. My* gastropub." He threw the rag he was holding down with too much force. "And I'm out."

Out of here…and out of her life, just like last night.

"What about your infiltration plan?" Ken asked. "What happened to the 'possession is nine-tenths of the law' strategy that you told me about the first day you took her to that storage unit? You're here. You're making changes. You're making money. Maybe she'll just give up the fight."

Or I will, Law thought glumly. It would be easy, a well-loved shortcut to the next life, full of…nothing because Libby wouldn't be there.

When the holy hell did that happen?

"She's not giving up anything," he said.

"You got that right."

Both men swung around at the statement, which came from the darkened kitchen hallway.

Libby.

How much of that had she heard?

"I'm not giving up a thing." She appeared in the doorway looking…fierce. Her blond hair tumbled over her shoulders like the mane on a breathtaking palomino pony. She wore a deadly black tank top, his favorite cutoff shorts, and a look in her eyes that said…oh damn.

She'd heard everything.

Chapter Twenty-One

is infiltration plan?

H   What did he think he could infiltrate besides her place of business? Her bed? Her life? Her *heart*?

"Hey, Lib." Law took a few steps closer, eyeing her carefully. Behind him, Ken nodded in greeting, his navy blue firefighter's T-shirt dusty from the work of taking that heinous back bar down. The bar looked great, though, she had to admit, until she remembered it was part of Law's *infiltration plan.*

"You're just in time to help him restock that bar," Ken said. "What do you think of what Law did here?"

What Law did to the bar *he didn't own.* Except...p*ossession is nine-tenths of the law.*

She hated when her mother was right.

"Nice," she said, purposely brusque. Then, to Law, "We need to talk."

Law drew back at her tone, but Ken instantly moved toward the door. "Yeah, well, I was just leaving," Ken said.

"Thanks for your help," Law said, turning to give his friend's hand a shake.

"Sure thing. Call me if you need anything." He glanced at Libby and gave a tentative smile. "You, too, Lib."

"I don't need anything but answers."

Ken gave Law a slight grimace and took off, leaving them standing face-to-face in the empty restaurant.

"Answers to what?" Law asked without moving. "Because if you just heard what he said—"

"We'll get to that." She took a slow breath, steadying herself. She knew this wasn't going to be easy, but she sure as hell wasn't going to stew one more hour without confronting him directly. "Let's talk about the picture that isn't Jake Peterson."

"What?"

She took a step closer. "Or how it is possible that I spent a year going in and out of that closet and never saw that shaving kit on the top shelf."

His eyes flashed, but he didn't say anything.

Oh God, don't let Mom be right.

Two more slow steps and now she could see his green eyes growing darker.

"Or let's talk about how convenient it was that the date Charity Grambling pulls out of thin air is nine months before my mother's due date."

"Convenient? For who?" He looked more confused than attacked, she could tell, but that didn't stop her from getting close enough to reach out and touch him. Not that she would. No, she curbed that urge, but used the proximity to truly read his reaction to see if he was lying.

He looked...honest. And good. And stunned by the attack she refused to stop.

"After we discuss all that," she said, "then you can address the, what was it? *Infiltration plan?*" Mom would have a field day with that one. After she got finished delivering a standing-ovation-worthy *I told you so* soliloquy.

"I didn't say that," Law said. "Ken did." But she heard the resignation and, essentially, the confession in his voice.

Libby finally tore her eyes from his and slowly scanned the dining room. Not a single inch of it was quite like it had been before he moved in. That was the infiltration plan and, damn it, he'd gotten her to *help* him.

He crossed his arms and sighed. "Look, Libby, I thought, at one point, that the best way for me to get what I wanted was to move in, take over, and show you what could be done. I'm not going to lie. I still do believe in what I could do with this restaurant. But once we found the DNA—"

"That you planted so that when it comes back without a match, you can claim Jake isn't our father after all."

His brows drew together in confusion. And no small amount of sadness. "Libby, seriously? You think I'd do something that…that low?"

"I don't know. Did you?"

"No." He blew out a breath and looked away. "But the fact that you even think that…wow. I didn't think that kind of thing could hurt so much anymore."

Her whole heart dropped, hitting her stomach hard. She'd made him feel worthless, which made her feel like crap.

"Libby, that toilet article kit was pushed against the wall on the top shelf. The only reason you saw it was because your head was tilted all the way back."

"In the throes of a climax that you gave me."

He gave a quick laugh. "Is that what I'm being accused of? False and misleading orgasm transmission? Is that Sam's legal interpretation?"

"Actually, no." She took another breath, maybe a hair less steady than when she walked in. "Sam never questioned the veracity of that bag. Or the picture."

"But someone did. Your mother?"

She closed her eyes as the truth hit. "My mother sees this in a different way."

"Your mother found some dude running out of your house at midnight, half dressed and covered with your scent. Wouldn't you lash out at a man you discovered leaving Jasmine like that?"

"My daughter wouldn't be so stupid as to sleep with a man who was…tricking her."

He winced. "I'm not tricking you." He turned away, busying himself with a row of bottles on the bar, thinking. Buying time. Building…a lie?

"Yes, your mother sees this differently," he finally said. "We've established that from day one. And I'd very much like to talk to her, because her take on Jake Peterson is really different from mine."

She eyed him. "But not wrong."

"*Different*," he repeated. "And I'm willing to talk to her. To share what I know and get her historical perspective without you filtering it. What the hell is she talking about that that isn't Jake in the picture?"

She shrugged. "She said it isn't him, just some guy she went out with to make Jake jealous and it didn't work. She doesn't remember his name."

"Some guy who happens to have Jake's exact, distinct nose."

"Some guy who happens to have a large nose, which isn't exactly a positive identification."

"But I don't understand," he said. "If she's trying to convince you that I have some dark ulterior motive of planting proof that you aren't Jake's daughter, why would I use a picture to try to prove that they were together and then have it confirmed—by *you*—that the picture was taken on or about the day you were conceived?"

She angled her head in concession. "That confused me, too. But I didn't date the photo, Charity did. Charity, who will do anything for you. And my mother thinks you have some courtroom antics up your sleeve where you'll go to that hearing and suddenly prove my mother was with another man, not Jake, and make her look like a liar."

His eyes widened as he came closer to her. "She's crazy."

Libby didn't argue. "She's...imaginative."

He reached for her hand and snagged it before she could pull away. "She can't do this to us, Libby. Don't let her."

"First of all, there is no us. Second, she can do anything she wants. Always has, always will."

"There was an us last night," he said quietly, the tone in his voice making her next breath difficult to take.

"There was sex last night," she replied. "I think we've both established that's all it was and ever will be."

"*You* established that."

She searched his face, looking for the truth, and what she saw was genuine.

Which screwed everything up, because she shouldn't have trusted him in the first place. But...she had. She did. She trusted him. Liked him. Wanted him.

Still holding her hand, he pulled her closer, a storm of emotion in his eyes that matched the one brewing in her heart. "Libby. Please don't do this."

"I'm trying to look at this situation from all sides and take my blinders off where you're concerned. Is that what I'm not supposed to do?"

"You took your blinders off last night," he said gruffly, slowly easing her to him. "And maybe you didn't like what you saw. Now you're looking for any excuse to push me away. And I don't want you to do that."

She let him press her against him, the solidness of him as

warm and appealing as the words. *Please don't be an act. Please.*

"I liked what I saw, Law," she whispered, holding his gaze. "I think that's the problem. I liked it too much. I liked it so much I...freaked out."

He exhaled as if the words were a balm to him. "You sure did."

"Sorry about that, but I'm not sorry about asking you these questions. I have to know. I have to look in your eyes and get the absolute truth."

He stared at her, unblinking, as if he were inviting her in. "I did not, in any way, shape, or form, plant that bag that belonged to Jake. I totally overlooked it when I cleaned the place, and you saw it, not me. I also fully expect the DNA test to come back with a match to prove you are his daughter."

"Why do you believe that?"

"Because you do." He frowned at her. "Don't you?"

"Yes, I do. I want to. I want her to be telling the truth, because..." She shook her head. "I don't think I can take another heartbreak of finding out who isn't my real father."

At the crack in her voice, he wrapped his arms around her, the pounding of his heart surprising her. He couldn't fake that.

"Nobody wants to break your heart," he said softly. "Including me."

Her throat tightened, and her eyes filled. "I want to trust you."

"You can," he said. "And I want to..." He hesitated as if digging for courage to say something. "I want...more." He barely breathed the last word.

"More?" she whispered back.

He swallowed, nodding slowly, a mix of terror and hope in his eyes. "You make me want more."

"More what?" She knew, though. She knew, and the same ripples of terror and hope were making her whole body vibrate.

"More time. More connection. More...more."

A smile pulled at her lips. "More more?"

"You know what I mean."

She did, and it scared her and thrilled her and made her feel totally off-balance. In a good way. "I was ready to believe the worst in you ten minutes ago," she whispered.

She reached up and touched his face, stroking the unshaved skin, counting the lines that life had given him, falling into those eyes that looked at her like she was...more.

Not a trophy. Not a toy. Not a conquest.

"But when I look at you, I don't see a man who'd connive to win something or break rules to get ahead or lie or cheat or steal or do anything that would be a shortcut to getting what he wants."

His expression softened, telling her the words had hit some mark. "Thank you," he whispered. "You couldn't have said anything to me that would mean more."

They both closed their eyes at the same time, the kiss pulling them together in the most natural way. Law's lips grazed hers, then pressed harder, as if sealing their quiet agreement of trust.

Somewhere, in the distance, a high-pitched sound started to whine. No, that was a guitar. Opening notes to a...song. An old song from the middle of the eighties...a haunting chord that made her want to sway into the kiss.

But he pulled away, frowning. "Now it works?" Law turned and looked at the jukebox, which stood gaping open like a big metal animal about to take a bite. "What the hell?"

"Pretty song, though," she said, easing him back for more kisses. "I loved U2."

He gave up on the jukebox and smiled at her. "I hated this song. Hated U2. Bunch of whiny boys."

She laughed. "*I Still Haven't Found What I'm Looking For*? This is a great song."

"Yeah." He lowered his face again. "This is a great kiss."

It was. Sweet and tender and—

He jerked away so suddenly she almost cried out. "*What's* the name of this song?"

"He's singing it now. *I Still Haven't Found What I'm Looking For.*"

His jaw slackened. "By U2."

"Yeah. I had the album. *The Joshua Tree.* I had every album by U2."

"U2. Which is the same as..." He stepped away, his attention riveted on the machine. "That's what he said, Libby. That's what Jake said."

A slow roll of goose bumps rose on her arms, traveling up to send a shudder through her. "What?"

Very slowly, he walked to the jukebox, as if he was half afraid of what he'd find.

"When he told me to find a will," he said. "He said, 'you, too.' Like the words. But maybe he meant a...a letter and a number." He pointed to the row of bright yellow buttons, the whole alphabet and ten numbers. "It was L5."

"But U2 is the name of the band."

"Holy shit." Visibly shaken, he leaned against the frame and looked into the opening of the jukebox. "He said, 'I still haven't found...'" He looked over his shoulder. "Was he talking about this song?"

"And that's where he put his will?" She darted closer, her heart hammering as she peeked into the machine, seeing an old 45-style record on a turntable surrounded by tubes, wires, a few cloth-covered speakers.

"This song or the slot where this song resides," he said, his arm all the way inside the jukebox now.

He bent over, determined and unable to see exactly where his hand was, his shoulder making the needle slide over the record and screech.

"Got it!" He bounced back to a stand and produced a business-size envelope so thin she doubted it held more than one piece of paper. "Libby, that night in the hospital. He told me *exactly* where it was, but…" His eyes widened as he read the front of the envelope.

"What is it?" she asked.

He looked up at her. "What did Charity say that guy's name was? The one in the picture with Jake and your mom?"

"Frank something?"

"Frank Rice, right?"

"Yeah. Why?"

He looked at the envelope again, then at her, his expression unreadable. "Libby," he said softly. "I found a will."

She reached for the envelope, but he just turned it around for her to read.

"*A* will," he said. "Not *the* will."

She squinted at the tiny words typed across the envelope.

The Last Will & Testament of Franklyn M. Rice, Sole Owner of The Toasted Pelican.

Chapter Twenty-Two

Hours later, the restaurant officially closed for business per Sam's orders, Libby and Law sat side by side in a back booth, facing Law's laptop. On the screen, Sam spewed yet another endless string of legal terminology at them on this, their fourth Skype session since they'd discovered the will.

The wrong will.

Well, possibly, the only will, Law thought.

The two papers they'd found in the envelope lay in front of them. Sam had a copy they'd scanned and sent him, but theirs seemed sacred somehow, or at least historic. Neither one of them touched the documents very much, but Law made notes on a pad of paper, and Libby leaned very close to him so that Sam could see both of them through the computer's camera.

Or maybe she leaned close because she wanted to. Needed to. He certainly wanted and needed the closeness.

Since they'd discovered the will, there'd definitely been a change, or maybe he'd call it an *intensification*, in where they'd already been going. Walls down, at least one complication removed, Libby was as close to him as she'd ever been, physically and emotionally.

Their discovery had changed everything. *Everything.*

If it was legitimate, it meant neither one of them could have this restaurant.

Law's gaze drifted over the two pieces of paper again, one typed on an old-school typewriter with one letter covered in white-out and fixed. The other, on thin creamy parchment, was labeled a Certificate and Deed of Ownership and clearly named Franklyn Rice as the sole owner of the Toasted Pelican.

And the truth hit Law again. This wasn't Jake's business to give away. He never owned the place. According to this will and the deed attached to it, the business belonged to Franklyn Rice and, upon his death, his heirs.

Well, where the hell were they?

"This is actually an addendum to another will," Sam said from the computer screen. "My research team says there was a will filed and administered fifteen years ago for Franklyn Moore Rice wherein his entire estate, except this property, was bequeathed to his wife, Rosalind Rice, who, at the time, resided in Atlanta. She has no known address now, but is not listed in any records as deceased. She'd be ninety-five years old."

"But what about his children and grandchildren?" Libby asked. "The will says the Toasted Pelican is never to change family ownership and must be transferred to his offspring or their heirs and…" She turned to read the words again, even though she had to have them memorized by now. "In the case of those heirs not taking ownership, the Toasted Pelican is to be closed and torn down. Until then, the business cannot change names, style, décor, menu, or ownership."

With every word, Law understood more and more.

This was the secret Jake alluded to before he fell into a coma. Not kids, but the fact that he didn't own the Pelican.

This was the reason for his lifelong hatred of lawyers—he was probably terrified of one walking through the door and taking everything away from him. And *this* was the reason he never changed anything and wouldn't let Law take over—he wasn't *allowed* to by virtue of this document.

Law dumped his head in his hands and swiped back his hair as snippets of things Jake had said over the years came back. Finally, it all made sense.

He'd been adamant—to the point of ridiculous—about never changing anything, not a decoration on the wall, not an item on the menu, which was why he kept Law out of the kitchen. He'd run everything with pen and paper and cash. No accounts, no investments, nothing official, nothing that could open up this can of worms and reveal the truth. He ran the business as if it were underground, because, in essence, it was.

Everything made sense, except…why would he keep that secret? Why not tell Law all those years later and the two of them do something about it? Why hide the proof in the jukebox and not reveal it until he was on his deathbed?

"What did he think I was going to do?" Law mumbled out loud, quieting the stream of legalese pouring out of Sam's mouth.

Libby put a hand on his thigh, giving another comforting squeeze, out of sight of the camera. He put his hand over hers and slid her a quick look.

He had to stop thinking about himself. Libby was screwed by this discovery. Even if she could prove Jake was her father, he hadn't owned the business in the first place.

They were no longer adversaries, but allies, and he didn't hate that. He kind of hated Jake for being such a stubborn old secret-keeping mule, but he didn't hate that the giant brick wall between him and Libby had tumbled with one randomly selected song on a jukebox.

L-5. Maybe Jake was watching down on him after all.

"I imagine Jake thought you'd continue on as he had," Sam said, yanking Law from his musings.

"No, he didn't," Law corrected. "He knew exactly what I wanted to do with the Pelican. We'd discussed it at length, but he refused to let me change a thing."

"Well, he built a viable business and made a considerable amount of money," Sam said before leaning forward and adding, "None of which, we assume, was shared with the owner."

"So now he's a criminal?" Law shot back. "For running the guy's business for, what, forty years? Fifty? When did all this happen, anyway?" The will was dated September 1972, and according to Sam's researchers—who were damn good—Frank's last known address on Mimosa Key was sold that same year.

"Assuming Jake took over or already worked there in 1972, he's run the business for well over forty years," Sam said. "Which could be hugely in our favor, unless he ran it illegally."

Law squinted at the screen. "Illegally?"

"We don't know what kind of arrangement they had," Libby piped in. "Maybe Jake sent him cash. Maybe Frank told him to just keep what he made. Maybe Frank, who Charity Grambling told us died after years of dementia, forgot he owned the business."

Sam moved out of camera range, his voice distant as he talked to one of the legions of associates, interns, and junior lawyers who seemed to do his bidding.

While he did, Libby and Law shared a look, giving him a chance to see she looked pale, tired, and a little vulnerable.

"You okay?" he whispered.

"Spinning."

"I know how much you like that."

She smiled and nodded. "Everything changed so fast."

"That's not a bad thing, Lib."

She angled her head. "Neither one of us gets the Pelican," she said. "And, hell, another fifteen minutes of kissing and I was ready to go for the Twisted Pelican and put my studio upstairs." She winked at him, but something inside Law slipped and fell and...hit smack into his gut.

A seismic shift, that's what happened.

The Twisted Pelican. That silly, crazy, off-the-wall idea would be...fun. It would keep them together. It would be the "fair and square" they both wanted.

A slow, low burn started in Law's belly as the idea started to take shape. An impossible, irresistible, insane shape, like when he'd put two totally unrelated ingredients in the same pan and magic happened.

"What were you saying, Libby?" Sam's question pulled them apart, forcing them to look at the screen where Sam was studying some legal-sized paperwork.

"I said that Charity Grambling told us Frank Rice had severe dementia." She glanced at Law. "Remember? It's possible he flat out forgot he owned the place."

"Or hid it," Sam said, turning a document toward the screen for them to read.

"What's that?" Libby asked.

"Decree of divorce, dissolving the marriage of Franklyn Rice and Rosalind Rice in January of 1973. And I have to say..." Sam gave a smug smile. "I couldn't have done better for Rosalind if I'd been her lawyer." He flipped a page. "She cleaned his clock. But she didn't get any restaurant on Mimosa Key."

"So she didn't *know* he owned the Pelican?" Libby suggested. "Or she thought he sold it to Jake?"

"Who would know that?" Sam mused.

"Charity Grambling," Law suggested. "She had a lot to say about this guy when she saw the picture, but we weren't interested. Her memory is pretty infallible."

Even with a screen between them, he could feel Libby and Sam somehow silently communicate, like twin language.

"Yeah, the picture," Sam said after a moment. "Mom doesn't think that's Jake."

Law closed his eyes and stayed quiet. It was Jake, but they had enough to discuss right then.

"Charity might know if there were heirs," he said as if Sam hadn't even mentioned the picture.

"So we can give them the business?" Libby asked.

"So we can make them an offer."

"You want to buy it?" Sam barked.

Law didn't reply, watching Libby carefully, gauging her reaction. Did she hear the *we* or just *make them an offer*?

Her eyes widened ever so slightly, a flicker of acknowledgment, followed by the tiniest flush of color. Maybe she heard the *we*.

Sam cleared his throat. "Look, let's not jump the gun here. For now, we still want to be handed ownership. Libby and I do," he added, slathering a lot of emphasis on that, proving that he caught the *we* as well. "I have five business days before that hearing. I'll put my firm investigators on the job to find this woman or the heirs, if there are any. If I do, then, and only then, will we discuss other legal avenues. I'm filing a motion to recognize concurrency estate management."

Libby moaned. "Sam, for crying out loud, English for the blonde, please."

"Jake ran the place long enough to make the legal argument that he owned it," Sam explained. "Think of it like a common-law marriage. Now, I need to research Florida case law, but if no one comes forward to argue this, and we file all the proper notifications and can prove due course of attempts to find the legitimate owners...Jake can get ownership and we're back to where we were."

"So we can still get the Pelican?" she asked, the first note of real excitement in her voice in hours.

"Assuming Law doesn't have any more surprises up his jukebox."

Law bristled at the implication, but managed to tamp down a response. Under the table, Libby's fingers curled through his in a silent show of support.

"Sam, you work on Frank Rice, and I'll handle this end of the issue," she said.

This end being Law. He didn't say a word, though.

"I talked to Mom this morning," Sam said, as if he understood exactly what *this end of the issue* was—a man they didn't trust like family.

Law would have to prove her wrong. And he knew he could do it. Knew he could give her what she wanted and what he wanted. It would take time and closeness and honesty.

"My mother has some interesting theories," Libby said, looking hard at Law. "Interesting and, I believe, wrong."

"She's on her way back to Miami." Sam leaned closer to the screen, directing his gaze dead center at both of them. "I hope for both your sakes that she's wrong. Because it sure seems like someone pulled a Hail Mary pass right out of the blue—again—and it changed the course of events. *Again*. What's next, Law? Proof that this Franklyn Rice is *your* father?"

Law winced at the dig. "This will and deed does not exactly play in my favor."

"But they did change our legal strategy and could slow things down. As of right now, we can't walk into that hearing and get ownership of the Toasted Pelican, regardless of what DNA shows or what so-called will you produce or not."

Law tensed, but Libby pressed into him. "Sam, I was with Law when this happened, and not even Donna Chesterfield herself could have acted that surprised. So let's talk later."

She tapped the keyboard and ended the call, turning in the booth toward Law.

"Thank you for the vote of faith and confidence," he said. "I promise you're right."

She searched his face, visibly fighting doubts. "You did have an actual infiltration plan, though, didn't you?"

"Yes," he admitted.

She pointed at him. "Listen to me, Law Monroe. You lie, cheat, steal, or break my heart, and I will—"

He shut her up with a kiss, long and sweet. When they parted, he put his hands on her cheeks. "I will not lie, cheat, steal, or break your heart. That wouldn't make me a very good…partner."

She eased back and searched his face, silent. "What exactly are you suggesting, Law?"

He swallowed, closed his eyes, and took a breath. "A partnership, Libby. If this property turns out to be owned by someone else, I think it's pretty obvious that person doesn't care about it. They have to have a price. I have money saved, quite a bit. It might not be enough to buy it all in a cash offer, but…"

"If I put in the rest?" she asked tentatively.

"Then we could have the Twisted Pelican. Yoga upstairs. Gastropub downstairs. And we both win."

She stared at him for a long, long time. "Let me think about that."

It was all he could ask for right then.

Chapter Twenty-Three

Charity Grambling adjusted her glasses and looked a little like she sucked on a lemon as she stared at the papers. "Well, I can't say these are words I utter very often, but this is news to me."

Law gingerly lifted the papers they'd decided to share with her. Sure, she was the town gossip and would tell the next fifty people who walked into the Super Min what they'd discovered, but that was fine. A lead to the Rice family could save them endless weeks and months in limbo if the judge didn't buy Sam's "common law" ownership plan.

Libby leaned on the counter and watched Law and the old lady banter a bit, admiring how Law let her flirt but didn't volley back. Must take a lot of self-control when a woman— even a withered old witch like Charity—was drooling all over you.

Under that former bad boy and current hot hunk lived a true gentleman, Libby mused. Someone…she wanted to…let inside. And not just in her body, though that was always top of mind.

No, it hadn't gone well for her in that regard. But…in the back of Libby's mind, the song that led them to the will played like, well, a broken record.

I still haven't found what I'm looking for...

But maybe she had.

As she listened to him tease whatever information he could out of Charity, Libby gave in to the crush on her heart and how tender it made her feel toward him. He wouldn't hurt that tender heart, would he?

He'd just promised her that, hadn't he? He'd just proposed a partnership, hadn't he?

"I will tell you this," Charity said, putting her hands on her hips. "That was one ugly-ass divorce, so I wouldn't be surprised if he did hide assets. I heard she accused him of everything short of murder. Quiet but nasty, that little Rosie. Course she's in her nineties now, so I'm like a kid next to her." She cackled at her joke, making Libby smile and earning a red-nailed finger pointed right in her face.

"Oh, you think it's funny, missy. Just wait until those overblown mammaries drop to your knees and all the estrogen drains out like you sprung a leak and you get like the Sahara down south."

Libby just closed her eyes, shaking her head.

"Won't be long now," she warned Libby. "Oh, you can snag these handsome silver foxes now, but you know what they really want is a twenty-five-year-old."

Next to her, she felt Law bristle and inhale for a response, but Libby put a gentle hand on his arm and refused to take the bait.

Charity turned her attention back to Law. "But you men." She sighed, devouring him from behind her specs. "You age so gracefully, it's not fair."

Law's muscles tensed under Libby's hand. He was clearly losing his patience with Charity. "And you're sure this Frank and Rosie had no kids?" he asked again.

"Not a one. My guess is Rosie was an ice cube in the sack and too busy spending his money to procreate."

No kids or direct heirs? That was good, unless he had them with another wife they didn't know about.

"Did he remarry?" Libby asked.

"Never heard, but I don't think she did. Lived like a queen off her alimony." She raised a judgmental eyebrow to Libby. "Can you *imagine*?"

"All right, thanks, Charity." Law slid a possessive, protective arm around Libby, purposefully leading her away. "We appreciate the information."

"Wait, wait, wait," Charity said, making them stop. "Just wait."

They turned, expectant.

The old woman took a slow, deep breath as if it pained her to say whatever she was about to say. "Rosie came in here once, years ago, after Frank was dead."

"And?" Law asked.

"She said she'd moved to Atlanta. Now I know that's a big city, but—"

"We know that." Law's voice was rich with edginess. "Thanks, anyway, Charity."

Charity shook her head, looking with strong disapproval from one to the other. "Do you know that together you're about ninety?"

"Then we're your age," Law mumbled, but Libby stepped forward, zeroing in on the old bag.

"What are you saying?" she demanded.

"That you're old for...you know."

Oh, she knew. What Charity wanted and would never have, if she ever did in the first place. "Are you saying we're too old to enjoy sexual intercourse, Charity?"

"Well, like I said, things don't work the same."

Libby tsked noisily. "Hate to break it to you, Char, but nothing's dropped, drained, or dried up on me, and I'm happy to report that Law is the most amazing lover I've ever had."

A little color rose in her old cheeks as Charity stole a lusty glance at Law. "I bet...he is."

"Five." Libby held up her hand, fingers splayed.

Charity frowned at her.

"Five orgasms last night." Libby wiggled her fingers to make her point, then turned to Law. "Come on, honey. We have time for six tonight. See ya, Charity!"

She went back to the door and slid her arm around Law, who didn't know whether to laugh or look pretty damn smug.

"Never in my life have I seen anyone shut down Charity Grambling like that," he said.

"What?" She looked innocent as she took the helmet he offered. "I was being honest."

He fastened the strap for her, kissing her nose. "Let's make it seven. Your place or mine?"

Oh hell. Why fight it? She was certain, strong, and couldn't care less what their ages added up to. Law made her feel alive in every way. "Let's ride back to the Pelican, get some stuff for a few days, and you can follow me back to my house."

"Libby." He drew back, feigning shock. "You're inviting me to stay? Overnight? With a toothbrush and all?"

"Only if you cook."

"Have to since Sam made us close the damn restaurant. In fact, when I get my stuff, I'll get some food from the kitchen and make you a feast tonight."

"Good."

He lifted her chin. "Guess who's gonna be dessert."

She leaned into him and kissed his mouth, getting additional satisfaction from knowing Charity was watching out the window. "You are, Lawless."

An hour later, pulling into her driveway with Law on his bike right behind her, Libby gripped the wheel and forced herself to take three cleansing breaths.

Could she do this? Could she open her house, her heart, herself to Law and let him all the way in? Not just her body, which, given the way she hummed with anticipation, was a no-brainer, but it had so quickly escalated to much more.

Now, it was her business and her dream. A partnership? The Twisted Pelican? Was this what she wanted?

She glanced in the rearview mirror and watched him get off the bike, giving his head a shake as he took off his helmet and worked out a crick in his neck. As it did every single time she looked at him, Libby's body reacted. Warm, tingly, needy. And they were going past physical attraction.

But here was another man giving her...hope. No, he didn't want her exclusively for her body, but she did have another carrot to dangle and he wanted that, too. What if all that didn't pan out? Would this be any different? Would this man be any different from the others?

Leaving her purse in the car, she opened the door and climbed out, needing the answers she sought before she welcomed him and made everything...vulnerable.

She walked straight up to him and asked, "Can I trust you?"

He drew back. "What brought that on?"

"I don't know. My life?"

His shoulders dropped with a sigh, maybe resignation, maybe frustration. Then he held out his hands, palms up. "Give me your hands," he said.

Slowly, she obliged, slipping her fingers in his strong, callused, burned and scarred fingers. He squeezed them and held their joined hands in the air between them.

"You can trust me. You don't have to sleep with me or enter into business with me, but you can trust me."

"I want to," she admitted.

"Which one?"

"All three. I want to sleep with you. I want to enter into business with you. And I want to trust you."

"Then what's the problem?"

She angled her head, surprised he didn't know. "I don't want to get hurt, in any way."

"Libby." He pulled her into him, wrapping both arms around her while not letting go of her hands. The position made her more vulnerable because she was unable to push him away. She had to trust him. "One day at a time, as we addicts say. One day at a time." He kissed her forehead. "And each day with you gets better."

She closed her eyes and felt the last walls come down around her. "Then let's—"

"Mom! Mom, there you are!"

They spun around as the front door popped open and Jasmine burst out, holding her phone. "Sam's trying to reach you," she called. "He thought I might know why you weren't answering your phone."

"I left my phone in the car." She backed away from Law and hurried toward Jasmine, noticing she was a little breathless and her eyes were bright with...something not good. "What is it, Jasmine?"

"The DNA test is in," she said softly.

"Oh." But Libby's blood chilled a bit, more at the way Jasmine was looking at her than the fact that she was finally going to know for sure.

But that's when she knew. Even before she heard Sam's voice, she knew.

"Yeah?" she breathed into the phone Jasmine gave her.

"A complete and total and massive mismatch," he said. "Not one strand of DNA in either one of our bodies matches the samples taken from that toilet article kit."

Balance slipped again as a whole different kind of dizzy rocked her world.

There was only one explanation. Well, two. Either Law lied about the shaving kit or Mom lied about Jake being her father.

Neither option made her feel very grounded at that moment.

"Okay, then," she said. "Well, moot point as far as the Pelican is concerned, because Jake didn't own it, anyway."

"What?" Jasmine choked.

Libby quieted her with a hand and listened to Sam drone on about a motion to...do something. But the only motion that mattered was in her head, which was light and spinning a little.

She handed the phone to Jasmine and walked into the house, with Law on her heels.

"Libby—"

She turned and held up her hand. "Hey, it's okay. He's not my father." *Or you lied.* But she refused to go back there because she believed him. "I should be used to this, right? I'm going upstairs."

She darted up the steps, but Law was right behind her. "Let's talk."

"Okay, later." She stopped at her room and put her hands on his chest. She sure as hell couldn't fall into bed with him now. "But I need to be alone for a while."

He searched her face, ready to argue, but something

stopped him. "A little while. I'll be downstairs when you're ready to talk about it."

She nodded, closing the door behind her. What was there to talk about? Who her father was?

She didn't trust her mother. She didn't trust science. She didn't trust the hairs from an old brush. She didn't trust the courts.

And, deep down inside, she still wasn't one hundred percent sure she should trust Law. Was that why she turned him away when she needed him the most?

She fell on her bed and gave in to a good, hard cry.

Law stood outside the half-closed bedroom door, leaning in to see that the room was dim, the shutters closed, and Libby was curled up under the covers.

He'd given her plenty of time to deal with the news. He'd stayed out on the porch with the young woman who was not only honest, she was bright, sensitive, and knew just how much this news had rocked Libby, maybe better than anyone else on earth.

But he was dying to talk to Libby, and went straight to her room when Jasmine left to go to her boyfriend's house. Not just because he knew damn well that Dopp kit was Jake's and that meant he also knew damn well that Libby was not Jake's biological daughter.

And not just to tell her that, in his opinion, the crazy-ass, pot-smoking actress mother was at the heart of this. Especially after Jasmine had explained a lot for him out there on that porch. Libby and Sam protected their mother, instinctively and constantly, and over the years, that had morphed into forgiving her for her mistakes and shortcomings. They all cut the woman way too much slack out of a familial love that, on some level, Law respected.

At least they hadn't left town or beaten the crap out of each other. Every family had dirt, but how they handled it was the real test.

In his opinion, Donna Chesterfield probably had no idea who the father of her babies was. She probably had a drunk night, a stranger hookup, and was too ashamed to admit the truth. That kind of thing was pretty scandalous in 1971.

But poor Libby just kept getting flung from father to father, from husband to husband, and now he wanted to tell her that he—

"I know you're out there, Law."

Now it was his turn, and damn, he didn't want to fling her anywhere. He just wanted to hold her and make her feel whole.

"So, can I come in?"

She moved around in the bed, making the covers sigh. Or maybe that was her. "Yeah. No lights, though. I look like hell."

"As if that's possible." He closed the door firmly behind him and walked to the bedside, trying to see her, but she kept her face in the pillow. "Let me see the damage," he said.

"No. I don't cry pretty."

He sat down on the bed. "Funny, neither do I."

Her shoulders moved with a dry laugh. "You never cry," she murmured into her pillow.

"That's where you're wrong, Lib. I cried last night."

She turned over and flicked some of her hair off her face and, whoa, yeah. Not a pretty crier. But despite the swollen eyes, blotchy skin, and rims of lost mascara, she was utterly beautiful. "You cried? Last night? Why?" she asked.

"Because you made me leave."

She choked and sat up a little. "You did? Oh, God, I'm sorry."

He brushed the rest of the stray blond hairs out of her face and ran his thumb over the black smudge under her eye.

"Maybe I didn't cry this hard," he said. "I didn't weep my makeup off, but I teared up a little."

She blinked, studying his face, looking for a reason to believe him, no doubt. "Because I wouldn't let you spend the night after we had sex? That's not very…well, that's not the sex-starved, hard-ass, booze-guzzling guy I once thought you were."

He laughed. "I'm dying for sex, my ass is hard as a rock, and I got pretty damn drunk last night."

"What?" Her face paled in horror. "You drank? After you left here?"

"Chill, yoga bear, I didn't drink. I said I got drunk." He leaned closer, tipping her chin up. "On you."

"You're a smooth talker."

"Actually, I'm not. I'm just being honest." He stroked her lip, his heart aching a little from the doubt in her eyes. "Libby, you've had some raw deals. This business with your father, whoever he is, and two bad marriages. I know you don't trust men. I know you feel like you never have a foundation. And I know I'm probably the last combination of 'male' and 'unstable' you want or need."

"True," she grudgingly admitted.

"But, baby, I want a chance."

She inhaled softly, still staring at him.

"Just a chance," he whispered. "Let me into your life. Your heart. Yes, your bed. And, hell, I'll take your yoga classes. And then, we'll see what happens. We can be friends. We can be lovers. We can be partners. Or we can be…"

She put her finger over his mouth. "We've been friends for a long, long time, Law. Let's move on to lovers."

"Oh yeah. Let's." He leaned closer and kissed her mouth, the salt from her tears breaking his heart.

He eased her back onto the pillow and stroked every single hair from her face so he could see it. "It might have been an ugly cry, but you're not an ugly crier."

"I don't care that I look ugly," she said, reaching up to grasp his neck. "In fact, I'm glad. That way I know it's me you want to make love to and not the package."

"It's you," he assured her, lowering his head for another long, wet kiss. "It's you, Libby."

He felt her moan under the pressure, sliding her fingers into his hair, deepening the kiss. He cupped her face, trying to keep himself from touching anything else just to show her how much it was her, and not her body, that turned him on.

But she rocked under the covers, and his hard-on felt only her body, and grew with need. She tugged at his T-shirt, which he yanked over his head and tossed. As he stepped out of his jeans and boxers, she shimmied out of her bottoms.

"Come in here," she said, pushing back the covers. He climbed into the bed with her, kissed her as he helped her out of her top and bra, and finally pulled her fully naked body against his.

Where it belonged.

"You left some condoms here," she whispered, stroking his chest, his stomach, and reaching to wrap her hands around his erection.

He grunted softly, closing his eyes as heat rolled through him.

"I'm optimistic like that." He kissed her again, then

worked his mouth down her chest to taste more of her. "Let's use them all."

"And send Jasmine out for more," she teased.

He lifted his head. "She went to Noah's house. But if you want we can call and send her to the Super Min and ask Charity for a few boxes. That's a conversation I'd like to hear."

Laughing, she pulled him back into her for more kisses. "Quit being so much fun and make love to me."

"Yes, ma'am."

"And don't call me ma'am or you might die. Our combined age is ninety, you know."

"Ninety-one," he corrected. "We're clearly on borrowed time."

"Then make the most of it," she ordered.

Still smiling, he closed his eyes and found more places to kiss and explore, more ways to make her moan and writhe and, of course, lose all control. It took less than five minutes to make her come.

"You have a hair-trigger orgasm response, Lib," he told her as he held her shuddering body.

"Only when your finger is on the trigger." She recovered enough to make her own path down his body, taking him into her mouth, torturing him by bringing him to the brink, and finally letting him climb on top and slide into heaven.

He filled her up, rocking into each stroke with his eyes squeezed shut, pleasure licking every inch of him. She smelled sweet and spicy and felt hot and creamy around him, and Law felt his whole body clutch with need.

Their tongues curled and imitated the movement of their bodies, in and out, sweet and wet, as his hands finally stilled and just held her shoulders for stability. Above her, he watched her face flush and listened to the tender pleas and promises that spilled from her lips.

Need pressed with each stroke, building in him, driving him, inflaming him. He finally had to close his eyes and hang on as she took him closer and closer to the edge. Pleasure swelled and overwhelmed him, but he fought the release until he opened his eyes and saw that she was right there with him. Frantic. Lost. Holding on to her last thread until it broke.

He came with her, a glorious, heady, raw sensation that made him throb even harder with each thrust. He'd never experienced that before. He'd never experienced anything like this before.

Catching his breath, he pushed up to look at her, that thought pounding in his head. Nothing like this. Nothing like Libby.

Slowly, she opened her eyes, and he could swear he saw his own reflection in the stormy blue-gray color.

It was a first, all right. First freaking love at forty-six. Who would have thought it was possible?

"Wow," he muttered as the reality slammed him like a cast-iron pan to the head.

"Yeah, wow." She laughed lightly. "Real words fail us."

But he knew the real word. He'd heard it all his life, but never had any idea what it felt like. Now he knew. It felt like Libby, like home, like peace and forever and contentment he'd never even thought was possible.

Talk about an infiltration plan. She'd climbed right inside his heart and taken ownership instead of the other way around. He wasn't going to be satisfied as Libby's business partner...he wanted to be her partner in every way.

Chapter Twenty-Four

In...and...out. In...and...out.

Each breath cleansed Libby's body more. And considering all her weight was on her head and forearms with her feet pointed straight in the air, she was remarkably balanced. An earthquake wouldn't knock her over now.

But that wasn't yoga. That was...Law.

Upside down, Libby smiled, embracing the perfection of the moment. Of the past six days, actually. She had never been happier in her life.

From the bed they'd shared for the better part of those six days, Law moved and let out a sleepy groan. "Where did you go?"

"On the floor. Doing a headstand."

"Naked?" She heard him shift and the mattress moan as he sat up. "This I gotta see."

She laughed and wobbled. "Not naked."

"Mmm. Sports bra and panties. Close to naked. How the hell do you do that?"

She tightened her core. "Breathing. Practice. Concentration, which you are ruining."

"Why are you out there and not in here, Lib? We have a big day today. We need to start it off with a bang."

She laughed but didn't tilt. "Yes, we have a big day today, and I need to start it off with my spine aligned, my circulation improved, and my heart rate at a nice pace."

"All that is waiting for you, right here in this bed." He slipped out and walked over to her, and he was naked. And hard.

She wobbled. "Damn you, Lawless."

He caught her legs and stood right in front of her, pressing himself against her upside-down thighs. "Here's one we haven't tried yet."

"A miracle considering we've spent the last week reenacting the *Kama Sutra*."

"You and your eastern influence." He kissed the tip of her big toe and let her go. "Don't move. Gotta hit the head."

As he disappeared into the bathroom, Libby found her balance again, closing her eyes to enjoy the rush of blood to her head and the cleansing that inversion always gave her.

"Shit." He popped out of the bathroom, wiping toothpaste from his mouth. "I don't have a freaking suit. It's at the restaurant with my bags, I think."

Slowly, she lowered her legs to the floor but kept her head down to avoid getting dizzy. "Do you need a suit?"

"I don't want to waltz into some courtroom in support of you and maybe have to talk to a judge about how the business has run in khaki shorts and a T-shirt."

The blood settled and moved out of her head, clearing it enough for her to think about the timing. "That would make us late to meet Sam."

But he was looking at her funny, his head at an angle, his eyes soft.

"What's wrong?" she asked.

"Nothing." He took a few steps closer and reached for her

hand, tugging her up. "Sometimes when I look at you, I can't even breathe."

She smiled. "All those yoga classes with me and you still can't breathe?"

"All these days and nights with you and I still can't...believe it."

"Believe what?"

"This." He wrapped his arms around her and pulled her into his chest, which was hard and solid and comforting and...home.

She laid her head on his shoulder with a sigh. "Believe it."

He stroked her hair with a slow, sweet, tender touch that sometimes made her heart fold even more than when his hands were hot and demanding. Anytime Law touched her, it affected her.

And this was no different. She lifted her face to look at him and gasped softly when she saw his eyes were moist. "Law? What's wrong?"

He shook his head, a silent denial of what she could see. "It was the mirror that got me."

"What?"

"I looked in the mirror," he said.

"And got a little choked up over all the laugh lines I've given you?"

"No." His voice was thick with emotion. "Most of my life, when I looked in the mirror, I had to brace for what would be looking back at me."

"Law, you're one of the best-looking creatures on earth."

"It has nothing to do with looks, and you, of all people, should understand that."

She nodded slowly, listening.

"For a lot of years, I looked at a man I loathed. A

hungover, wretched, dried-up soul," he said, his voice ragged. "Then, for a decade or more, I didn't see him, but the man in the mirror was hollow, with no…luster. Jake died, and I saw grief and frustration and emptiness. And then…now…" His voice cracked, and so did Libby's heart.

"Now what do you see?" she asked.

He tipped her chin as if he needed to get her face closer. "It scares the hell out of me, Libby, but I see…hope. A home with you. A business, a life, a future."

She felt her eyes fill, too.

"I see something I never, ever want to quit." He closed his eyes, and a tear squeezed out.

"Oh, Law." She wrapped her arms around him and held him tight. "I see it, too."

They kissed, a whole new kiss, an open, honest, heartbreaking kiss that Libby would never forget as long as she lived. Slowly, he backed her to the bed, because there simply wasn't any other place to take this.

Outside her door, she heard footsteps on the stairs, the sound of Jasmine going down to the kitchen.

"Jasmine's going with us," Libby said. "But she's driving herself in case she has to cut out early. Why don't I drive with her and you take my car and meet us there after you get your suit? Sam wanted me to come a little early, but you don't have to."

He frowned. "Why do it that way?"

She pushed him the rest of the way to the bed. "So we have time to seal that beautiful declaration you just made."

"You want a declaration?" he said.

"What I want is you on that bed." She nudged him back. "And my fabulous idea buys us some time."

But he didn't move, looking at her so seriously for a man who was about to get quick and dirty morning sex. "But I want to make a declaration." He took her face in his hands. "I've never told anyone this, ever. You are the first woman I've ever said this to."

All Libby could do was stare as blood pumped in her head, all the benefits of the inversion gone just by looking into his eyes.

"I love you," he whispered. "I *love* you."

She pressed on her chest, stunned and joyful and so, so happy. "Law. I can't even breathe."

"All those yoga classes and you can't breathe?" he teased, echoing her words.

"All these years and finally, finally…" She closed her eyes. "I love you, too."

They fell on the bed together and made that love official.

Upstairs in the darkened room that had, on more than one occasion, protected him from the world, Law sifted through a stack of dry-cleaning bags he hadn't looked at in months. God, maybe more.

A suit! Thank you, God. He ripped at the plastic, realizing the last time he had this suit on was Jake's funeral.

Well, that was fitting. As he tossed the plastic down, he noticed the world-famous Ritz-Carlton logo hit the floor. Damn, he hadn't turned down the job yet.

He'd gotten the official offer by email days ago and had even shown it to Libby, teasing her about the possibility of accepting it.

But over the last few days, they'd worked out a much

better business plan than him working for the Ritz in Arizona. Now they had a real plan.

Stripping out of the clothes he'd worn, he glanced around the space that would be a yoga studio after they closed this deal. Yes, they had contingency plan after contingency plan in place. If Sam won the judge over today, she'd own it and they'd split it. If he lost and some heir showed up, they'd make an offer. If they had to wait a year, they'd move forward with the combo place, anyway or, hell, find something else.

By now, they were committed to the Twisted Pelican. And after this morning, he thought with a smile, they were committed to each other. And Law couldn't be happier.

He froze in the act of buttoning his shirt, frowning at a noise downstairs.

Was someone down there? Still barefoot and wearing only a shirt and pants, he walked silently to the door he'd left open, cocking his ear toward downstairs.

He heard a thump, and a footstep, and another thump, and a footstep.

What the hell?

Staying silent to be sure he had at least the element of surprise on his side, he walked down the stairs, certain the sound was coming from the dining room. Shoot, he'd walked in the front door and hadn't locked it behind him. Someone thought the place was open? At seven in the morning?

He got to the bottom step and listened to the distinctive sound of something rubber hitting the dining area floor, then a slow step, then a repeat. He turned the corner, passed the closet, and stepped into the doorway to peer into the dimly lit area.

There, crossing the room, was a little old lady with a walker.

"Can I help you?" Law stepped into the dining room, blinking at the hunched-over silhouette against the front window's morning light.

She turned to him. "Oh, there you are. I hoped you'd be down nice and early."

He recognized her from the other night. The old ladies from Naples. Regulars, but he didn't recall her name. She was the oldest of a group he'd chatted with the second night he and Libby were serving dinner. "I'm so sorry," he said gently, coming closer, wondering if maybe she thought it was seven at night and not in the morning. "We're not open for breakfast."

Brown eyes, clouded with age but still surprisingly sharp, peered at him from behind thick bifocals. "I know that. I came to talk to you. I've been here several mornings this week, but the place is never open. And then you closed for dinner. I'd like to know why."

And he'd like to know why he had to deal with this. "We had to," he said vaguely, blinking when she stopped the walker in front of a booth and positioned herself to sit down. "And, really, I have an appointment and can't be late."

She plopped her narrow frame into the booth and scooted back, then tapped the table with a solid rap. "Sit down, Lawson."

Ire poked at his gut like a two-pronged fork. "I can't, Mrs...."

She flipped a sizable bag off the handle of the walker and brought it close to her body as if she thought he might try to take off with it. "Everyone just calls me Rosie."

"I can't, Rosie. I..." *Rosie?*

She pulled a piece of paper from the side of her bag. "We have a business transaction to conduct, and it's my guess you'd like to have this signed, sealed, and delivered before that court hearing in Naples starts in less than an hour."

All the air escaped him in one long whoosh.

This was Rosalind Rice...former wife of Franklyn Rice and, quite possibly, the legal owner of the Toasted Pelican. He didn't even think about not sitting down across from her.

"You've been coming in here for a long time," he said, the realization certainly not the strangest thing about this meeting, but still, it stunned him.

"Oh yes. I would sneak in when Jake was still alive, but considering he was thirty and I was fifty when he met me, it's no surprise he didn't recognize me now."

She spread some papers in front of her, but looked at him. "What?" she asked, reading his expression of disbelief. "You're surprised I came in here? I had to be sure the Pelican was running exactly as my ex-husband ordered it to. And, until recently, it was. And then I met you the other night." She lowered her glasses and showed a spark in her eyes. "You are quite a charmer and a great chef."

"I am..." Law leaned back on the booth, rooting around for some way to make sense of what was happening. "Confused. Why didn't you come forth sooner?"

"Oh, those lawyers," she said, stroking a puff of white curls. "They think I'm ninety-five and stupid. It's like they never met a shrewd woman before. Did they not see my divorce settlements?"

Plural. He let it go and waited for more of an explanation.

"Frank did not hide this particular asset very well, though God knows he tried. He honestly didn't hide anything very well, but that's why I ended up with the lion's share of his vast fortune and the good Lord took his mind and memory away and let him die in an old-age home with nothing but social security and a string of mistresses." Bitterness cut through her voice. "Anyway, what did I need with this stupid old restaurant?"

"Then why didn't you talk to Jake when he was still alive? Why not give him a chance to buy it from you?" Could have saved a lot of misery, but something told him this old woman thrived on misery. "Was it because the deed said it can only be owned by Frank's heirs?"

"Pffft." She flicked her hand. "I forget I own it half the time. That's how unimportant it's been to me. Then Jake died, and my lawyer notified me, and we took just a little too much time moving forward." She gestured toward her bottom. "Hip replacement. Anyway, by the time I was healthy enough to come in here and discuss selling it, some 'shell company' had taken over, which is a real hoot if you ask me, and no one had any idea who that was other than some guy named Sam in Miami."

Law gave a wry smile. "I know exactly what hitting that brick wall feels like."

She sniffed. "Well, then that 'notification' appeared in some paper that's read by no one but first-year law associates in sixth-rate law schools. Does this Liberty Management think I don't have Harvard-educated lawyers working for me?"

"I don't think they know you exist. Or your former husband." In fact, Sam's research machine had come up completely empty-handed while trying to locate this woman.

"Well, I do. Obviously, after three marriages, I have new names, and when you have money like mine and you're a day over ninety, you keep a low profile." She leaned forward. "Men can be gold diggers, too, you know." She winked. "Are you interested?"

"In that paper."

She nodded. "Well, my lawyers looked at all the business

this Liberty Management was filing with judges and whatnot and came up with a simple plan to just meet this upstart on the courtroom steps and head them off at the pass."

"To do what?" he asked, already worried about what Libby was going to run into when she and her family arrived at the courthouse.

"Oh, they'd wave the deed and Frank's pathetic will that I'm sure there's a copy of around here somewhere…"

Somewhere like the jukebox.

"And then we'd just tell them to go away."

Law's jaw loosened. "That's what they're going to do?"

"No. You're going to buy the place."

He blinked at her. "I am?"

"Assuming you have money in your pocket."

"Probably not enough, but—"

"Do you have a dollar?"

He nodded.

"Good, then you have enough." She turned the paper toward him. "This is a bill of sale that will stand up in court. There might be some official stamping that needs to be done, of course, but my lawyer will arrange that when you arrive."

"You're selling me the Toasted Pelican for a dollar?"

"One dollar. I'm told that's the minimum allowed to 'gift' a business in the state of Florida."

Nothing computed. Nothing at all. "Why?"

"Oh yes, it's because you're young and handsome and have big dreams for the place, but it's more than that, too." Her eyes misted, and she leaned forward. "You remind me of Frank, in a good way. In the way that I fell so hard for before…before it all broke apart so brutally."

Was this even possible? Everything was done and easy and cheap? This was one contingency plan he and Libby had never thought of—but she would love it. And he'd better stop talking, start signing, and get over to the Collier County Courthouse ASAP.

"Are there any stipulations?" he asked. "Like I can't change anything, or it has to be exclusively a restaurant, or...anything at all?"

"Well, yes," she said. "You need to keep the name because I was the one who called it the Toasted Pelican."

"Really? After a drunk bird? Or the one who loved toast?"

"Tsk, as if I'd be so simple. The brown pelican is endangered, or it was back in the day. And I dearly loved animals, and I wanted one that would never be extinct. So I named it after the brown pelican in hopes that it would last forever. Some things don't, you know."

No, many things don't, he thought. And he couldn't be happier. "But some things do last forever." Like Law and Libby and this place and their lives. "So you're good as long as the word 'pelican' is in the name?"

She lifted a dubious brow. "You drive a hard bargain, Lawson." Then she nodded. "Fine."

"And there's no other catch?"

She gestured to the bottom of the document. "Please take your time and read the fine print. If you choose to do so, however, I will need coffee and a sandwich, because I'm feeling peckish, and legalese makes me positively sick to my stomach."

He grinned, looking down at the thick paragraph of single-spaced words that looked like Sam had vomited them on the page. Jake would have had a few choice things to say about those paragraphs.

Law skimmed. The only words jumping out at him were *heirs*, *null and void*, and *destruction of property*. He frowned, remembering the will he'd found. "Frank had a stipulation that only his heirs could ever own this place, or it would be destroyed."

"I'm his heir, and that sentence?" She pointed to the very one with a gnarled, veiny finger. "That eliminates the validity of his will."

So she had read the fine print.

"Do you have ham? Because if I have to sit here one minute longer, I will need a ham sandwich."

But he had to get to the mainland and fast. "There's a convenience store on the corner."

"I'd rather die of malnutrition than speak to that woman."

He laughed. "Then let's move fast. I can send you home with a sandwich. Where do I sign, Rosie?"

By the time Law was halfway across the causeway to Naples, he'd formed one last plan. When he presented Libby with this amazing new twist in their life story, he might do it...on one knee.

She'd lose her balance and fall right into his arms...forever.

Chapter Twenty-Five

As Libby, Sam, and Jasmine climbed out of Sam's Escalade in the parking lot of the Collier County Courthouse, a horn honked loud and long.

Libby whirled around, her gaze landing on a bright yellow Volkswagen Beetle parked in the next row.

"She beat us here?" Libby asked, tamping down the disappointment that the honking was from her mother and not Law.

"I wasn't sure she'd come at all," Sam said, putting the car in park. "She's absolutely convinced Law switched the DNA, and she didn't even want to be here."

"Not even for moral support?" Libby unbuckled her seat belt and glanced at Jasmine in the back. "This whole thing was her idea."

"Oh, you know Gran," Jasmine said. "It all depends on what role her inner director told her to play this morning. We may get super-supportive Mom or scorned lover or determined fighter with a cause."

Libby rolled her eyes and greeted her mother, who'd chosen a wildly colored maxi dress that made Libby doubt she was playing any of the parts Jasmine mentioned. "Quirky hippie actress Mom?" Libby asked.

"Where is he?" Mom asked, looking past all of them.

Ah, she was the accusing mom, no doubt looking for the evidence-tampering chef who she and she alone knew was a liar. Well, she'd hated him ever since they'd found the picture of her with Jake, and no doubt it was because Law knew that Jake wasn't a jerk and her mother had been coloring that truth all along.

"He's not here yet," Libby said. "But he will be."

He mother sniffed as if she didn't believe it, but Sam ushered them all toward the bright white building with massive black windows. "Come on, our hearing starts in twenty minutes."

After they got through the metal detectors, Sam nodded toward the elevator and Libby looked once more into the parking lot.

"He'll be here," Jasmine whispered. "He probably got caught in Naples traffic."

"Or he's already waiting inside," her mother said. "With the *new* will in his hand. Oh, surprise, surprise. Jake left him everything. That other one was a forgery."

Libby shot her a look. "You're wrong about him," she said simply.

"Was I wrong about Carlos?" she muttered. "Or Parker?"

Jasmine leaned closer on the other side. "Just breathe," she whispered to Libby. "We're going to be fine. And he'll get here. And, Gran, you chill. Mom's happy. Don't you want her to be happy?"

"I want her to be safe from men who will ruin her life."

"You were ready to lick him like a human ice cream cone when you met him."

"He was almost naked. I was dazzled."

"Join the club." Libby squeezed her daughter's hand and held it through the elevator ride. When the doors opened, a man standing outside Courtroom C turned and looked expectantly at them.

"Mr. Chesterfield?" he asked.

Sam hesitated and frowned. "Yes?"

He extended his hand, a cool smile on a distinguished face that exuded power and confidence. "I'm Michael Sanderson of Sanderson Neville Bainbridge and Simmons."

"Ooh, that's a mouthful," Jasmine joked under her breath, but Libby gave her a quick look to hush her, already not liking this interruption.

But Sam seemed impressed, drawing back with raised eyebrows and adjusting his glasses like he did when he was meeting someone important. "Oh, Mr. Sanderson. What a pleasure to meet you. What brings you to Collier County? To Florida, for that matter? And…how do you know who I am?"

"I represent Mrs. Bickford."

"Pardon?" Sam asked.

"Rosalind James Rice Stuart Bickford."

"Is that another law firm with too many names?" Jasmine leaned in to whisper. On Libby's other side, Mom stiffened like someone poked her in the back.

"No." Libby sighed as the name registered. So it wouldn't be *that* easy. Maybe Rosie had a price. She glanced at the elevator, willing it to open and Law to appear.

Sam took a millisecond to gather his thoughts before speaking, but the older man moved closer and gestured toward another door. "I've taken the liberty of reserving a conference room to discuss the case. It seemed only fair before my motion to dismiss is read by the judge."

"Motion to dismiss?" Libby murmured.

Mom was still stiff as a board, and Libby half expected her to blame Law for this. But she was ghostly white, staring at the man.

Sam frowned, looking uncertain of the situation, something one rarely saw on her always cool and collected brother. "I'm sorry. I wasn't aware of a motion to dismiss."

"We just filed it this morning."

"A little late, isn't it?"

"Not technically, Counselor. Follow me."

Sam bristled at the order and shot Libby a look, but no one said a word. The conference room was freezing and bathed in a yellowish fluorescent light that made her mother's face look like someone had poured a gallon of milk over her.

"Are you okay?" Libby asked softly.

She closed her eyes. "I shouldn't have come," she muttered. "Can I leave?"

"Mrs. Chesterfield?" The lawyer came right up to Mom, reaching his hand out. "Good of you to be here."

Libby wanted to ask why was it good, but the whole thing was just too surreal to speak.

"You certainly didn't have to be present," he continued. "But I'm sure my client will appreciate your supporting her position and decision."

What position and decision? And why would Donna Chesterfield's presence matter to this old lady who they weren't even sure was still alive? Libby and Sam shared an equally confused silent exchange, but Mom averted her eyes and looked like she'd pay big money for an escape hatch.

"What is this motion to dismiss?" Sam asked without sitting down.

Sanderson didn't respond, but took a seat where papers were already lined up in neat piles. "It's simpler, now that the property has been sold."

"Sold?" Libby, Sam, and Jasmine all spoke at the same

time, and even Mom sat up and seemed to come back to the living.

He reached for a document in front of him. "Sold this morning, paperwork is complete, I'm waiting for the buyer and a notary to arrive, and—"

"How can it be sold?" Libby exclaimed. "We weren't given a chance to make an offer."

"Not only that," Sam said. "Judge Reinhart issued a temporary deed of ownership to Liberty Management Corporation."

"He did indeed, and that expired last night at midnight, as you well know."

Did she? A low-grade panic bubbled up in Libby's gut. "So it's over? It's sold? No chance of an offer to anyone?"

"I'm waiting for the buyer to arrive at any minute, when I'll call in the notary, but he met with my client this morning, and they both signed a very amicable and simple real estate exchange agreement, which, as I understand it, has been in the works for a while, ever since my client met the new buyer."

White sparks popped behind Libby's eyes. "How can that be possible?" she demanded of Sam.

"The agreement did expire less than twelve hours ago," Sam said. "And anyone with prior knowledge of the agreement could have arranged to sign the property over in the few hours between midnight and..." Sam looked at his watch. "Five minutes from now."

"Who would know that?" Libby asked.

Her mother snorted. "You can't make an educated guess?"

Libby whipped around and glared at her. "Law was in bed with me until seven o'clock and will be here any minute. I sincerely doubt he had time to arrange a secret rendezvous—"

The door popped open with so much force it smacked into the wall as Law burst into the room. "Don't start without me."

"Law." Libby almost leaped over the table that separated them, relief rushing through her.

"Mr. Monroe?" Sanderson stood and offered a hand and a smile. "We were just talking about you."

All that relief turned ice cold. "We were?" Libby croaked.

"My client was delighted you accepted the offer," Sanderson continued. "Although, at that price, it would be tough to turn down. Am I understanding correctly that you are acquainted with the Chesterfields?"

Law gave a quick laugh. "Pretty well." He glanced at Libby's mother, who was practically sputtering now. "Well, some of them."

Libby pressed her hands to the table and willed blood back into her brain. "You...worked out a deal with Rosie?"

Law turned to her, his eyes bright, fighting a smile. "I did. It's done and, damn, the price was right. We can make everything top notch now and exactly how we want—"

"Um...excuse me." Sanderson held up a hand. "*You* purchased the property, Mr. Monroe. The contract was quite clear."

"Clear enough. Especially the one-dollar price point. Check it out, Counselor." Law tossed a piece of paper on the table so it slid in front of Sam. "Rosie paid me a visit this morning, told me she was impressed with my cooking, made me a deal I couldn't refuse."

Libby blinked and tried to process what he was saying, but failed. He saw Rosie? This *morning*?

"How convenient," her mother said. "They met right after he got out of bed with you, Libby."

"Mom."

"Gran."

"I'm sorry, but look how cocky he is."

"Cocky?" Law choked.

The argument was lost on Libby as her mind and heart went to war. Was her mother right? Had she once again trusted a man she shouldn't have? It *was* convenient.

Convenient that he forgot a suit. Convenient that he was the only person outside of their family who knew the temporary ownership expired at midnight. Convenient that he somehow *met the owner in the restaurant while it was closed* and signed a deal.

Doubts strangled her. As hard as she tried to swallow them away by remembering what they'd shared that morning, she couldn't. Not completely. Still silent, she pressed her hands to her mouth and tried with everything she had in her to trust him, but…she was failing.

Come on, Libby. Come on. Believe him.

"The fact is," Sanderson continued, "the place is yours, but Ms. Chesterfield is not to have anything to do with it or profit from the business in any way. And that is quite clear in the contract you signed."

Libby sat back, mostly from the force in the man's words, looking over at Sam, who was vehemently shaking his head as he read. "There's nothing about her in this contract."

"No, there isn't," Law said. "I'd have noticed that."

"She's right there," Sanderson replied. "You both are, Sam. See clause two, point seven, line nine. Purchaser is expressly forbidden to share ownership or profit with any biological heir of Franklyn Moore Rice."

For a long, painful, heart-stopping moment, no one spoke.

Except Libby's mother, who whimpered.

Finally, Jasmine leaned forward. "Are you saying that this old, dead Frank guy is my mother and uncle's biological father?"

The lawyer's gray brows furrowed as he shifted his attention to the woman sinking deeper into a cowering ball.

Libby dropped back into her seat with a thud. This was not happening. It was not. Not again. *Not again.* Trust Law? She couldn't trust her own mother. She couldn't trust *anyone.*

"Thank you, Mr. Sanderson." Her mother's voice was rich with sarcasm as she slowly stood, gathering herself the way she did before a big onstage monologue. "Thank you so very much for this special family moment."

Libby couldn't turn. Her head was so heavy, she couldn't look at her brother or Sanderson or Jasmine or even across the room where Law still stood. And she especially could not bear to look at her mother. She just stared at the wood grain in the conference room table and listened to her pulse pound in her head.

"My lover was a married man." She used her Donna-onstage voice as she ground out the words like she was chewing glass. "My mistake was great, but his power was greater. He wanted me to have an abortion. No, no. Let me be clear. His *wife*, your esteemed puppeteer of a client, wanted me to have an abortion. When I refused, she tried everything, including offering money to one Jake Peterson to marry me. And guess what?" She stepped back from the table, commanding every eye in the room now. "He said yes."

"Because he loved you," Law murmured.

She gave a dramatic flick of her hand. "If that's true, I was too blinded by another man. So I refused that charade because I wanted one thing and one man." Her voice trembled. "Frank Rice. But he…" Her voice hitched. "He wouldn't leave his wife for me."

She exhaled and put a hand on Jasmine's shoulder, who covered it with her own. "It's okay, Gran. We all make mistakes."

No, Libby thought. It's *not* okay. Another father—and *this* one—was not okay. "Why did you lie?" Libby asked on a rough whisper.

"Because Rosalind proceeded to make my life a living hell, threatening to ruin my father's business, wreck my mother's reputation, and accuse me of all manner of atrocities."

"Forty-five years ago," Sam reminded her.

She shook her head as if it had been forty-five minutes. "She will always have power, and if you don't believe me, look at exactly what's going on in this room. Anyway, I finally left, the loser. I think she thanked Jake for his kindness by letting him continue to run the Pelican and keep the profits. Of course, their marriage ended, but I had already found Mike by then. But she stole any chance I had at happiness with Frank."

"Mom!" Libby choked on the word. "The guy was thirty years older than you and married to another woman."

"And miserable. She was cold and hateful and calculating and only wanted his money." She pointed at the lawyer. "Correct me if I'm wrong, but did she not divorce the other two rich men for millions, also?"

He shook his head once. "I won't speak about my client. And while your history is, uh, unique—"

"And true!" she shot back.

"That may be," he conceded. "The fact is, Mr. Monroe signed a crystal-clear contract. He just said so himself. The terms are straightforward, and the price was obviously a factor. However, if anyone who is a biological heir of Frank Rice's is in any way associated with the business, the contract is void and the restaurant will be torn down."

"How the hell would I know who's his heir?" Law demanded.

"Not to mention that's the most ridiculous thing I've ever heard spoken in a courthouse," Sam said, pushing the document back down the table. "I will tear that agreement, and you, to shreds, sir."

"That will take time," Sanderson replied.

"We have it," Sam volleyed.

"Not really. Look at clause four, point one, line three. The business transfer must take place in fourteen days or is null and void. No court in the county will hear this in fourteen days."

"Why?" Law demanded. "What difference does any of this make to her?"

"She hates me," her mother replied. "I don't blame her, but she hates me, and she hates Libby and Sam even more. She doesn't want any of us to be happy, since she's not. She knew you two were together." She gestured to Libby and Law. "I'd bet any amount of money that she knew and did this whole thing on purpose."

Sanderson snickered. "Quite ambitious for a woman a few years away from one hundred."

"Rosalind Rice is a destroyer!" Donna cried out, clearly high on her own performance now. "She lives to destroy other people's happiness. I put nothing past her."

Except you slept with her husband. And what did that say about both her parents?

Libby squirmed in pain, but her mother pointed at Law. "And I put nothing past you, Mr. Monroe, including being in cahoots with that horrible woman. From the minute you walked into this, you've been pulling surprises out of thin air and pretending they were just coincidences. You found a picture that only Rosie could have had, since it was taken with her camera. I know, I was there. You wormed your way into the business, and now you're sleeping with my daughter."

Jasmine choked softly. "Kettle. Pot. Black."

Law's gaze narrowed at the woman as his jaw locked. "You are wrong."

"Prove it," Sam said. "How did you orchestrate this chance meeting this morning?"

Law startled at the new attack from a different side of the table. "She came into the restaurant. I was upstairs getting this suit."

"You didn't know for the past week that you stayed at Libby's house that you'd need a suit?" Libby's mother demanded. "You don't lock the door when the business is closed? You happened to have this meeting in the one open hour between the expiration of the agreement and the hearing?"

"Stop it!" Libby jumped to her feet, whipping around to her mother. "Stop trying to wreck my life."

"I'm not, Libby. I'm trying to protect you from exactly the kind of agony I endured."

She slammed her hands on the table, fire in her blood as it boiled over. "I'm not sleeping with another woman's husband. I'm not lying to my kids for their entire life. I'm not putting half the blame on a dead man who professed to love you and the other half on a man who…who…" She finally turned to Law. "Who professed to love me."

For a moment, the entire room was dead silent, and Libby realized she was waiting for Law to jump over that table and confirm that he did, indeed, love her.

But he just stared at her, silent. Too silent.

"I need answers, too, Law," she added, her voice softer now. "Why didn't you get the suit ahead of time? We talked about it. How did she get in? She doesn't have a key. And you sit down and sign a contract without so much as a phone call to me?" She heard her voice rise and crack, but she managed not to break down.

He just looked at her. "You honestly doubt me?"

Did she? She didn't want to. She wanted to believe him, but…something deep inside her wouldn't let go and trust. Probably some hideous gene she inherited from her father the adulterer and mother the homewrecker.

"Never mind," he said before she could answer. "You know what? Save yourselves a lot of trouble." He bent over the table and snagged the document he'd brought, lifting it to his face and staring at Libby over the top. "I'm out a dollar and my pride." He tore the paper right down the middle, opened his fingers, and let the two sides flutter to the floor. "I quit."

He left, and everyone in the room talked at once. Sam threw legal terms. Mom whipped out I-told-you-so's. Jasmine reached to console Libby. And that old bag of wind Sanderson actually took out a cell phone to call his client.

But Libby stared at the door, frozen.

"Mom!" Jasmine elbowed her. "You're going to let him go? He's the best thing that's ever happened to you."

She turned to her daughter, trying to find a word, an explanation, anything to counter the truth. But there was none. He *was* the best thing to ever happen to her. She jumped up from her chair and rounded the table, only to have her top snagged by her mother.

"You're going to run after him? He couldn't even provide

a lie to get him out of this. We confronted him and he ran. He can't be trusted."

She looked from her mother to her daughter. Two other generations of Chesterfield women. Which one should she listen to? There wasn't any doubt.

"You know who can't be trusted, Mom? You." Libby pointed at her. "You're the liar, you're the one who changes history, and you're the one who let one mistake screw up her entire life. Act your way out of this one. I have a relationship to save."

She tore out the door and hissed a curse as the elevator doors clunked to a close. No, *no*. She wasn't going to lose him.

Turning, she spied the stairs, shoved the door open, ran down, and practically flung herself into the lobby just in time to see him walking out the front entry.

She bolted and shouldered the glass door as he reached the top step of the courthouse.

"Law!"

He stopped but didn't turn.

"Please." She fought for a breath, trying to hold herself back from running to him and throwing her arms around him. "Please."

Finally, he turned, smacking her in the heart at the misery—and tears—in his eyes.

"I believe you," she said on a ragged whisper.

"But you didn't. There was that moment that you didn't." He could barely say the words.

"I was in shock. I was trying to process everything and—"

"You thought I might be lying. You thought you couldn't trust me. You thought I wasn't worth you or us or all our plans."

"For one second, Law."

He shook his head, hurt all over his face. "One second too long."

Her jaw dropped. "Is that fair?"

Taking a deep breath, he looked over her shoulder at the courthouse. "Damn, Jake was right about lawyers. But he wasn't right about your mother." He gave a dry laugh. "He dodged a bullet there."

Libby drew back, breaking inside. "Law, please. You can't just...*quit.*"

He looked at the ground for a moment, giving her a second to drink in the fact that he did find a suit and tie—and looked insanely good in both—so it wasn't like he'd had time to run off and have a secret meeting. Why did she doubt him?

"I can't live on the knife's edge of trust," he finally said, meeting her gaze. "We made love this morning. In my opinion, we sealed...this thing. I told you I love you. I can count on one hand the number of people who've heard me say that, and I'd still have a few digits left over."

"Law, I'm really sorry. I mean, I found out about this guy being my father and it hit me so hard, I..." The excuse sounded lame, so she let the words trail off.

"The first thing, Libby. The very first thing that happens, and you don't trust me."

She swallowed, knowing he was right.

"I don't want to take the easy way out, but I sure as hell don't want to live a life where I have to prove myself all the time. I suck at that, frankly. Either you trust me one hundred and ten percent, or you don't."

"I do."

He angled his head. "Not when it mattered. Not when I needed you most."

Her heart folded in half. "Law."

"Look, I'd put my money on Sam. He'll work out some deal with that old bag, or she'll die, or something will happen. And you should have your place and your dream."

"But..." *You are my dream.* The look in his eyes kept her from admitting that. The cool, distant, already gone look. She'd seen it before and knew what it meant. "What about your dream? The gastropub? The..." *Life we could have together.*

He shrugged. "Wasn't Jake's to give me. It was your father's business all along. And, in some weird way, your mother is absolutely right. That guy owed you something, since you are his and he wouldn't take responsibility for you. So get your brother to work his magic and you get...Balance."

She stared at him, the pain in her chest almost unbearable.

He pulled her keys out of his pocket and held them out. "I'll get an Uber home."

Hope marched up her spine, making her straighten. "Home? Will you be there when I get back?"

He smiled and shook his head. "I didn't mean your home. I mean back to my bike, which will take me wherever I'm going next."

"Which is..."

He shrugged. "Arizona, I guess."

"Law...*no.*"

"Hey." He reached out and gave her cheek a stroke. "You'll be fine. And I'll...see you at the next reunion or something."

The words twisted and sliced, making her close her eyes at the pain.

When she opened them, he was halfway down the steps and headed across the parking lot. He stopped long enough to take off his suit jacket, flip it over his shoulder, and stride like a man of confidence and strength on to the next phase of his life.

While once again, Libby was left standing on courtroom steps, unsteady, alone, and picking up the pieces of her heart.

Chapter Twenty-Six

A full moon at midnight spilled light over the dozens of islands and canals on the northeast corner of Barefoot Bay. Law lay flat on his back across the dock, his face turned toward the moonlight, his chest rising and falling with the kind of full-bodied breaths he'd learned from Libby.

Oh, there he went again. Back to Libby. Where he'd been this whole long, hard, hot day.

He'd imposed on Ken for the truck again, got his meager belongings from his friend's garage, and packed his clothes, chef's coat, and knives in a duffel bag he swung over the back of his bike. Then he shot an email to the Ritz telling them he'd be there in a few days and...got as far as Beckett's dock.

How different would his life have been if he hadn't gotten on that skiff with his brother that day? How different if Beckett hadn't been drunk, or if Law had been paying attention, or *if he hadn't left*?

He waited for the usual kick of guilt and a dunking in self-hatred, but it didn't come. Libby had changed that, somehow. She'd shown him his worth...until she didn't.

Hey, who could blame her? He should have called and

told her what he'd done. No, he shouldn't have even signed the paper without telling her and having her sign, too. Hell, if the two of them had sat down with Rosie, they might have changed the old lady's mind about Frank's biological heirs.

Maybe it wasn't too late...

He turned his head to stare up at the moon, the ache gnawing as it always did at this hour. The need to numb the pain. The need to hide from the sound of his father's voice. The need to cook something amazing. The need for Libby.

And there he was, back to her again.

Addiction was a powerful thing. It made a body ache in the most palpable way, a physical hurt, a hole in the chest, a need that only one thing can fill.

He'd gone and gotten addicted to Libby Chesterfield. He let out a sigh and closed his eyes, hearing her voice, feeling her touch, reliving her declaration of love.

But a sound drowned out his imagination—a distant engine heralding a car not so far away. He hoped it would drive right by and not stop when whoever was in it saw a motorcycle parked at the end of the dock. Wouldn't be the first time some do-gooder got nosy and wanted to be sure everything was okay.

Because everything was not okay.

The engine grew louder, along with the faint screech of music from a car radio, which had to be stupidly loud if he could hear it this far away. Kids, no doubt. Looking for fun, for trouble, for booze.

The noise grew increasingly louder, making him turn in anticipation of a car that must be a half mile down the road, but was still ruining the peace of the night by blasting hard rock. In a few seconds, headlights bathed the whole area in halogen white as the car came around the corner and the music cut through the night air.

Damn stupid…wait. Oh God, *wait*. That wasn't just *any* music. So that mustn't be just *any* driver.

It had to be her.

His heart squeezed, and he pushed up a few inches, squinting at the beams of light that blinded him with a direct glare.

The engine quieted, but that only intensified the music. The opening notes to a song he immediately recognized echoed over the still waters and through the humid air.

She cut the lights and suddenly there was nothing but moon shadows and the bleeding notes of an electric guitar. And the sound of a car door slamming.

Libby.

The storm is on the inside…deep within my heart.

Oh hell, it sure was.

Every time I look at you I'm just torn apart.

The last line wasn't just Eddie James on vocals. A figure came around the front of the SUV, long, blond hair catching some of the light, the voice he'd just been hearing in his head singing along.

"Baby, you're a force of nature, I just got to say."

She reached the first wood plank, and he could finally see her face. Her eyes were clear and direct. Her lips moved with the next line.

"'Cause every time you kiss me…" She took a few slow steps to the beat, her long legs bare except for cutoff shorts.

He met her halfway. "I am blown away," he finished, whispering the words that caught in his throat.

The next verse started, but they stood stone-still, about two feet apart.

She tilted her head up, cocked a brow, and held out her hand. "I came to dance with you."

All the fight melted away. All the numbness he'd been seeking turned to a sparking, hot sensation of...Libby. Nothing in him, not one molecule of man in his whole body, wanted to live one day without her.

And she came to him. *Knew* he'd be here. For some reason, that did him in. He took her hand and eased her a step closer. "Watch out for the belt buckle, Lib."

"That's not what I want from you." She let out a sigh as she slid her hands around his neck. "Sing to me."

"That's what you came for?"

She put her head on his shoulder and started to sway. "Sing, Law."

Pressing his hands against her back, he picked up the next line.

"The wind is whipping outside and the rain is falling down..."

He could feel her smile against him. At his terrible voice? Or just because she was as happy as he was?

"Lightning streaks across the sky and..."

"Bees are underground," she filled in.

"Those damn bees," he whispered.

"Always stinging us."

"Trying to ruin everything by buzzing nonsense in our heads," he added.

"Planting little bee seeds of distrust."

He laughed softly. "When all we want is the honey."

She stilled in his arms and looked up at him. "Lawson Monroe, I love you."

He blinked at the unexpected statement, letting the impact of it warm him.

"And that means," she continued in a whisper, "that I

trust you. I made a mistake, and might make more, but I can't do this without you. I don't want to. I love you, Law. Don't leave." She swallowed and grasped his neck a little tighter. "Please."

He wasn't leaving. He knew it deep in his gut when he walked across that courthouse parking lot. He knew it when he threw himself down on this dock. And he knew it when she walked toward him tonight.

He wasn't leaving. He wasn't quitting Libby.

"Please," she whispered again when he didn't answer.

"You're right," he said softly. "Leaving would be taking the easy way out. I need to stay here and…learn song lyrics and…twist my body into yoga poses and…make you comfort food and…"

"Run a restaurant."

"If we had one."

She relaxed a little in his arms. "We do. I bought one today, as a matter of fact. Except I just want the upstairs and need a partner and chef for the downstairs."

A frown pulled as he gauged her expression to see if she was joking or not. Not. Definitely not. "How?"

"Never, ever underestimate the power of my mother's acting skills."

"They are impressive," he said.

"Honestly, she wasn't acting when you were there. That's the real story. But she gave Meryl Streep a run for her money when she talked to Rosie."

"What? They *talked*?"

She inched away, another laugh in her eyes. "It turns out there was even more fine print in that contract than Sam, of course, dug out. Rosie wanted an apology."

"She did?"

"Clause…something, paragraph three, line six. It was

buried in legalese, but when Sanderson got her on the phone, she admitted that's what she wanted. Heartfelt repentance."

"And your mother apologized to her?" Damn, he wished he'd stayed for that. "For sleeping with her husband?"

"Apologize is too tame a word," she said. "She groveled like an Oscar was on the line. It took all we had not to stand and applaud. Tears were shed, forgiveness was begged for, and then she pulled out the big guns. A plea for mercy before Rosie left this earth for another place...a better place. At least, it would be better if Rosie sold me her restaurant for a dollar."

"And it worked?"

"Plus her legal fees. I mean, the woman wants to go to heaven, but didn't want to be a complete pushover. Plus, she hated old Frank more than his mistresses. Apparently, there were many."

"And what about you?" Law asked.

"Me? I didn't do anything to incur the wrath of Rosie except be born."

"Did your mother apologize to you for all the lies over the years?"

She sighed and lifted her shoulders. "With much less flair. Look, she's wretchedly ashamed of what she did and how hard she worked to cover the truth, including implicating Jake when he was clearly not a bad man at all. She said, looking back, he had shown a lot of interest, but she couldn't reciprocate."

"Why did she lie about him?"

"She was truly afraid of Rosie's power if she named Frank as our father, so she put Jake on the birth certificates to protect herself. But she was also convinced that Rosie didn't know about the Pelican being owned by Frank. Apparently, it was an investment he'd made under the table, buying it from the guy who originally built it as a shack to serve beer to the men building the causeway in the forties. My mother thought only she knew that Frank had purchased it, and in her eyes, Frank owed us a parting gift for not taking responsibility for his own children. She didn't know if Frank had sold it or given it to Jake, but when he died, she hatched this plan."

Law shook his head. "She's wild, Lib."

"She is, but she's my mother. And we have a lifetime of stuff to work out, and we will, more or less. I've got Jasmine, who is far more of a blessing to me than a normal mother would have been. And now I know who my father was. Sanderson can get us medical records and a family history, so…" She gave a smile. "Law, I don't want to wallow in it. I want to move on."

He nodded, appreciating the maturity and wisdom of that decision. "So you got it. You got the Pelican."

Her face fell. "*We* got it, Law. Don't you see? That's why I'm here. That and the fact that Jasmine would have come herself once I told her you were here."

"How did you know?"

She tipped her head. "Because I know you."

He let that wash over him. No one, except maybe Jake, ever cared about him enough to know his habits and weaknesses. If that wasn't love, what was?

"Law, I don't want to do this without you." She gripped him tighter. "I don't want to do *anything* without you. I screwed up so bad today when I questioned you, but I know, I mean, I *know* you love me. I trust that is true, and I believe in you and in us, and—"

He silenced her with a kiss, a deep, meaningful, all that he had in him kiss. Her words became a moan, and the moan became a whimper until she was quiet and kissing him back.

"Libby." He took her face in his hands and looked right into her eyes. "I've made a lot of mistakes in my life. One, right here, in these waters." Her eyes shuttered at the mention, but he didn't stop. "But I will not make the mistake of letting you go. Not now, not ever. I love you. I really, really love you."

"I love you, too," she whispered. "And more than that, I trust you."

He pulled her close, and they danced to the closing notes of their song, hanging on to each other and the moment when the rest of their lives started.

Epilogue

"It's like déjà vu all over again." Emma DeWitt—well, Solomon now, after the sunset ceremony on the beach a few hours earlier—looked into the mirror to meet the gazes of the two women behind her. The three of them had slipped out to the brides' dressing room for a break from the festivities and lingered for just a moment in the peace and quiet.

Libby smiled back at Emma and then put a hand on Beth's shoulder. "Not exactly déjà vu. You two may have gotten married on the same weekend at the same resort, but last night's wedding was totally different from this one."

"Right, Ken and I had all those hot firefighters and house builders," Beth joked, her hand on her baby bump, as it had been all night during her own wedding just twenty-four hours earlier.

"There's plenty of heat here tonight, too," Libby said. "Not that I'm looking," she added and then pointed to Emma. "And you certainly aren't."

"I only have eyes for my husband," she said, a huge smile making her golden-brown eyes dance with joy. "Two hours and I already like saying that."

Libby's heart jumped a little, too. *Husband.* The word

held such meaning for her, such weight. She was close to using it on a daily basis again. She and Law had spent almost two months building their business and planning their life. Making it official was all that was left.

But after back-to-back weddings full of joy, promise, and high hopes, something was still stopping Libby from jumping into those all-too-familiar waters. It wasn't fear. It wasn't doubt. It certainly wasn't Law—he'd have dragged Libby up next to Mark and Emma to take vows with them if she'd have agreed.

Was she still not ready to commit to him?

"Oh, there's heat here." Emma turned from the mirror, the silky cream-colored dress she wore swishing with the move. "If you mean the Legends Table."

"The what?" Beth asked.

"When we were doing the table planning, Mark called it the Legends Table," Emma explained. "I mean, when you put Jesse MacDonald, Ben Santiago, and Adam Slater at a table and invite the lead singer of the Lost Boys to sit there between sets, you've got a table full of timeless legends."

"And gorgeous men," Beth noted.

"I know who Ben Santiago is, of course, since he's been synonymous with baseball for as long as I can remember," Libby said.

"And I don't follow NASCAR, but I know Jesse MacDonald is racing royalty, but who's the other guy, Adam Slater? Besides a dead ringer for that Gibbs guy on *NCIS*?" Beth asked.

"Adam Slater is the astronaut who spent almost two years on the space station," Emma told her.

"Oh, that's where I saw him, on the Today show!" Beth exclaimed. "He wrote a book about raising a kid from space. Hilarious and handsome."

"How does Mark know all these superstars?" Libby asked.

Emma rose and smoothed her dress to head back out to the beachfront reception. "*Single* superstars," she corrected with emphasis. "Sexy, single, silver superstars."

They laughed at the former ad copywriter's penchant for alliteration, but certainly couldn't disagree.

"Mark's been skydiving with Adam the Astronaut, as I call him, and was on a fundraising board with Jesse," Emma continued. "But we met Ben at one of Lacey's parties a few months ago, and the guys became friends. He's moving to Barefoot Bay to manage the Bucks next season."

"Ben Santiago is still single?" Libby asked. "I don't know why I remember him being married."

"He was, but not anymore," Emma said. "And probably single not for long."

"Oh…I hear the band starting," Beth said, gesturing for them to get back. "Are you going to throw your bouquet?"

Emma squished her features. "It seems a tad silly at this age, don't you think? I mean, my friends are all married."

"Libby's not," Beth teased, leaning into her with the familiarity of a friendship that had blossomed quickly. "Yet."

Both women looked at her, and she felt the pressure to squeal and give a date. But there was none. No squeal, no date. And no desire for either one.

Why not?

"Everything's okay, isn't it?" Emma asked, obviously reading Beth's expression.

"Better than okay," Libby assured them. "I'm insanely in love with Law. We're both like…" She shook her head. "It's perfect. He's moved into my house, and Jasmine's moved in with Noah. *That's* the wedding I want to go to next."

"Are you going to be happy living together?" Beth asked softly. "Is that what you want? Because Law has told Ken in no uncertain terms that he wants to marry you, like yesterday."

She laughed. "Things were a little busy around here yesterday."

"You know what I mean. That man is ready to roll."

Libby sighed. "I know, and I want the ceremony, the vows, the officialness of it all, but..."

Emma took her hand. "You don't want another divorce."

"I won't divorce Law," she said, knowing the statement went beyond hope and into fact. They were solid, connected, and better with each other.

"Then what's stopping you?" Beth asked.

She looked from one to the other, searching her own heart. "I honestly don't know."

Emma slipped her arm around Libby's waist. "Take your time," she said. "You'll know when it's right."

She smiled at both of them, every trace of wistful envy she'd felt when they'd found forever happiness all gone. She had hers...she just didn't have the ring.

Which she suspected Law had already bought.

"Okay, Mrs. Solomon and Mrs. Cavanaugh." Libby linked arms with her two friends as they left the resort to walk back to the party on the beach. "Enough about me. This is your weekend, and it's time to dance. And please don't throw that bouquet."

Emma put her head on Libby's shoulder. "You don't need to catch it. You just need to jump in and take the plunge."

"And there's the gulf," Beth teased.

"In this dress?" Libby fluttered the red silk sheath that skimmed her knees with a flirty hem. "Not a chance." She nudged them along the tree-lined path, the three of them walking to the beat of the next song.

"Listen to that Eddie James sing. He's still fantastic," Emma mused.

"And still has women wanting to throw their panties at him onstage," Libby said.

"Then he better get ready to be buried in them," Emma said, "because Willow's dad said that the Lost Boys are considering doing a reunion concert series at the new stadium now that baseball season has ended. If they can find a permanent bass player, that is, because Keith Harte will not come back."

When they reached the canopy-covered party area, they spotted their three men in a group, talking to the very "legends" they'd been discussing.

"Now, that is a feast for the eyes right there. All of them."

"Especially ours," Beth said, smiling at Ken as he talked to one of the men.

"Oh, come meet these men," Emma said, steering them that way, but Libby's gaze went straight to Law, who looked downright sinful in a suit, his tie loosened, his laugh so easy and genuine with his friends.

He immediately caught sight of her and held her gaze long enough to make her delightfully unsteady.

He left his group and approached hers, sliding his hands around her waist to extricate her. "Here's my lady in red." She let him pull her to the side. "She'll be with you shortly, ladies. Go drool over the famous hunks."

"We're too married to drool," Emma joked as they left.

Immediately, Law blocked Libby's view with his sizable shoulders, still holding her waist. "They're going to play our song any minute," he whispered. "I talked to Eddie."

She smiled up at him. "So I can't talk to the legends?"

He laughed at the term. "You'll have plenty of chances. Ben's moved here, Adam has decided this is the place to raise a kid alone now that he's retired from the astronaut corps, and Eddie's signed up for a fall concert series. Jesse Mac says he's enamored with the resort and will be coming back, too." He eased her closer. "But this legend has plans for our song."

"Plans..." Her voice faded. She knew what his plan was.

"Yeah." He touched her chin and lifted her face to his. "Might be cliché, but I want to do it right."

"To our song. On the dance floor."

He puffed out a breath, a little disappointment darkening his eyes. "Gonna be kind of anticlimactic now, yoga bear." He stroked her cheek with his thumb. "You're not ready yet, are you?"

"I am," she said quickly. "I'm so ready. I love you, Law, and I want to be with you forever. But two men have gotten on one knee and, can I just say, I thought the whole position was kind of demeaning."

He croaked a laugh. "How about I do a down dog? Would that work for you?"

Smiling, she looked to the right, taking in the panorama of a beautifully orchestrated wedding. "It's so much white and lace and champagne and cake," she whispered. "All those flowers and tulle feel...wrong to me. What matters are the vows, the promises, and the two people saying them."

He drew back, his eyes clear with understanding. "Libby, it's not marriage you don't want. It's the *wedding*."

"Yes," she agreed. "You're right, Law." The realization hit hard. "I don't want a wedding. But I want to be married to you. How can we do that?"

He looked at her, thinking hard for a moment. And then a

slow, sexy smile curved his lips. "I know how." He slipped his arm around her and turned, walking in the other direction.

"Where are we going?"

"Vegas."

"*What*?"

"Vegas. Tonight. Let's go pack, find a flight, and go."

She choked softly, but walked with him. "Now? Tonight?"

"Why not? We'll drive up to Tampa and catch a red-eye."

Glancing over her shoulder, she looked back at her friends enjoying a conversation, Law's idea so preposterous that...that it wasn't.

Vegas was exactly what she wanted. No fuss, no muss, no wait, no planning, no stress. Just Libby and Law making promises to each other that they would both keep until death parted them.

It was perfect. "Do you think Emma will understand?"

"I think all four of them will understand. They've just been through two of these things."

"I love the idea, Law." His name caught in her throat as she slipped her arm around him. "And I love you."

He tucked her closer. "Then you better marry me."

"Is that the proposal, Law?"

"Not yet. Reach into my right pants pocket."

"Oooh. I know what's in there, and I like it."

"Humor me, Lib."

"All right." She dipped her hand into his pocket, her fingers curling around a small box. Her heart kicked up. "Is that it?"

"That's it." He slowed their steps. "You want it?"

"Yeah. I want it and I want you." She pulled the box out slowly. "Don't do the knee."

"No knee. No big deal. And…"

She flipped it open, instantly in love with the tiny emerald ring that was the precise color of Law's eyes.

"No diamond."

She could barely speak. "It's beautiful."

"I wanted it to be different than anything you've ever had before."

She looked up at him, her eyes swimming with tears. "It is. You are. This marriage will be."

He took the ring and slipped it on silently. "There," he said softly. "This ring is staying right here, forever." Then he wrapped his arms around her and pulled her close. "And so am I."

Did you read every book in the Barefoot Bay series?

THE BAREFOOT BAY SERIES

Don't miss Roxanne St. Claire's latest popular series, The Dogfather, which is chock full of hot guys, cute dogs, true love…and one great big Irish family you will adore!

Daniel Kilcannon is known as "The Dogfather" for a reason. It's not just his renowned skills as a veterinarian, his tremendous love of dogs, or the fact that he has turned his homestead in the foothills of the Blue Ridge Mountains into a world class dog training and rescue facility. Ask his six grown children who run Waterford Farm for him, and they'll tell you that their father's nickname is due to his uncanny ability to pull a few strings to get what he wants. And what he wants is for his four sons and two daughters to find the kind of life-changing love he had with his dearly departed wife, Annie. This old dog has a few new tricks…and he'll use them all to see his pack all settled into their happily ever afters!

Every book in the Dogfather series features a rescue dog on the cover and a portion of proceeds are donated to the Alaqua Animal Refuge, where the covers were photographed. And every story has a dog at the heart of the romance…front, center, and sometimes right in between. If you love dogs and romance, this series is for you!

THE DOGFATHER SERIES

More Books by Roxanne St. Claire

Prior to writing the Barefoot Bay series, Roxanne wrote romantic suspense in two popular series, and several stand alones. All titles are still available in digital versions and many are available in print.

THE GUARDIAN ANGELINOS (ROMANTIC SUSPENSE)
Edge of Sight
Shiver of Fear
Face of Danger

THE BULLET CATCHERS (ROMANTIC SUSPENSE)
Kill Me Twice
Thrill Me to Death
Take Me Tonight
First You Run
Then You Hide
Now You Die
Hunt Her Down
Make Her Pay
Pick Your Poison (a novella)

STAND-ALONE NOVELS (ROMANCE AND SUSPENSE)
Space in His Heart
Hit Reply
Tropical Getaway
French Twist
Killer Curves
Don't You Wish (Young Adult)

About The Author

Published since 2003, Roxanne St. Claire is a *New York Times* and *USA Today* bestselling author of more than fifty romance and suspense novels.

In addition to being an ten-time nominee and one-time winner of the prestigious RITA™ Award for the best in romance writing, Roxanne's novels have won the National Readers' Choice Award for best romantic suspense four times, as well as the Maggie, the Daphne du Maurier Award, the HOLT Medallion, Booksellers' Best, Book Buyers Best, the Award of Excellence, and many others.

A recent empty-nester, she lives in Florida with her husband, and still attempts to run the lives of her young adult children. She loves dogs, books, chocolate, and wine, especially all at the same time!

www.roxannestclaire.com
www.twitter.com/roxannestclaire
www.facebook.com/roxannestclaire
www.instagram.com/roxannestclaire1